AN UNDENIABLE ATTRACTION

"There are no first editions in here," Bennett explained. "The few I own are kept in a vault."

"I see." Cyndi knew she sounded breathless because she *was*—breathless and suddenly weak and irritated at herself for her excited reaction to his nearness.

"Do you?"

A quiver rippled through Cyndi at the now whispery sound of his voice. He stood so close to her she could feel his warm breath ruffle her hair, could inhale the aroma of the wine he'd drunk with dinner and the even more potent combined scents of spicy cologne and healthy male.

"Yes . . . yes . . . I . . ."

"Cynthia." Ben's voice was nearly nonexistent, just a shimmer of sound teasing her ear.

She felt more than heard him, vibrated to the note of hunger and passion in that shimmer of sound.

He grasped her shoulder and turned her around to face him. "I'm going to kiss you, Cynthia."

Her head jerked up and she stared into Ben's eyes . . . only to discover herself reflected in their smoldering depths.

"No," she whispered.

"Yes," he said, lowering his head.

A jolt went through Cyndi, as if she were electrified, when his mouth covered hers. His kiss was no tentative foray, no hesitant test, but a commanding possession of her mouth.

Cyndi's starved senses went wild in response to the sheer boldness of his sudden display of unleashed passion. . . .

Books by Joan Hohl

COMPROMISES

ANOTHER SPRING

EVER AFTER

MAYBE TOMORROW

SILVER THUNDER

NEVER SAY NEVER

SOMETHING SPECIAL

MY OWN

Published by Zebra Books

EVER AFTER

Joan Hohl

Zebra Books
Kensington Publishing Corp.

http://www.zebrabooks.com

ZEBRA BOOKS are published by

Kensington Publishing Corp.
850 Third Avenue
New York, NY 10022

First Printing: August, 1997
10   9   8   7   6   5

Printed in the United States of America

Prologue

What was she doing with this guy?

Cyndi peeked around the edge of the door on the changing cubicle; the man posing as her husband sat waiting for her to emerge from hiding and model for him. His demeanor projected indulgent patience.

Straightening, she stared at her reflection in the long mirror. She had never worn or owned a dress like the one he had chosen for her to try on. In fact, she had never owned a designer label of any kind.

The dress looked expensive, which it was—to her mind, dreadfully expensive. Feather-light, a bit of froth, chiffon no less, its style updated classic, the mauve and pink confection gave the appearance of abundant material, draping her bosom in a deep V, hugging her torso at the waist and then swirling to an inch below the knees.

Cyndi had read more than a few books—in reality, hundreds. In her opinion, the only description that fit this particular bit of cool summer attire was that it was the perfect frock for an afternoon tea or lawn party.

And, so far as Cyndi knew, summer afternoon tea or lawn parties were no longer a happening thing. Except, she mused, grinning, maybe in England, on the estates of the landed gentry.

Yet, Ben had declared the dress perfect.

For what? The cover of a magazine? Cyndi wondered, frowning at the near stranger frowning back at her from the looking glass.

To her way of thinking, the perfect summer attire was a pair of shorts and a tee shirt, accessorized with strappy sandals or sneakers. Or, for special occasions—few of which she had ever enjoyed—such as an evening out at the theater or dining in a fine restaurant, perhaps a cotton sleeveless dress.

But, then, what did she know? Cyndi made a face at her reflected self. What chance did a girl from the hills of Western Pennsylvania have to know or learn about, how the other, much better off, half lived and dressed?

Books. Everything anyone wanted or needed to know could be found in books.

The problem was, Cyndi rarely read *those* kinds of books. She enjoyed novels, the romantic kind that held out hope for the future, as opposed to literary tomes, which seemed to address only the seamier side of life: the lost, the lonely, the down-and-outers.

Of course, the characters in the books she read were often attired in smart clothes with designer labels, but that was fiction, a lot of it glamorous romantic fiction, and she knew the difference.

Cyndi had grown up poor; she had firsthand, in-her-face knowledge of the down side. She had chosen to rise above it all by ignoring it.

And that was what she was doing with this guy, she

reminded herself, taking another quick peek around the edge of the door at him. He continued to wait, his expression blasé, as if he had all the time and money in the world.

He wasn't hard on the eyes, either, Cyndi mused, not for the first time running a slow look of appraisal over him.

To her eyes, Bennett Ganster was one good-looking hunk in the prime of his masculinity. He wasn't hand-some in the conventional sense; his features were too defined and hard edged. The set of his strong, squared jawline bespoke purpose and determination. His lips were on the thin side—another note of steely purpose? And yet, his mouth had definite allure, a promise of paradise on sultry nights.

Startled by the direction her thoughts were taking, Cyndi shifted her gaze to his form; that wasn't half bad, either. In truth, it was darned attractive.

He stood around six feet, every inch of him muscled, toned. He was hard and rangy looking. Attired in a suit, white shirt, and necktie, as he presently was, he exuded vitality, dynamic maleness.

Cyndi had noted—how could she not?—the slow, smoldering sidelong looks given Ben by females, both young and old. She had only seen him dressed in conser-vative attire, so she could just imagine the impact he'd have when dressed in a torso-hugging pullover and skin-tight jeans.

Of course, had Ben not been easy on the eyes, and a persuasive charmer to boot, she wouldn't have been here, inside this cubicle, trying on clothes with price tags that made her heart race with shock, causing tremors in her hands when she touched the garments.

What was she doing here? she again asked herself, beginning to feel a coil of panic twist in her stomach.

She didn't belong. She was out of her depth and sinking fast.

Ben's grand scheme was plain crazy; she was stupid for ever having listened to him.

But she had, and here she was, miles away from home with a man she didn't know, a virtual stranger, pretending to be his wife.

Stupid barely described it.

What the hell was she doing in there?

Bennett slanted a glance at his watch. How long did it take to slip out of one outfit and into another, for God's sake? She had been in that changing room for almost ten minutes.

She should have let the clerk assist her, as the woman had wanted to do. But, no, Cynthia had insisted she could manage by herself. So, why wasn't she managing a little faster?

Bennett was careful not to reveal his growing impatience. He had promised himself that he would go slow with her, considering her lack of experience ... in almost everything.

But there were limits to endurance, and he had just about reached his.

It wasn't so much her lack of experience but her stubbornness that bothered Bennett. Hell, she had even argued against this shopping excursion.

He hadn't believed there was a woman alive who would balk at being gifted with a complete new wardrobe. But Cynthia had, from the moment he had made the suggestion at the hotel over breakfast, right up to and including their entrance into the upscale shop.

She didn't need anything, she had said.

Ha! Bennett had been hard pressed to keep the exclamation to himself. For if ever there was a woman who needed everything, it was Cynthia.

Bennett knew that it was sheer dumb luck that he had stumbled across her in the first place. And his brainstorm to pass her off as his wife, for the sole purpose of keeping his mother calm and happy, was a stroke of genius. Convincing Cynthia had been the hard part.

He had thought she would jump at the chance to escape that run-down home of hers located on the far side of the outskirts of a nowhere little town. Not to mention the drudgery that made up her day-to-day life.

His offer had been generous, in fact, a lot more than generous. In exchange for her pretending to be his wife until such time as his mother's health improved, Bennett had offered her a lovely home, her own bank account, and the opportunity to achieve her most cherished desire, that of furthering her education with the college courses of her choice.

He knew it was the offer of college that had won the victory for him.

He suppressed a sigh. It didn't make sense. Cynthia had accepted his offer of a college education without hesitation, yet she'd dug in her heels over the comparatively minimal cost of a new wardrobe.

She had fought his suggestion of a shopping spree from the beginning, maintaining her own clothes were good enough. He'd disagreed. In the end, he had chosen each and every article. Though Cynthia had exclaimed in dismay at the expense, she had, with voiced reluctance, finally accepted the lingerie and casual attire.

In his unspoken personal opinion, she made a suitable appearance in the lightweight shorts and tops, the swirly skirts and blouses. Though he had ordered a dozen of each of the lingerie items, in assorted colors, he had allowed her to have her way in the choice of just a few of the outer items; after all, summer would soon be over, and she would require fall and winter attire. Bennett didn't even want to think about how she'd react to that future shopping expedition.

They had just started on the more formal clothing. She was taking forever to try on the first of his selections. She had objected so, he couldn't begin to imagine how she'd react to evening wear.

Her attitude just didn't seem normal to him.

Go figure.

Giving a mental shrug, Bennett eyed the closed dressing-room door just as it swung open and Cynthia appeared in the sheer, mauve and pink number . . . which he had deemed perfect for one of his mother's Sunday afternoon thingies—or whatever she called her little gatherings—if she ever resumed her social activities.

He opened his mouth to compliment her, but the words got stuck in his throat. Cynthia had looked appealing in the casual clothing; but then, he had known she would. Her figure was good, if a mite too slender for his taste. And she was attractive, pretty, though in an unsophisticated, too innocent way that had left him unmoved.

Or so he had thought.

In actuality, the sight of her, somehow managing to look elegant, beautiful, and sexy as hell in a dress which caressed her breasts and swirled around her hips and legs, tantalizingly defining her figure, stunned him, stole his breath, rendered him speechless.

She had flipped her newly sheared hair behind her ears, away from her face, leaving a few loosened strands to curl at her temples, bringing into relief the purity of her facial bone structure, the delicate length and arch of her neck.

Though speech eluded him, a little voice inside his head was making itself heard, clamoring a warning that this charade wasn't going to be as smooth and easy as he had told himself it would.

Cyndi waited for Ben to speak, say something, anything. The longer he sat there, staring at her, the edgier she became.

He hates it, she thought, standing absolutely still to keep from fidgeting.

His expression, cool, remote, sent a quivering bolt of discouragement and disappointment through her.

She fought back a groan of dismay with a mental jab of reality.

She had known—of course she had known—the dress was not her style; it was too high class.

But, dammit, he had insisted on her trying it! The least he could do was admit he'd made a mistake.

Finally, her nerves snapping, tears threatening, she took the initiative.

"Do you like it, Ben?"

"The name's Bennett," he reminded her, for the umpteenth time, even though she persisted in shortening it to Ben, while he persisted in using her given name of Cynthia. "And, ah . . . yes, it's, eh, very nice."

Very nice? The damn dress sported a three-hundred-dollar price tag—and that with twenty-five percent off—and all he could come up with was 'it's nice?' Never mind offering an apology for making her try on the *nice* dress in the first place.

Cyndi's stomach heaved, and she heard a frantic whisper inside her rattled mind.

How had she gotten herself into this situation?

Chapter One

Cyndi was a dreamer.

When she'd been little, her mother had always said with gentle indulgence that she either had her nose in a book or her head in the clouds, spinning daydreams.

Cyndi accepted her mother's assessment with good nature, because it was true.

What was also true was that her given name was Cynthia. But, as she had always considered herself ordinary—and the name Cynthia too extraordinary for a girl from the hills of Western Pennsylvania—she much preferred the nickname Cyndi, which was a good thing, as she had been called that for as long as she could remember.

In point of fact, Cyndi knew there were folks who didn't know or didn't recall or didn't much care that her given name was Cynthia. It didn't matter to her one way or the other, she was content being Cyndi.

The name Cyndi fit her situation in life and the people within it. While the mountainous landscape was beautiful, especially in the autumn when the trees blazed red and gold and russet, the lifestyle of many of those living in it was harsh, especially in the winter when driving storms swept the mountains.

Undoubtedly, there were those, in the surrounding towns and communities, who lived well, enjoying comfortable middle-class existences with all the modern conveniences.

But for those living in the mountains and foothills and the tiny hamlets therein—families like Cyndi's—mere survival was a daily struggle.

There were few luxuries. Some were grateful for even the bare necessities. Everyday life, and the living of it, was hard, at times brutal. And yet, Cyndi was not and had never been actively unhappy, very likely because she was a dreamer. She loved to read, devoured the written words of her favorite or chanced-upon authors when she could get ahold of a new—to her—book. She lost herself, her lot in life, within the pages of novels, short and long.

She believed in happily ever after.

It certainly wasn't that, at the advanced age of twenty-six, Cyndi expected to see her Prince Charming charge into the little village in a white Jaguar and awaken her dormant sensuality with a soul-stirring kiss. She was much too realistic for that. Having lived with cold reality each and every day of her life, she knew better.

But Cyndi did believe in the possibility of happiness and of genuine love, a bond everlasting. Not that she had seen an awful lot of proof of such a love, or that she had ever been in love herself, for she hadn't. She had always believed her own parents had experienced such a love. Though undemonstrative, they had displayed a deep, abiding caring for one another.

So, Cyndi believed in the possibility of such a deep,

abiding love for herself, and she felt positive she would recognize it if and when it came along.

She didn't . . . not at first.

It was a same old, same old kind of day.

The midsummer sun spread early warning signals of the brilliance about to crest the horizon when Cyndi quietly slipped out the back door of her home. Pausing on the narrow, rickety back stoop, she drew in deep breaths of the cool, pine scented morning air.

It was going to be another hot one, she decided, skimming a glance over the bluing sky, hot and dry, with no rain in sight, not a hint of relief from the unremitting heat.

It would be even hotter in the diner.

Her roving gaze settled on the silver oblong structure. A short distance from the house, which wasn't in much better condition than the stoop, the diner sat back from the road, to one side of the old gas station. Like the house, both structures were past their prime, long past. The diner dated back to the late forties.

"Dinner in the diner, nothing could be finer . . ."

The words of the old song floated through her mind. Cyndi smiled; she could think of a lot of things that could be finer, a decent restaurant, for one.

Not that the diner wasn't decent. It was. She made sure of that. The place was her bailiwick, her responsibility. It provided the lion's share of the family income. The gas station was her father's domain. The profits from it were minimal, but it gave him something to do.

Carl Swoyer had a bad back, a congenital condition with a long, unpronounceable medical name. Other than prescription painkillers, which they could seldom afford, there was no known treatment for the condition.

Cyndi's father lived with it, enduring in stoic silence. She ached with pity for him, and worked all the harder, at times manning both the diner and the pumps, in addition to keeping, or at least trying to keep, their house in order.

It wasn't easy. The domicile was cramped for space, with three small rooms down and three up, plus the tiny bathroom her father had added on to the house just off the kitchen.

Up until her father had constructed the addition, the year Cyndi was in the second grade, they had had to troop out back, to the little house with a crescent moon carved out of the loosely hinged door.

Tiny though the bathroom definitely was, Cyndi had given silent thanks for it for some years after her father completed it, even when she'd had to wait in line to use it.

There were five of them in residence, had been since her mother died from pneumonia mere months before Cyndi graduated from high school. Her mother's death had shocked every one of them, from her father down to the youngest member of the family, and it had drastically changed Cyndi's life, her plans for the future.

Cyndi had excelled at her studies and had earned a full scholarship to a highly accredited liberal arts college. Tears of sorrow streaming unnoticed down her face, she had accepted her high-school diploma, while saying a sad farewell to any hopes of furthering her education, to her dreams of a better life.

Because she loved books so much, she had aspired to be a college librarian. Instead, she had abandoned her work and had shouldered the responsibility of becoming a surrogate mother to her three younger siblings, in addition to running the diner and helping with the station.

Of course, with her acceptance of these duties, Cyndi had little time to indulge in personal relationships, romantic or platonic. So, she got her romance vicariously, from the books she read, and told herself if she became really desperate for friendship, she'd get a dog.

Therefore, she was still a virgin at the advanced age of twenty-six. The condition didn't bother her, since she had yet to meet any man she considered interesting and exciting enough to gift with her innocence—other than that one boy in high school she had gone dreamy-eyed over. But Bruce Harte really didn't count, since all he'd managed to accomplish with his groping hands and crude mouth the one time they had been alone together had been scare her and turn her off further experimentation.

Up until the previous couple of years, when her sister Jess, the youngest of the brood, had taken over inside the house, she had done nonstop hard work. Fortunately, Cyndi possessed an abundance of energy, and she never got weary. Oh, it wasn't that she never got physically tired, she did, often. In that respect, she was quite normal. But she was not susceptible to the emotional bone-weariness of utter defeat.

She was hopeful, a romantic, an optimist; traits she had inherited from her father. There had been occasions during the previous eight years when she had wondered if those traits might eventually do her in, but she had not complained.

Well . . . at least not much, she reflected, a reminiscent smile curving her lips. Taking on the chore of raising three siblings, the youngest just ten, the two middle kids normal, active boys, had required love—and a lot of patience.

And now the boys were gone, both into the armed services—Carl Jr. into the Air Force, David into the

Navy—upon graduation from high school. So it was just Cyndi, her father, and her sister Jess—christened Jessica; their mother, also an avid reader, had had a thing about fancy female names.

Yes, life was now a good deal easier, Cyndi acknowledged, making for the diner at a long-legged stride in order to open the place for business at the exact posted time of 6 A.M.

She was up; the sun was up; it was time to pull her head out of the clouds and get to work. There was already one customer, a regular, waiting.

For the first hour, as usual, business was brisk, made up entirely of local men grabbing a fast plate of bacon, eggs, and home fries before heading for work.

While cooking and serving, she traded banter with the wise-cracking ease of long familiarity.

By a few minutes after eight, Cyndi was busily occupied with the daily chores of scraping down the grill, washing the dishes, and wiping the counter, the small booth tables, and every other flat surface in the confined space.

It was steamy in the diner. Damp tendrils of sweat-darkened honey brown hair were stuck to her damp forehead and neck. But on the whole, Cyndi was content. The morning rush was over. She hummed to herself as she worked.

All in all, life wasn't too bad.

Bennett Ganster was on an unplanned vacation, meandering, simply driving, no definite destination in mind. He hadn't particularly wanted a vacation, although he knew he needed a break, had needed a break for some time, most especially after the worries and pressures of the previous eight months, ever since the night his widowed mother had suffered a fairly mild, yet frightening, heart attack.

Made aware so suddenly of his mother's mortality, Bennett had overreacted, insisting she leave her own home and move in with him so he could properly look after her.

The very fact that Frances Ganster had acquiesced to having her son take over her life, and determine her living quarters, said much about her own fears concerning her health.

Bennett had long since accepted his mother's independent bent; it was a given. Yet he could not tolerate the thought of her remaining in her own home, cared for by a housekeeper who, though spry, was nevertheless several years into her seventies.

In addition to staying on top of his work, that of owner and CEO of a thriving and growing chain of innovative and unusual bookstores, Bennett had overseen the removal of his mother from her home and into the large house he had inherited from his paternal grandmother.

Only after she was comfortably ensconced in Bennett's home did his mother grow fractious. Possibly because of his open concern, Frances began fretting about the possibility of her imminent demise, and she became fixated on her lack of grandchildren.

She continually voiced her desire to see her son, her only child, married and settled. In point of fact, she had first given voice to this desire soon after Bennett celebrated his thirtieth birthday, two years before.

At the time, Bennett had merely laughed off his mother's less than subtle hints about his finding a nice, suitable young woman for himself. He had gone on his contented way, satisfied with his life as it was—without binding strings.

Then, in the aftermath of her heart attack, Frances

redoubled her efforts, expressing her longing aloud, and often, to see and hold a grandchild—while she could still see and hold one.

Bennett didn't want a suitable wife; he didn't want a wife, period. Some of his best friends had wives, not only suitable but attractive, a few flat-out gorgeous and most charming and good company.

He genuinely liked the majority of his friends' wives. But, in his unstated opinion, they all had one glaring flaw. Each woman felt her husband devoted far too much time to professional pursuits and not nearly enough to his family, most particularly his spouse.

And so, when Bennett heard the word "wife," he thought of the word "nag." He had no intention of shackling himself to any woman, despite his mother's wishes.

Lately, however, his mother had abandoned any pretense of subtlety. She had kicked her marriage-and-grandchild campaign into high gear.

The arrival of Frances's younger sister, Louise, on the scene had given Bennett a break of sorts. Not only had Louise distracted Frances from doing her wishful thinking aloud, she had relieved him of the constant concern and worry he suffered during the hours he had to be about his business.

But Bennett had not expected to be summarily ordered out of the house, his house, and on his way for some rest and relaxation. Though he had argued, he had lost.

"Go on, take off for a while," Louise had advised—in a tone of command. "Have some fun."

"Fun?" Bennett had stared at his aunt in disbelief. "How can I have fun by running away when Mother—"

"But you wouldn't be running away," Louise said

over his protests, laughing at him. "I'm sending you away—for your own good, of course."

"Yes, we're sending you away," Frances had chimed in, backing up her sister. "You look worse than I do, for heaven's sake." She'd run a critical gaze over him. "As Louise said, get some rest, relax, have fun, and who knows"—she shrugged—"you might even meet someone interesting."

Bennett had given up the battle.

After six days of aimlessly driving over the hills and dales of Pennsylvania, he had not had a moment's worth of fun. He did not feel rested, nor, fortunately, had he met anyone of the female persuasion, interesting or otherwise.

Then again, he hadn't been looking for anyone. Bennett had a . . . friend, a close female friend, with whom he could relax over a quiet dinner and later relieve his sexual tension in bed, sometimes his, sometimes hers.

Her name was Denise. She was a stunningly attractive, curvaceous woman, a five feet, four inch dynamo.

Bennett and Denise shared a perfect understanding, and mutual desires. Like him, she had her own agenda. She was on the fast track in pursuit of her career goals. The word "marriage" could send her into hyperventilation.

While Bennett might have considered inviting Denise along on his unscheduled vacation, he was not given the option, since she was away on a business trip to the West Coast.

And so, he was on his own. Although he appreciated the pastoral beauty of his home state, the summer green of the rolling countryside, the intricate patchwork designs of the farmers' fields, he was nevertheless tired of staring at unfurling ribbons of road, wired from drinking endless cups of coffee. As if that weren't enough, he was suffering an acute case of sexual frustration.

Bennett knew there were opportunities; he wasn't unconscious of the occasional sidelong glance of appraisal cast his way by an interested female, actually at nearly every restaurant, motel, and hotel where he had stopped along his uncharted and erratic route.

For reasons other than, but not excluding, concerns of health, he simply was not interested in a quickie, slam-bam-thank-you-ma'am foray into casual sex. It was not, never had been and never would be, his style. So, his growing irritation was aggravated by frustration.

He had asked himself, repeatedly, why, instead of choosing to drive aimlessly along the byways of his home state, he had not booked himself onto the first flight to the West Coast. The absence of a coherent answer to the query merely abraded his discontent.

After too many days of introspection, Bennett was not in the best of all possible moods.

"Am I having fun yet?" he asked himself, in an unfunny-sounding snarl.

Heaving a sigh, he glanced down . . . and started. The needle on the gas gauge hovered over the quarter mark.

How had that happened? Bennett frowned. He never let the level go below half. And here he was, on a blacktop road winding around the back of beyond. He had seen few houses, never mind a service . . .

At that moment, Bennett rounded a bend in the road and found himself approaching what might pass for a service station, of sorts. At first glance, it appeared to have come into being around the time the automobile came into use.

On closer inspection, it didn't look much better, nor did the old-fashioned diner to the back of it. The whole scene reminded him of a movie set from the thirties.

If Bennett had ever thought about it, he'd have presumed such ancient-looking, round-topped boxy gas pumps had disappeared from the scene, relegated to the trash heap or perhaps positioned outside rustic antique stores.

At any other time, he wouldn't have stopped, but would have kept going, in search of a real service station. But this wasn't any other time, and he hadn't a clue as to the distance or location of another gas station.

There was no help for it. Bennett knew he had no choice in the matter. He pulled the car to a stop alongside one of the pumps, stepped out, and took a slow look around. The place was less than prepossessing. He could, and did, sum it up in a word . . . "run-down."

He started for the old weather-worn station just as a man stepped out. The man didn't look much better than the station. He was slightly bent, as if from a weight almost too heavy to bear, and he looked tired, almost frail, beaten by life.

" 'Morning," he called, shuffling toward the pumps. "Looks like we're in for another skin burner, for sure." He angled his head to glance up at Bennett. The good humor glowing from his washed-out blue eyes proved the adage that looks could be deceiving. "You need a fill or directions?"

"A fill."

Nodding, the man shuffled to the car.

Following, his facial muscles tightening as he tamped down a compassionate urge to spare the man the effort by pumping the gas himself, Bennett exchanged small talk with him while the tank was filling.

"Where you headed?" asked the man, arching an eyebrow.

"No where in particular," Bennett answered.

"Well, you found it." He laughed. "This is about as nowhere as you can get."

Smiling, Bennett paid the man, then turned to eye the diner with disfavor.

"You can trust it," the man drawled, correctly reading Bennett's dour expression. "The food won't poison you."

"I'll move my car up," Bennett said, but the man stopped him with a jerky head shake before he could take a step.

"You can leave it." He chuckled. "There's another pump, and I don't expect there'll be a run on business at ten-thirty on a weekday morning."

His smile turning wry, Bennett nodded, murmured his thanks, and headed for the diner, hoping the man was right and the food wasn't too unpalatable.

Cyndi immediately noticed the car that pulled to a stop alongside one of the two antiquated pumps. It was an expensive, current model, and she didn't know many people with new cars, let alone *expensive* new cars. Come to that, she didn't know many people with cars, period. Most of the folks she knew drove trucks, none of them new.

The car, a sleek, midnight blue, was gleaming in the now blazing sunlight. It wasn't a Jaguar, for certain. But it wasn't hard on the eyes, either.

She was asking herself who it could be when the driver shoved open the door and stepped out. *He* wasn't hard on the eyes, either.

Her hand paused in midair, clutching the salt shaker she'd just refilled. Cyndi watched him, a knowing smile curving her mouth on seeing the twist of disdain curling his lips as he glanced around the run-down—looking property.

His broad shoulders moved in a barely discernible shrug, and then he ambled toward her father, who had just stepped through the open door of the station.

She liked his rangy, loose-limbed gait, Cyndi decided, while disliking the overconfident set of his shoulders, the arrogant thrust of his jaw, and the condescending expression on his sharply defined face as he talked to her father.

Who the hell did he think he was? she asked herself, her eyes narrowing in anger as she saw her father nod, then shuffle toward the car at the pump. Her narrowed gaze shifted back to the stranger in time to see his expression change, become indecisive.

Was that a flicker of compassion she had seen flash across his strong features? she asked herself, watching intently as he exchanged a few words with her father. No, she quickly revised, noting his sour look as he turned to face the diner. He hesitated, a wry smile curving his mouth, then, with another tiny shrug, headed for the diner.

Cyndi was furiously wiping away at the already spotless countertop when he entered. She didn't glance up until she heard the homemade screen door bang shut behind him.

"Isn't this place air conditioned?" asked the stranger, his tone harsh with disbelief.

"Good morning to you, too," Cyndi said, her tone sugar sweet. "And I never respond to the obvious."

He raised dark auburn eyebrows over intent, equally dark eyes . . . and darned attractive they were, too.

"Meaning, since there's a screen door, there's obviously no air conditioning. Right?"

"Very good," she commended, somehow managing to keep her tone bland.

He raised an eyebrow.

Setting the cleaning rag aside, she straightened to her full five feet, seven inches, met his disparaging stare head-on, and infused a note of briskness into her voice.

"What can I get for you?"

Chapter Two

"I suppose it's too early for lunch," Bennett answered, studying the smart-mouthed woman.

She looked hot, as well she should, considering the temperature inside the diner seemed to be somewhere in the neighborhood of a hundred degrees. Her face was flushed, dewy with perspiration. Her shoulder-length hair, a honey brown color, had a limp, wilted look, and though she had pulled it back into a pony-tail, errant strands had escaped and lay plastered to the sides of her face and neck.

Although Bennett considered her a mite too slim, the woman possessed feminine appeal, nothing like Denise's classic beauty, of course, but more of a young-girl prettiness.

She was fairly tall, perhaps four or five inches taller than Denise . . . and a lot thinner. Set in the slightly squared oval of her face, her features were regular, if unexceptional. Her lips were full, and rather alluring in shape. Her nose was slim and straight. Her eyes were spectacular, bright and alert, hazel green with gold and brown flecks.

Overall, she wasn't bad to look at.

"Makes no difference to me." She shrugged. "You want lunch, I'll cook you lunch."

Accommodating, he thought. But then, why shouldn't she be willing to serve him whatever he wanted? She was in business to make money, wasn't she? Besides, it wouldn't be her stomach under attack.

"A cheeseburger?"

"Sure. Why not? Some folks eat steak for breakfast." She grinned, displaying straight, white teeth, their perfection marred only by a tiny chip off the corner of one in front. "And, anyway, a burger's no greasier than bacon."

Uh-huh. Bennett's stomach lurched—in a demand for food or in protest against the grease? Telling himself it was hunger, he gave a quick nod.

"Right," he agreed. "I'll have the burger, with lettuce and tomato . . ."—he raised his eyebrows—"if you have them on hand?"

"I have them." Her mocking smile underlined her dry tones. "You want fries with that?"

Feeling strangely chastised by being made aware of the note of condenscension in his voice, he offered her a smile of apology, and a tone of respect. "Yes, please."

She accepted his offering with a flashing smile of her own, and flourished a hand in invitation. "Why don't you take off your jacket and hang it up over there?" She swiped the back of her hand over her forehead, brushing back the clinging strands. "It's hotter than blazes in here."

"It certainly is," he said, shrugging out of his suit

jacket, which had felt comfortable in his air-conditioned car. "How can you work in here?" he asked, shaking his head as he went to hang the jacket on one of the short rows of hooks on the wall next to the door.

"I'm used to it." She had turned to go to the freezer to get the meat patty, but paused to toss a grin to him. "My father always says a body can get used to anything, even hanging, if you hang long enough." She slapped the patty onto the grill. "Where do you want it?"

Pondering the despair implied in her father's grim saying, Bennett frowned at her question.

"Where do I want what?"

"Your food. You gonna sit at the counter or in a booth?"

"Oh." He shrugged. "The counter." He slid onto a stool—the only one without a tear in the vinyl covering. His gaze idle, he glanced around the confined area behind the counter, noting with relief the spotless condition of everything. His eyes widened as his gaze came to rest on a milk-shake mixer that looked as old as the diner. "Does that thing work?" he asked in a tone of wonder and sheer disbelief.

She shot a confused look at him. "What thing?" she demanded, indicating the interior with a sweep of the spatula in her hand.

"The milk-shake mixer." Accustomed to the thick concoctions currently passed off as milk shakes, consumed with a spoon and not through a straw, Bennett could almost taste the smooth combination of milk and ice cream occasionally found in trendy new old-fashioned ice cream parlors.

"Well, of course it works," she said indignantly. "It wouldn't be there if it didn't." She peered at him intently, as if reading his expression. Then she smiled. "It makes perfect shakes. Want one?"

"Yes." Bennett smiled back at her. "Chocolate."

"With malt?"

"Yeahhh."

She laughed.

Deciding the light, spontaneous sound of her laugh was not at all unattractive, he joined in with her, feeling the long weeks of accumulated tension slowly ease from him.

Her timing was close to perfect. While the burger and side of fries were cooking, she set out two plates, preparing one with lettuce, slices of tomato, a long pickle spear, and a tiny paper cup of mayonnaise. While the fries were draining and the cheese melting on the burger, she made the shake.

"Sorry, but I forgot to ask how you wanted your burger cooked," she apologized as she set the plates and tall milk-shake cup in front of him. "It's well done." She lifted her shoulders in a light shrug before continuing, "But, that's probably the safest, anyway, considering all the medical warnings recently about undercooked meat."

Distracted by the process of applying lettuce, tomato, and mayo to the burger, Bennett gave a vague nod of agreement. Picking up the sandwich, he took a big bite, began to chew, then closed his eyes, as if in sheer bliss.

His praise came after he swallowed. "Heavenly. The best burger I've tasted in"—he shrugged—"forever."

"Why . . . thank you." She laughed, and the heat flush already coloring her cheeks flared with pleased embarrassment. "I . . . I'm glad you like it."

"You're welcome." Bennett smiled, suddenly realizing how pretty she was, with her pink cheeks, her sparkling eyes, and her sweet mouth curved in laughter. "Ms., Miss, Mrs. . . . ?"

"Miss. Swoyer. Cynthia." She grinned. "But folks around here call me Cyndi."

Reaching across the counter, he extended his right hand. "Bennett Ganster," he said, mildly surprised at the softness of her smaller hand. "I like Cynthia better," he went on, even more surprised by the strength of her grip.

She laughed again. "And I like Ben better."

He frowned. "Nobody has ever called me Ben."

"Well, somebody does now," she said, shrugging. "How's the milk shake, Ben?"

He gritted his teeth at her deliberate use of the nickname, but answered truthfully. "Delicious. I haven't tasted a real milk shake in years. Not many places make them anymore, it's mostly those thick things."

"It's the only kind we make, but then, we're not very progressive here." She laughed. "I guess we're about thirty years behind the times."

He shrugged. "Progress has its price."

Her expression sobered, and she sighed. "Yes, it does, and I wish I had the rate of exchange."

"Business slow, is it?" he asked, not in the least curious, but just to make conversation.

She gave him an arch look, then glanced around the diner. "It's summer, the traveling season, people going places. How many customers do you see?"

Bennett shrugged. "Point taken. But I'd have thought you'd see plenty, with the mountains; a lot of people like the mountains."

"Yes, a lot, and many of them go to the mountains, to resorts with comfortable rooms and planned activities." She indicated the area with a negligent wave. "There are no resorts around here. The others, the folks that go to the mountains to camp, rustle up their own meals. We see the occasional back-to-nature types. They seldom eat in restaurants or diners.''

''Times are tough all over,'' he commiserated.

She laughed. ''Times have always been tough here. Most folks are just scraping by.''

''Then why stay?'' Bennett asked, not wanting to offend her, yet certain that were he in her position, he'd have been long gone.

''It's home,'' she said. ''Most folks around here wouldn't be happy anywhere else.''

''Most folks,'' he repeated, picking up a hint of wistfulness in her voice. ''You included?''

She sighed. ''No . . . but don't misunderstand,'' she was quick to add, ''I'm not unhappy, it's just . . .'' her voice trailed away, and she shrugged. ''So,'' she went on with a forced brightness. ''You a traveling salesman or something?''

Bennett shook his head, and swallowed the bite of french fry in his mouth. ''I'm on vacation.''

She gave him a strange, overall look. ''You always wear a suit on vacation?''

Bennett frowned; he hadn't thought of it like that. He had just dressed every morning, the way he dressed every other morning. He shrugged. ''Habit.''

''Uh-huh.'' She held the sober expression for an instant; then she laughed.

He laughed with her.

''Where are you vacationing from?'' she asked, in an obvious curve around the strangeness of his attire.

''Philadelphia,'' he said, going along with her ploy to change the subject.

The mention of the city had a startling effect on her. She appeared at once enthralled by the sound of it. Her eager expression, the sudden glow in her eyes, had a startling effect on him.

Bennett mentally shrugged off the odd sensation of stirring interest, marking it down to lonesomeness, the need to interact with another person after days spent alone in his car.

"Do you work in an office inside one of those tall, mostly glass buildings?"

Amusement, and something else, something different, some emotion he couldn't quite identify, was stirred into the mixture brewing inside Bennett's mind. She was suddenly so animated, vivacious and avid for information, he hated having to disappoint her.

"No." He shook his head, strangely saddened by the dimming of the glow in her eyes. "My office is on the second floor of the flagship store of the small chain of bookstores I own."

Instantly the light sprang back into her eyes, even brighter than before. "Bookstores!" she exclaimed, in tones of hushed, awed reverence. "You own your own bookstores?"

"Yes." He couldn't help himself, he had to laugh; she looked so incredibly excited and impressed. "You like books?"

"No." She gave a quick shake of her head, setting the limp honey brown ponytail swinging. "I *love* books—and bookstores," she clarified, her voice rich with excitement. "Did you actually say you own a whole chain of them?"

"A small chain, only six, all in Southeastern Pennsylvania," he clarified. "Nothing like the major, big-name chains."

"Only six?" She laughed. "I could lose myself for months and months in only six bookstores." She sighed. "I don't get to the bookstore very often. We have only one around here, and that's in the town of

Hillsboro, nineteen miles from here. My sister works in town, and sometimes she stops into the store for me"—she smiled—"but, as she's not interested in the fiction I like to read, she just grabs up a couple of books for me, then heads for the cookbooks, to see if there's anything new; there seldom is. It's a new and used store, you see . . . mostly used." She shrugged.

Bennett grimaced; the subject of used bookstores had been one of controversy for some time in the business.

She appeared perplexed by his sour expression and, not wanting to get into the pros and cons of it, he steered the discussion toward one of her other remarks.

"I'm not sure I fully understand your problem," he said, a frown replacing his grimace.

"What problem?"

"About getting to the bookstore. Nineteen miles is nothing today," he pointed out, risking to yet again state the obvious. "Rather than depend on your sister, why don't you go to the store yourself? It's a short run for most people."

"Maybe for the people you know," she retorted. "It isn't for us—my family. Gas costs money."

On the face of it, her assertion was ludicrous; her father owned and operated the station. Bennett started to smile, then thought better of it as the underlying meaning of her statement registered.

She had said times were tough, had always been tough. It hit him that Cynthia hadn't been parroting a common or general complaint. Her statement had been literal, and dead serious.

"Ahhh . . . yeah, I know," he muttered.

But he didn't. Other than a surface knowledge of the numbers of people living in actual poverty or on the edge of it, some forced to the street, he had no actual frame of reference for need.

Bennett had never wanted for anything. Though his family were not by any measure wealthy, they had always been, and still were, a few notches above middle-income comfortable.

Caught, as it were, with his ignorance exposed, he was uncertain exactly how to proceed.

Displaying a depth of perception he couldn't claim for himself, Cynthia spared Bennett the embarrassment of papering over the awkward moment with platitudes.

She simply changed the subject once again.

"While still in school, I had hopes of spending my life surrounded by books."

"You wanted to work in a bookstore?" He laughed, not at her or her ambition, but in grateful relief.

"No." She was gracious enough to laugh with him. "I had hopes of, dreamed of, working in a library, preferably a university library."

Bennett frowned, confused, and sent a quick glance around the diner. If Cynthia had a college degree, then why in the world would she—

"I never got to college," she said, correctly reading the question in his expression.

"But there are—were—student loans available, weren't there?" he said, presuming expense as the cause.

She shook her head. "I wouldn't have needed a loan; I had earned a full scholarship."

"But then, why—" he began.

"My mother died in my senior year of high school," she broke in to explain. "She had contracted the flu near the end of that winter." She paused, swallowed, then went on in a voice devoid of color. "She fought the virus until mid-March, caught pneumonia, and then, too weakened to continue, lost the fight."

"I'm sorry." The sentiment sounded inadequate, but Bennett didn't know what else to say.

"Thank you." Her voice was as flat as before.

"Even so," he argued. "You could have—should have—gone on to get your degree."

"No." Her eyes were soft, wistful; her voice was firm, determined. "I couldn't. Dad argued with me for weeks about it." She smiled; it was gentle, as soft as her eyes. "He argued, and coaxed, even insisted I go. But I knew all along that I wouldn't change my mind."

Bennett frowned.

"I'm the oldest of four, you see," she said, again answering his unvoiced question. "The youngest, my sister, was ten, my brothers twelve and thirteen. As I'm sure you must have noticed, my father has a back condition." She enunciated the medical term of the congenital, deteriorating disease. "I . . . couldn't," she repeated, her shoulders moving in a barely discernible shrug.

She didn't elaborate, but then, there was no need. Bennett got the picture. Cynthia had sacrificed her education and her future on the altar of family love and dedication. He felt certain she would probably wind up marrying some local swain, then toiling to keep her head above constantly rising debt while raising a family of her own, her hopes and dreams buried beneath the weight of sheer survival.

Bennett's speculative thoughts made him uneasy. Here he'd been, disgruntled and feeling sorry for himself, believing he was under pressure since his mother's heart attack. In actual fact, he had been fortunate.

He hadn't lost his mother, thank God, nor had he been forced to give up his own career.

"Of course, you couldn't," he finally agreed, his uneasiness growing beneath her steady regard. "So, you are daughter, sister, mother, homemaker, and"— he inclined his head, indicating her station behind the counter—"chief cook and bottle washer."

Her laugh was spontaneous, unexpected, and delightful. "Gosh, sounds kinda grand and important, doesn't it?"

"Yes," he said, smiling. No, he thought, inwardly grimacing. To him, it sounded crushing.

"And your father," he went on, recalling the man and his bent form. "There's no treatment?"

She gave a quick shake of her head. "No, only pain-killers, which cost the earth."

"And which you can't afford."

Her lips tightened, and her eyes took on a fighting glitter. "I can afford them. I . . . all of us kids would have gladly done without to supply him with the medication. Dad wouldn't hear of it." Memory robbed the glow from her eyes. "Now it no longer matters."

Her final remark made no sense to Bennett, and while he was well aware that it was none of his concern or business, he couldn't contain the question, "Why not?"

"It seems that with this particular disease, the pain diminishes at some point in middle age. But the crippling is irreversible." She blinked, rapidly, several times. "His back will be bent, his spine curved, as it now is, for the rest of his life."

"That's . . . too bad." Once again, Bennett knew his expression of sympathy to be lacking. But what the hell else could he say? he asked himself.

"Yes, it is," she agreed. She sighed, then went on

in a lighter tone, "Dad, to his credit, takes it in stride, but then, he's an incurable optimist."

An optimist? The man who maintained a body that could get used to anything, even hanging if it hung long enough, was an optimist? It didn't fit. By it's very negative content, the maxim indicated despair.

Bennett started to shake his head; then he had a flashing memory of the gleaming light of humor in the man's eyes. Maybe it did fit. Maybe optimism, with a dash of dark humor, was how the man had decided to play the hand life had dealt him.

Mr. Swoyer stood tall, even with his back bent, his spine permanently curved.

Though he was tall in height, his body fit and healthy, his spine straight, Bennett felt small in comparison.

"Can I get you anything else? Coffee? Some dessert?" Cynthia's brisk voice broke into his self-derisive thoughts. "My sister baked blueberry pies for today, and I can assure you she makes great pies."

"No. Thank you." Shaking his head, Bennett polished off the last of the milk shake, still pondering what he had perceived as a contradiction.

There was none, he concluded. He simply had misjudged in the first place. It was now obvious that rather than from a sense of despair, Cynthia's brave father used such sayings in a courageous and spirited form of defiance.

Yes, that explanation did fit.

Watching Cynthia clear the now empty plates and cup from the counter, Bennett felt certain he had hit upon the truth, simply because the proof of it moved efficiently before his eyes.

She was definitely her father's daughter.

The really strange thing was, Bennett couldn't for the life of him figure why in the world it should matter to him in the first place. It was highly unlikely he would ever see her again.

Chapter Three

She'd probably never see him again.

Standing motionless behind the counter, Cyndi watched as the midnight blue car moved away from the gas pump and onto the blacktopped road.

The sound of her own curious, unconscious sigh of regret startled her.

What did it matter if she never saw him again? He was just another stranger, another customer, and, except when he laughed and lowered his guard, a rather arrogant one at that.

But she had sorta liked him anyway.

Bennett Ganster was more than good looking, and there weren't an awful lot of men—in reality none—like him cluttering up the immediate landscape.

Ships passing in the night.

The thought made her laugh.

"Cyndi, you read too much," she told herself aloud. "It's starting to make mush of your mind."

Grinning, she turned to walk to the sink, to wash the passing *ship's* dishes.

But random thoughts of the man were not so easily dismissed. Throughout the remainder of the day, she caught herself at the odd moment picturing the way he looked, his slow smile, his low laugh, his long body, his broad shoulders, his direct dark eyes, the crisp look of his auburn hair.

And his hands. Ben Ganster had the most elegant, yet wholly masculine, hands. Attached to wrists that were narrow, their bones prominent, his hands were broad, the fingers long, slender, the nails short, blunt.

Strange, Cyndi had never before noticed the attractiveness of any man's hands. They were merely a necessary and useful appendage. But she had immediately noticed Ben's hands, and had felt a deep, inner quiver of response on sight of them.

Why? She couldn't help but wonder.

Tactile hands. Caressing hands. Strong hands. Hands possessing the sensual power to stroke a woman into mindless pleasure.

The stuff of women's dreams—or fantasies, she chided herself, repudiating the quivering sensation.

Each time she caught herself engaged in the "Ben" daydreaming, Cyndi advised herself to grow up.

The diner officially closed at six; she usually swept the occasional last lingering customer out the door by six-thirty.

"Hi." Jess flashed a grin at Cyndi when she entered the kitchen through the back door. "You look as wilted as the marigolds in the flower bed."

"That's about how I feel," Cyndi said, swiping the

back of a hand over her damp forehead and dropping like a stone onto a kitchen chair.

Jess stood, bent over the kitchen table, rolling out pie dough with an ancient wood rolling pin.

"I can't say you look much fresher," Cyndi went on, pointedly glancing at her sister's flushed and sweat-shiny cheeks. "What kind of pies are you baking now?"

"Not pies, apple dumplings." The dough flattened to her satisfaction, Jess straightened and set the rolling pin aside. "I though it would be a change for the customers."

"They'll gobble them up," Cyndi predicted, then qualified with a grin, "That is, if Dad doesn't beat them to it."

Jess grinned back at her. "He's already given me fair warning; he claims my dumplings are almost as good as Mother's."

"They are," Cyndi said, confirming their father's praise. "And that's some compliment, because I remember, and Mom's dumplings were scrumptious."

"Why . . ."—Jess gave a small, but pleased sounding laugh.—"thank you, Cyn."

"You're welcome, and you deserve the praise," Cyndi responded, laughing with her sister.

It was odd, but while Cyndi enjoyed cooking, and running the diner, it certainly hadn't been her life's ambition. On the other hand, Jess loved to cook, and most especially to bake. She produced heavenly pies and cakes, yet she had declined Cyndi's offer to take over in the diner, claiming it would be unfair of her to usurp her sister's position. Jess fed her culinary need to create by producing mouth-watering desserts for home and diner.

"Busy at the store today?"

Since before the previous Christmas, Jess had been

working in a small, family-owned department store in Hillsboro, the town Cyndi had mentioned to Ben Ganster. She drove the nineteen miles back and forth five days a week in their father's old Ford truck they affectionately called the black bomb.

"No." Jess shook her head. "We're in the middle of summer slack. Young Mr. Adams said business probably won't pick up till it's time for back-to-school shopping."

Young Mr. Adams, first name Jeffrey, had a third behind his name, and at age thirty-one, he wasn't all that young anymore. He was the only son of Mr. Jeffrey Adams, Junior, and the only grandson of the first Mr. Jeffrey Adams, the founder of the family business.

Cyndi wryly noted that her sister seemed to be mentioning the younger Adams, and present heir, a bit frequently lately. In truth, the man was good looking, although he didn't cause as much as an interested flutter in her.

"You've got a crush on him, don't you?" she said, giving in to an impish urge to tease.

"What?" The flush on Jess's cheeks spread to her neck and ears. "No! Of course not," she insisted, too strongly. "He's way older than me, thirteen years older. And . . . and . . ."

"And?" Cyndi prompted, fascinated by the betraying play of emotions her sister unintentionally revealed.

"And . . . anyway, he's . . . he's . . ." Jess hesitated, visible pain in her eyes, her voice. "He's way above me. I mean . . . I'm not good enough for—"

"Wait—a—minute," Cyndi cut in, her voice rife with outrage. "Don't you dare put yourself down like that. You're a beautiful woman, a truly nice person, and good enough for any man, and don't you ever forget it."

"I guess I should have gone to college."

"Why?" Cyndi demanded, blinking in confusion at

her sister's sudden veering from the topic. "Though Lord knows you could have—and in my opinion, should have—with the grade average you maintained in high school." She frowned. "I don't get it. You didn't want to go to college, not even that culinary school your guidance counselor recommended. It was your choice to go to work instead." She shook her head. "I really don't understand where you're coming from, Jess. You said you enjoy working in the store, interacting with people. Why are you now questioning your decision?"

"Well . . . I've been thinking that maybe I should have gone, to acquire a little polish or something. You know . . ." Her voice faded on a wrenching sigh.

Hearing her sister's sigh brought a sharp pang to Cyndi's chest and fired her normally placid temper. Her hazel eyes spitting angry sparks, she leaped out of the chair, and launched a defense.

"Polish or something? What's wrong with your own natural outgoing personality?" she demanded in a choked, gritty voice. Not waiting for an answer, she rattled off another question. "What you're saying is you've convinced yourself you require a dash of sophistication to appeal to a certain man . . . right?"

Jess hung her head, lowered her eyes, and mumbled, "I . . . I suppose so."

"Uh-huh." Cyndi produced a very unsophisticated snort. "Let me tell you something, Jessica Marie Swoyer." Circling the table, she grasped her sister's chin and raised her head, forcing the sad-eyed girl to face her. "Mr. Jeffrey Adams is no better than you are, with or without the third behind his name. And if he thinks he is, then he's a snob and a cretin, and not nearly good enough for you."

Planting her hands on her hips, she glared into her sister's eyes, waited for a response . . . and waited. The first tear that spilled over to roll down Jess's flushed cheek brought a tight, lumpy feeling into Cyndi's throat.

Damn the man, she railed in silent fury.

"Has he said something?" she snapped. "Has he insinuated that you're beneath him in some way?"

"No!" Jess shook her head. "No, he . . . he . . . Oh, Cyndi, he doesn't know I exist!"

Cyndi stared at her in blank incredulity. "Then what in the world is all your angsting about?"

"Well . . ." Jess broke off to sniffle. "I just thought, maybe, if I had gone to college, improved myself, you know, he might have taken notice."

Wonderful. All that thunder and fury for nothing. Cyndi drew a long, calming breath. She felt like a blithering idiot.

"I see," she muttered. "And here I thought he had insulted you. I was ready to punch him out for you, teach him a lesson. Silly me." Pivoting, she retraced her steps around the table and flopped noisily onto a chair.

"I'm sorry." Jess sniffed again. "And you're not silly, you never were. I'm the one being silly," she offered, contritely. "Isn't that so?"

"A tad."

"I overreacted?" Her anxiety evident, Jess picked at the rolled dough.

Cyndi's lips twitched. "A bit."

"You're laughing at me," her sister accused, pouting to conceal the smile quivering on her mouth.

"Would I do that?" Cyndi grinned.

"Yes." Her pout gave way to the smile.

"No hard feelings?"

Jess shook her head. "No."

"Then would you stop mangling that dough, before it's overworked to the consistency of shoe leather?"

"Oh!" Jess shot a startled look from Cyndi to the

pastry dough, and then back to Cyndi. "Oh . . . my gosh . . . my dumplings!" she cried, stricken. "They'll be ruined!"

The horrified expression on her sister's face did Cyndi in, and though she fought the laughter crowding her throat, she lost the battle.

Laughter bursting from her, Cyndi sprang from her chair and ran around the table to throw her arms around Jess.

"Aw . . . c'm'on, honey," she said, between laughing and gasping for breath. "It's all right. You'll see." Still chuckling, she released the now also laughing Jess, and wiped tears of laughter from her eyes.

"I feel like a ditz," Jess muttered, slanting a disgusted look at the finger-marked pastry.

"I'm sure it's savable," Cyndi assured her, turning to the sink to wash her hands. She glanced at the clock while drying them, and grimaced. "And we'd better do it right smartly, too. Dad'll be closing the station soon, and he's going to be expecting to find hot dumplings waiting for him."

"Oh, gosh, you're right." Jess's sky blue eyes, so like the color their father's used to be, flew to the clock, then back to Cyndi. "I don't see how we can possibly make it, have some ready for him by the time he gets here . . ."

She broke off, spinning around to rush to the fridge to remove the prepared filling mixture of apples, cinnamon, and other spices. Her step brisk, she returned to the table.

"But we'll be close," she said breathlessly, her manner efficient, her grin confident.

"What can I do?" Cyndi asked, watching Jess smooth the edges of the mangled dough before spooning the apple mixture into the center of the pastry.

"Start rolling out . . ." she began, then she stopped, shoved the mixing bowl into Cyndi's hands, and circled around behind her. "You spoon and wrap the pastry, I'll roll out." She flashed a teasing grin. "No offense but, you have a tendency to overwork pastry dough."

Talking and laughing together, Cyndi and Jess had prepared one tray of eight dumplings and slid them into the oven. They were working on the second tray when their father came in through the kitchen door.

"Evenin', ladies." He gave his customary greeting.

"Hi, Dad," they chorused, simultaneously pausing in their work to offer smiles with their greeting.

Cyndi felt an accustomed twinge of pain in her heart as she watched her father shuffle across the room and carefully lower his curved body into the chair she had recently vacated. If she should live to be a hundred, she knew she would still experience the same rush of sympathy whenever she saw or thought about her formerly vigorous father.

He sniffed, drawing in the aroma of baking apple dumplings. A smile of anticipation curved his lips.

"Can I get you a cup of coffee, Dad?" Cyndi offered, hoping to distract him.

"Do I get a dumpling with it?"

Cyndi and Jess exchanged chagrined glances.

"Ah . . . mmm, the dumplings aren't quite ready yet, Dad," Jess said, quickly adding, "It'll only be another couple of minutes."

Angling his head, he shifted a look between the two women. "What were you two doing all this time?"

"Talking," Cyndi said, giving a dismissive flick of her hand. "Girl talk . . . you know."

A teasing light sprang to life in his washed-out blue eyes. "Telling Jess about that stranger who stopped by today?"

"Stranger?" Jess was immediately alert, and curious. "What stranger?"

Cyndi stifled a groan. She hadn't planned on mentioning him; so much for her plans.

"He was just a man . . . traveling." She hoped Jess would let it go at that.

She should have known better. Her eyes avid for information, Jess pounced.

"What do you mean, he was just a man?" she demanded. "Who was he? Where did he come from?" Her eyes gleamed with interest. "What did he look like?"

Cyndi shrugged. "Well . . . he was just a—" She was cut off by her father.

"I guess you'd call him a good-looking man, well dressed, tall, seemed to be in fine physical shape." He always noted a man's outward physical condition.

"Really?" Jess actually purred, casting a glittering glance at her sister.

"Oh, come on—" Cyndi again began, but was once again cut off by her father.

"Had a kinda stern look about him though."

"Stern?" Jess repeated. "How so?"

Cyndi heaved a sigh of impatience. This was getting too ridiculous.

"I don't know how to explain it, exactly . . ."

"Formidable," Cyndi interjected, figuring it had to be her turn to interrupt. "Formidable, arrogant, and intimidating."

"Ohhh . . . Formidable, arrogant, *and* intimidating." Jess produced a delicate shudder. "How exciting."

"Will you get real?" Cyndi jeered, rolling her eyes. "How in the world can you think of someone who projects such a negative appearance as being exciting?" she demanded.

Yet, she had found him so . . . and more, she acknowl-edged in silent chagrin. When he had bothered to put forth the effort, Ben Ganster was the most exciting and interesting man she had ever met. Not that she had met all that many, but Cyndi certainly wasn't about to admit to it.

Fortunately, the oven timer began ringing, diverting her sister and father from the subject of Ben Ganster.

For a few minutes conversation ceased. Working together like well-choreographed dancers, Cyndi and Jess removed the aromatic tray of dumplings from the oven, finished putting together the second and third trays, slid them into the oven, then served one of the hot apple pastries and a cup of coffee to their patiently waiting, eager father.

He dug into the dumpling.

Jess dug into Cyndi.

"Tell me more," Jess pleaded.

"More what?" Cyndi played dumb.

"You know what," Jess said, tossing a chiding glance at her sister while continuing to roll out still more circles of the pastry dough. "More about that man, the formida-ble, arrogant, intimidating stranger."

Cyndi shrugged. "What's to tell?"

Jess tossed her another look. "Oh, like, what did he say? Where did he come from? Where was he going? That kind of information."

"Said he was just driving," Carl Swoyer inserted in between mouthfuls of pastry. "Going no place in partic-ular." He swallowed and grinned. "I told him he had found it."

Jess laughed. "You've got that right."

Although she didn't want to, Cyndi had to laugh too; there was no arguing with the truth.

"So, where was he from?" Jess persisted, diverting a

glance from her pastry to her father and sister. "Did anyone ask?"

"Philadelphia," Cyndi supplied the answer, knowing her sister wouldn't quit until it was forthcoming. "He said he was from Philadelphia."

"Ohhh," Jess sighed. "I'd like to go to Philadelphia someday."

Thinking she'd like to be almost any other place just then, Cyndi grasped the moment to distract Jess from the man under discussion. "You could be leaving for Philadelphia this fall, if you had applied to that cooking school your guidance counselor recommended," she reminded her.

"I know." Jess gave a careless shrug, while resting a gentle and concerned look on her happily munching father.

"Then why didn't you?" Pushing his now empty dish aside, Carl angled his head to level a probing stare at his youngest child.

"Well . . ." She shrugged again. "You know."

"Uh-huh." He nodded. "But I still want to hear you say it."

Tired, sweating like a field hand, Cyndi leaned against the old and chipped porcelain sink, resigned once more to hearing yet another form of the argument her father had given her eight years ago about her decision to forgo college and remain at home.

Jess tried a dodge. "Well, I already had a good job, a job I really enjoy."

Won't wash, Cyndi thought.

"So you've said before," Carl observed, a skeptical smile shadowing his lips. "But I can't help but wonder if it's the job, the work, you enjoy," he went on, his voice dry, "or the man you work for."

Bulls-eye. Cyndi smiled.

Jess fidgeted, her fingers again picking at the pastry. "Okay, so I like Mr. Adams," she muttered. "But I also like the work."

"I believe you," Carl said. "But, to my mind, that's not the question."

Neatly laid trap. Cyndi silently applauded her father's tactics, recognizing them from past experience.

"Well, then, what is the question?" Jess cried, rushing right into his trap.

He didn't hesitate to spring it. "Do you love it, as much as you love the work you've been doing here at home"—he paused while his gaze swept over the baking paraphernalia—"after regular working hours?"

Jess didn't answer for long seconds, during which she glanced at Cyndi in a silent plea for help.

In turn, Cyndi glanced at their father; he smiled in understanding, but offered no assistance.

She was on her own, she thought. And then she decided, Wrong. She wasn't on her own. She had been there, done that, and bought the tee shirt.

She looked at Jess . . . and shrugged.

Jess got the message. She fiddled with the pastry dough. She shifted. She sighed. And then she faced her father and softly said, "No."

"You should have gone to school."

"But I couldn't leave you and Cyndi here on your own!" Jess cried out in her own defense.

Carl shifted his gaze to Cyndi and shook his head in despair. "The very same reason that you gave me."

"But the situation was altogether different then, Dad," Cyndi objected. "The kids were too young—Jess only ten—and I couldn't just up and leave you to take care of them, the station, and the diner." Thinking she was beginning to sound like a cracked record, since she had earlier given this same explanation to Ben Ganster, she nevertheless forged ahead. "I couldn't do it."

"And neither can I," Jess jumped in to say, knowing a cue when she heard one.

"But the situation's different now, Jess." Cyndi turned her gaze, and a frown, on her sister. "The boys are gone. Dad and I can handle things here. There's no reason why you shouldn't—or couldn't—attend that cooking school."

"But—"

"That's right," Carl cut Jess off, then shifted to pin Cyndi to the sink with his intent stare. "But the same reasoning applies to you. You could have gone to college, you *should* have gone to college. *I* could have—and still can—handle everything here."

"How?" Cyndi and Jess demanded in unison.

He shrugged. "I could've got someone to help out."

"Who?" Again, the women spoke at the same time.

"Emily Davidson."

Emily Davidson? For a moment, Cyndi stared at her father in perplexed astonishment, not only because of the name he had given but the certainty in his voice.

Emily Davidson—née Walters—was a neighbor who lived with her father a mile or so along the blacktopped road, farther up into the mountains. The same age as Cyndi's mother, Emily had married young, and had moved to Hillsboro with her husband, who had been a self-employed roofer, subcontracting out to various home builders and contractors.

As Cyndi had heard the story, Emily and her young husband had been married only a few years when he had made a fatal misstep on the job. He had pitched off a roof, and succumbed to the subsequent head and internal injuries.

Childless, alone in a town that was still unfamiliar to

her, Emily had sold everything she and her husband
had owned, packed her personal belongings, and
returned to her parents' home.

Emily's mother had passed away while Cyndi was in
junior high, and a few years later her father had suffered
a crippling stroke. Emily had cared for him ever since.

Cyndi had always felt rather sorry for the woman,
who was attractive and pleasant, with ever dwindling
prospects of a life, husband, and home of her own.

Apparently, Jess had been as startled as Cyndi by the
name their father had so confidently tossed into the
mix. Jess stood beside the table, gazing at him in blank
wonder. Cyndi was the first to find her voice.

"Emily Davidson?" she exclaimed after the lengthy
silence. "But she has her hands full looking after Mr.
Walters."

"Even so, she could've and would've helped with the
kids and the diner then. She still would help with the
house and the diner."

"But how do you know that?"

Carl gave Cyndi his patient-father look. "I asked her,
of course."

"But—"

"Cyndi," Carl broke in, "Harold Walters isn't nearly
as helpless as he lets people believe." A smile feathered
his lips. "The only person he hasn't fooled is Emily.
She knows the situation . . . more'n likely, better than
him."

What could she say? Cyndi asked herself, glancing at
her sister.

Jess remained equally speechless; but then, what
could *she* say?

If it was suddenly obvious to Cyndi that her father
had been seeing and talking to Emily a lot more than
either she or Jess had imagined, what was there to be

said? But it was now clear as crystal, at least to Cyndi, that her father's visits to the Walters house a couple of times a week had entailed more than playing checkers with the infirm old man to keep him company.

And she had her suspicions. From the expression on her sister's face, Jess did, as well.

Could it be possible their father had wanted them to go off to college for a reason other than the furthering of their educations? a reason of the heart as well as of the mind?

Cyndi was tempted—very tempted—to simply ask him if he had been keeping company more with the daughter than the father, but she refrained. If their father had wanted his daughters to know the details of his personal life, he'd have confided in them. Since he hadn't, she figured she had no right to demand he do so at this late date.

She looked at her sister. Jess raised her eyebrows and shrugged. Cyndi was well aware of Carl, the faint smile still curving his mouth, monitoring the silent communication between her and Jess.

Silence, still and watchful, shimmered on the aromatic, apple-cinnamon–laden air, and then Carl grinned.

"Worked it out, have you?" He shifted his gleaming gaze from Cyndi to Jess.

"You and . . . er . . . Emily are . . . ah . . . good friends?" Jess blurted out, disingenuously.

Cyndi winced at the euphemism.

Carl laughed. "No. We're lovers." He laughed again at the obvious shock induced in his daughters by his bluntness. "We have been lovers for over four years now." A teasing light danced in his faded blue eyes. "Up until then, we were just good friends."

"Dad . . . really, I don't—" Cyndi began.

"You're both adults," he said, once again cutting off her stumbling words. "You both know the facts of life. And, the fact of my life is, I am not yet fifty"—his smile turned wry—"even if I do look ten years older than that."

"No!" Jess exclaimed.

"You do not," Cyndi said, and not as a sop to his ego. It was true that, although his spine was bent, giving him the appearance of an older man from a distance, up close his face was amazingly unlined and youthful.

His smile softened. "Thank you, ladies. Strange, but Emily doesn't think I look a day over forty."

Cyndi had always liked Emily. She liked her even more now; apparently, the woman possessed discernment as well as good judgment.

"Anyway, to get back to my point," he continued. "I'm a normal man, with all the built-in urges of the animal. And Emily's a lovely, warmhearted woman." He sighed, and raised his eyebrows. "Any questions?"

"Mother?" Jess ventured in a small voice.

"I loved her." He cranked his head around to look at Cyndi. "Do you remember?"

"Yes." Cyndi's voice was soft, so was her smile. Memory swirled, and she blinked at a sudden rush of moisture to her eyes. "You always called Mom your queen."

"Yes." He inclined his head. "She always will be my queen, and she still rules a part of me. But she's gone . . . and I'm alive." He hesitated, as if unsure about saying more, then he murmured, "I call Emily my . . . er . . . countess."

"Not princess?" Cyndi teased, trying to lighten the somber atmosphere.

"What?" His eyes mirrored her teasing. "And be unfaithful to my princesses Cyndi and Jess?"

"Oh, Daddy, I—" Jess was interrupted by the oven timer.

"Look after your dumplings," he instructed, pushing himself upright. "I'm gonna get a bath and then head up the road to visit Mr. . . ." He paused in the doorway leading to the narrow hallway, and straightened, as best he could. "I'm going to visit my countess."

He left the room—left his daughters with food for thought, and virtually speechless.

Cyndi and Jess didn't discuss their father's revelations. Quiet and pensive, they worked together, and when the baking was finished, they went to their own respective rooms, each obviously consumed with her own thoughts.

Chapter Four

Bennett sat slouched in the molded plastic chair, staring vacantly at the flickering TV screen. There was a movie playing; he hadn't a clue as to what the film was about.

He didn't know what he was about, either.

After leaving the diner—and without conscious direction—Bennett had driven along the blacktopped road, then had made a turn at the sign marked HILLSBORO, 19 MILES.

To his surprise, he had found the town had a quaint, kind of nostalgic appeal. It also had a fairly new and modern motel, part of a well-known chain. It even had an on-site coffee shop and bar and grill.

Soon after checking into the motel, he left again to check out the town. Bennett couldn't miss the family-owned department store Cynthia had mentioned, it was the largest building on the main street. Unearthing the bookstore proved a little more difficult.

But eventually he found it—and found it wanting,

nondescript. The store, incongruously and erroneously named Books, Books, and More Books, New and Used, was located off the main street, in what had previously been the small living room of an equally small, nondescript private home.

In Bennett's admittedly biased opinion, the store's selection of books, new and used, was not only inadequate, but pitiful; the new books were old, the used books, older. Though he looked, searched, he could find nothing of much value, monetarily, intellectually, or pleasurably.

Little wonder Cynthia had expressed a wish to run rampant through libraries and spend weeks in his stores, Bennett mused, shaking his head as he exited the cramped place.

Restless, he then strolled along the streets of town, asking himself what in the name of hell he was doing there. It was the middle of a work week. He wasn't working. It was the middle of the afternoon. Actually he knew precisely what time it was; he'd glanced at his watch at regular intervals. And, although the entire town possessed a quaint ambiance—sort of—it wasn't his town.

He returned to the motel. The room was clean, the decor functional. It did have the one luxury of cable TV. But, like many book people, Bennett was a reader, he wasn't a watcher.

He called his mother.

"Well, Bennett, how are you?"

He gave a silent sigh. It wasn't his mother; it was his aunt—the instigator of this damned vacation.

"Compared to whom?" he responded, not quite successful in keeping the note of bored cynicism from his voice.

She laughed, proving his private theory that it was next to impossible to deflate a dedicated Pollyanna.

"Oh, Bennie, you're so amusing."

He ground his teeth. If necessary, he could tolerate the nickname Ben—though he scowled each time Cynthia called him that, he rather liked the sound of it from her—but he cringed at Bennie. Fortunately, his Aunt Louise was the only person who had ever called him that, and Bennett didn't see her all that frequently.

"Happy to be of service," he said dryly. "Recalling that mother had an appointment with the heart specialist this afternoon, I called to ask how she is doing."

"Very well," Louise assured him. "In fact, she is doing fine. Her doctor said he's pleased with her progress."

"May I speak to her?" he said, hanging on to his rapidly dwindling patience.

"Of course, here she is now."

"Bennett, how nice."

He felt a rush of relief. His mother did indeed sound fine, almost her former chipper self.

"Where are you?"

Good question, he thought, skimming a glance around the neat, yet unexceptional room. "Right now, I'm in a motel in a small town called Hillsboro, in Western Pennsylvania," he answered. "The mountains are beautiful," he tacked on, feeling he should say something positive.

"Are you having a good time there?" Frances's voice was bright with anticipation and hope.

Oh, super. Naturally, he couldn't repeat his thoughts aloud. Bennett suppressed a sigh. Deciding that hedging was better than an outright lie, he answered, "It's . . . interesting."

"Oh, good, but . . ." She hesitated.

He braced himself.

"Have you met anyone, any person in particular who is interesting?" she asked, much too casually.

He was on the verge of confessing that he hadn't, when an image flashed into his mind. "As a matter of fact, I have," he said, glad she couldn't see his smug smile. "Her name is Cynthia," he went on, soothing his conscience with the assurance that he had found her interesting, just not in the way his mother meant.

"Lovely name," Frances said, her tone fairly oozing satisfaction. "May I presume, then, that you might not be home next week as planned?"

Oh, hell. Bennett clamped his lips on a groan, and chastised himself for having mentioned Cynthia's name. Oh, well. He gave a mental shrug; let his mother presume what she wished, he decided.

"I'm . . . er, not sure yet," he stalled. "I need to call Connie, find out how she's doing in the office."

Frances trilled what in effect was a light laugh of dismissal. "Bennett, Connie has been your secretary ever since you've been in business. I feel certain she is more than capable of dealing with the day-to-day details of the book business for a few weeks."

Easy for her to say, he thought, suppressing a burst of irritation. His mother didn't have a clue about the details of the book business.

"Yes, well, I'll give her a call anyway. I've been checking in every other day," he said, relieved for the shift in the discussion from Cynthia to business.

He should live so long. Frances was not so easily diverted from course.

"Whatever," she said, displaying impatience. "Tell me more about this young woman . . ." She paused, as if struck by a sudden thought. "She is a young woman, isn't she, Bennett?"

Bennett simply shook his head, did some quick mental

calculations, and answered, "Yes, Mother. She's in her mid twenties."

"Perfect," she responded, in what could only be described as an actual purr. "Does she live there, in the town?"

"No." He knew his answer wouldn't satisfy, so before she could demand more, he expanded. "She lives some nineteen miles outside of town, farther up into the mountains. Her father owns a service station and . . . er, restaurant there," he explained, nearly choking on the embellishment of the truth. "I stopped to fill the gas tank and to have lunch."

"It's not the most romantic meeting I could have imagined." She laughed. "But it is original."

If you only knew, he thought, laughing with her as he envisioned the antiquated station and diner. But he wasn't about to offer the information that the place had been original some forty or fifty years before.

"I wasn't looking for a romantic meeting," he pointed out. "If you'll recall."

"Too clearly," she retorted, then immediately qualified, "but isn't that when exciting things happen . . . when you're least expecting them?"

Exciting? Right. Bennett didn't voice this cynical thought, of course.

"Seems like it," he agreed, simply to avoid disagreeing. In fact, he knew he'd agree to almost anything rather than upset his mother.

However, convinced the conversation could only go downhill from there, he deemed it wise to end it—before he dug himself deeper into the hole of prevarication.

"I'm going to hang up now, Mother. I want to call Connie before she leaves for the day."

"Oh . . ." Her disappointment came through, loud

and clear. "But I hoped you'd tell me more about Cynthia."

Bennett heaved a silent sigh. "There's not much more to tell, Mother." His reasonable tone concealed his dwindling patience. "I just met her."

"But you will keep me informed?" In truth, it wasn't a request, but an outright order.

He bristled . . . but caved. "Yes, of course. I'll call you again in a day or so."

After enduring her extended goodbye, and disconnecting, Bennett stared moodily at the phone. He felt like hell. Why had he done it? he railed in disgust. Why had he mentioned Cynthia's name?

Actually he knew full well why he had brought her name into the conversation, and he accepted the responsibility for having done so. It was appeasement, pure and simple.

But then, in retrospect, he acknowledged that there was nothing simple about it.

In a clichéd move, he had boldly stepped forth, out of the frying pan and into the fire.

Good work, Ganster, he derided himself. If you had half a brain, you'd be smart enough to be dangerous.

Lifting the phone receiver, he vented his spleen by punching in his office number.

"Good afternoon, Ganster Books," he heard in Connie's cigarette-smoky voice. "Sorry, the gangster isn't here."

"That's Ganster." He gave a loud, long-suffering sigh; Connie delighted in calling him "gangster," which just highlighted how well they knew each other.

She laughed. "I knew it was you, Bennett."

"How?"

"I'm psychic?"

"Or I'm predictable," he suggested wryly.

"No, Bennett," she disputed his suggestion. "You're a lot of things—dilligent, dedicated, and at times perhaps a little dictatorial, but never predictable."

"Uh-huh," he grunted. "Dictatorial?"

"I said, perhaps a little."

"I heard you. Don't you want to throw in tyrant?"

"Would I accuse you of that?" She sounded all wide-eyed and innocent.

He didn't answer.

She laughed.

He shook his head in despair, for an instant considering the threat of unemployment, but instantly rejecting the idea. She knew as well as he that she was as close as one could get to irreplaceable.

"So, are you up to your eyebrows in emergencies?"

"Nothing I can't handle," she said in tones of supreme, and not misplaced, confidence.

He sighed again. He was doing that a lot lately. "Okay, if I'm not needed there . . ."

"Of course you're needed here," she interrupted with a display of impatience. "But I can hold the fort while you take a break." Now she heaved a sigh. "I swear, Bennett, you are not to be believed."

"What's that supposed to mean?" he demanded.

"You know damn well what I mean," she shot back. "From your attitude, one would think you were banished instead of on vacation . . . a vacation, by the way, that you really needed."

Chastised by his secretary. What was the world coming to? A reluctant grin softened the strain of his tight lips.

"It was as obvious as that, huh?"

"Yes." While her voice was adamant, Bennett imagined he could see the smile curving her lips. "You've been running yourself ragged for months. You really did need to get away for a while. Why don't you just relax and enjoy the break?"

Enjoy. He'd been hearing that word a lot recently. Was it the buzzword of the month? Bennett's grin widened.

"If you say so," he responded, his voice dry as day-old toast. "I'll get back to you in a day or so."

"Why?" she dared to challenge.

"Because I own the business," he retorted, laughter woven through his stern tone.

"Oh. Okay. 'Bye."

Bennett heard a click and then the dial tone. His laughter erupted as he replaced the receiver.

What now? It was still too early for dinner; too late for a midafternoon snack.

He settled into the chair and flicked on the TV to do a little channel surfing. To his untrained eye, there appeared to be an inordinate amount of scenes depicting couples in various states of undress, groping one another while thrashing about on a bed or a couch or, in one instance, on the floor.

Was this the kind of stuff people were watching in the afternoon? he marveled, slightly shocked despite his maturity and sexual experience.

Bennett grimaced with distaste, but then, he had never viewed a porno film, nor taken in an X-rated movie. He personally considered sex a private matter between two consenting adults, not a spectator sport.

But the brief glance he had of the couple did remind him of his own celibate state; he decided it was not a comfortable state to live in.

How long had it been since he and Denise had shared a bed and each other?

Two weeks? No. Three. No. He shook his head, in negation and disbelief. Due to the circumstances of his mother's illness, and their conflicting and erratic schedules, it had been a couple of months since they had been together.

No wonder he was tense, wired, and frustrated.

Bennett sighed with the realization that he should have flown west to be with Denise, if only for a few days . . . and nights.

Too late now, he told himself, sighing again.

He flicked to another channel. A blue, fluffy puppet was stuffing its mouth with cookies. Flick. A white-jacketed chef in a tall hat was putting the finishing touches to an elaborate, delicious-looking, probably calorie-laden dessert.

He finally settled on a channel running an old movie. It soon became apparent that the film was a romantic comedy from Hollywood's heyday, one of those innocuous films with improbable plot twists, designed to draw the protagonists together and separate them in turn.

It didn't matter to Bennett. He wasn't paying attention to it anyway, but the background noise banished the silence from the room.

Bennett's butt withstood the hard plastic chair for all of ten minutes, then it sent out a complaint that drove him to his feet to pace.

The movie reeled on.

Standing at the window, he counted the cars in the motel parking lot.

Enjoy echoed inside his head.

Cursing aloud, he drew the drapes together over the window, stripped, then headed for the bathroom.

The movie continued to unwind.

A hot shower had a similar effect on Bennett.

The film was over, a beer commercial running, when he flicked the TV off on his way out. There had been a happy ending. Bennett knew this, even though he hadn't seen it; he recalled that, back then, those types of movies always had happy endings. And the customer had usually left the theater feeling good, upbeat, satisfied.

The thought recalled something he had said to Cynthia: progress had it's price.

Bennett feared a measure of that price was innocence.

Bypassing the motel coffee shop, he got into his car and cruised around the town, looking for a restaurant. He finally pulled onto the parking lot of a decent-looking roadside steak and seafood place with a bar and grill. It was on the outskirts of town.

The place was crowded, primarily with couples. C and W music swelled from the jukebox. There were no frills, but the place was clean, the servers were friendly and efficient, and the food was excellent. Bennett's steak was delivered as ordered, medium rare, pink in the middle. The baked potato was done all the way through. The beer was cold. Laughter and music surrounded him, while closing him out.

After paying the check, and overtipping the waiter, Bennett left the bar and grill feeling physically full and emotionally empty. He was, in a word, lonely.

Dejected—and feeling stupid for it—Bennett returned to the motel, determined to start for home in the morning. He had had just about all he could stand of *enjoyment*.

Bennett woke early with the weird idea playing around the edges of his mind. He had no clue as to where the idea came from, what had sparked it.

Had he dreamed it? he wondered, while dressing, then getting his stuff together. Although he hadn't paid much attention to the romantic plot, could the ridiculous idea have been spawned by the movie he'd left playing on the TV before he went out for dinner?

Maybe that was it, he mused, double-checking the bathroom to make sure he hadn't forgotten anything before leaving the motel.

Or maybe the idea had been instilled in his subconscious by the titles on some of those old historical romance novels in the store he'd visited yesterday afternoon.

Whichever, the idea was too improbable to work in real life. It could only work in a light romantic comedy or a historical romance of the heavy-breathing variety.

Besides, he ruminated, only half-conscious of heading out of town in the direction from which he had entered it. No nineties woman would so much as consider it, least of all a certain young woman named Cynthia Swoyer.

Still . . .

Chapter Five

It was going on eleven, and Cyndi hadn't had a customer since a little after eight, when that trucker who had taken a wrong turn came in for coffee and directions.

She was bored. The place was clean. For want of something to do, she was leaning on the counter, frowning over a synonym in the daily paper's crossword puzzle, when the sound of a car pulling up in front drew her gaze to the windows. The car was familiar; fairly new and midnight blue.

Ben Ganster!

A thrill streaked through her, and her heart did a little skip-jump as she watched him slide out of the car and stride to the screen door.

What could he be doing here again? she wondered, straightening away from the counter with a show of composure she was far from feeling. She had felt certain she'd never lay eyes on him again.

The screen door creaked. He stepped inside. Cyndi drew a slow, calming breath.

"Hello." He smiled.

The calming breath became lodged in her throat. She swallowed, drew another quick breath, and managed a weak smile in return.

"Hi. Lost again?"

Ben shook his head, laughed.

Oh, glory. The sound of his soft laughter rang a loud warning bell inside her head; it was too attractive, too masculine, too much for her to handle with equanimity. So, of course, she concealed herself behind cynical flippancy.

"Slumming, then?"

Abruptly, his laughter ceased. His features tightened. A chill expression chased the warmth from his dark eyes.

"Do you really believe that, Cynthia?" Frost rimmed his tone, and sent a shiver down her spine.

"Cyndi," she said absently, giving a quick shake of her head in denial. "No, not really." She heard the note of genuine contrition in her own voice. "I'm sorry, Ben."

"Bennett," he shot back at her with cool, controlled deliberation. "Apology accepted."

"Thank you." Cyndi refrained from saying his name. "Then, if you're not lost, what are you doing here?" She flashed what she hoped was a conciliatory smile. "At the edge of civilized PA, I mean?"

"Would you believe I was motivated by a craving for another chocolate malted milk shake?" The warmth was back in his voice, and his eyes.

Cyndi felt the tingling heat from the tip of her toes to the top of her head. Afraid to trust her voice to her parched throat, she gave him a skeptical look in response.

"No?"

"No," she echoed.

He heaved a sigh. "I thought not."

"Well, then?" she prompted, intrigued by him personally and by his purpose in returning.

Until then, Ben had remained standing just inside the screen door. Giving her another devastating smile and an elegant shrug, he moved forward, closing the distance to the counter, causing a delicious sense of anticipation to go ricocheting through Cyndi.

What the heck!

What was it about this man? she asked herself, suppressing an impulse to shiver. Not since her freshmen year of high school had Cyndi experienced such intensity of interest and response to a male. At that time, the male in question had been a senior and the quarterback of the high-school football team, and *he* had never given the slightest indication that he knew she was alive . . . until that one awful night.

Whereas this man, this Bennett Ganster, not only gave a clear indication of an awareness of her as a living entity, he displayed a keen interest in her with his smile and the warmth of his gaze.

He wanted something. Cyndi hoped she was wrong . . . but feared she was right.

In her experience, admittedly limited to that jerk in high school, men always wanted something when they turned on the charm.

The intuitive certainty that Ben had targeted her for a specific purpose dulled the immediate sense of pleasure she felt on seeing him again.

Quashing a sudden and overwhelming urge to move

back, away from the counter, Cyndi held her ground—
and his probing dark-eyed stare.

"Coffee?"

Coffee? For an instant, Cyndi gazed at him in
bemusement, mentally thrown by his question. Then
realization dawned, and she felt like an idiot.

"Yes, of course I have coffee," she said, frowning to
cover her chagrin at her brief lack of comprehension.
"Made it fresh a little while ago." She raised her brows.
"Do you want some?"

"No, I was just curious to know if you had some," he
replied in a teasing drawl. "Yes, I want some. If it's not
too much trouble," he said, a hint of a devilish smile
playing at the corners of his mouth.

"No trouble at all." Cyndi grinned. What else could
she do under the circumstances? It was either grin, or
reach across the counter and touch that smile with her
fingertips.

He grinned back at her.

Her knees went weak.

Feeling strange, excited, light-headed, she turned
away to get the coffee—and to get her rattled self under
control.

"Would you like something to go with that?" she
asked, placing the heavy coffee mug on the counter in
front of him. "My sister baked apple dumplings last
night."

"Apple dumplings? Home baked, from scratch?"

"Yes." She had to laugh at the expression of near
awe on his face. "From scratch."

"Incredible."

"Not really." Her voice was dry. "Believe it or not,
there are still people in this country who bake pastries
and even cook their own food."

The look he gave her was as dry as her voice. "But their numbers are dwindling, I suspect."

"Yet another bit of the price for progress?"

He sighed. "I suppose."

"So, do you want a dumpling?"

Ben was shaking his head before she had finished speaking. "No, thank you. If I had known . . ." He shrugged, looking rueful. "I ate a large breakfast this morning."

He glanced down at the cup, frowned, stared into the dark depths of the brew, not unlike a fairground's fortune teller making a performance of reading tea leaves, Cyndi reflected, the feeling growing inside her that he wanted something and was working himself up to the point of asking.

"Uhhh . . ." he paused, shrugged again. "My mother recently suffered a heart attack."

What? Cyndi stared at him. Coming, as it had, from out of nowhere, his comment left her blank, bewildered, and blinking.

"I'm . . . sorry to hear that," she murmured, after a tiny, wit-gathering hesitation. "Is she going to be all right?"

"Yes." Ben nodded, took a tentative sip of his coffee, then went on. "Oh, she's not fully recovered yet. She'll have to be careful for a while . . ." He sighed. "In fact, maybe a long while, but she has made remarkable progress."

"I . . . uh . . . good . . ." Cyndi paused to draw a quick breath, uncertain how to respond, and confused as to his purpose for confiding in her in the first place. "I'm . . . er . . . glad to hear she's making progress."

"Thank you." He took another sip from the mug, then cradled it in his hands, as if for warmth.

The seemingly casual action put her senses on alert.

The temperature was already in the nineties, and he cradled the cup as though he needed to draw warmth from it? Not likely, Cyndi reasoned. What she decided was that Ben was attempting to draw courage from his grasp on the heated mug.

If her deduction was sound, she concluded, it begged the question of what he might need the courage for.

She was curious. Naturally. She wouldn't be normal if she weren't curious. But Cyndi wouldn't pry or even probe for an answer. It was not her style. Curious as she most definitely was, she would hold her silence and wait for him to explain.

She didn't have to wait long.

After a few moments of apparent contemplation, Ben decisively set the mug down, drew an audible breath, then offered her an uneven half-smile.

"I ... er ... have a proposition to make you," he said, then adding quickly, "But not what you might think."

Of course, what she had thought of was a proposition both illegal and illicit.

"No?" Cyndi asked coolly.

"No." He gave a swift, hard shake of his head. "I have in mind an employment proposition."

"Prostitution is employment," she pointed out, her cold voice reflecting her disappointment and disillusionment. "Of an unsavory kind."

"I was not referring to that, Cynthia," he said, his tone sharp with denial and, to his credit, his expression one of appalled shock.

"I'm glad to hear it." While she managed to keep her voice bland, without inflection, Cyndi felt somewhat amazed at the strength of the relief washing over her. "I'm also waiting to hear precisely what you were referring to."

"I'll explain in a minute," he said, lifting the mug and draining it. "May I have another coffee?"

"Of course." Turning away from the counter, she grabbed the glass carafe, poured out the steaming dark liquid, and dropped two tiny containers of half and half next to the mug. Then, without missing a beat, she returned the pot to the heating pad and said, "Explain."

"Thanks." Ben nodded. "Okay, but let me give you a little background first."

"Sure." Her expression wry, she glanced around at the empty booths and the counter to either side of him. "It's not like I'm being rushed off my feet at the moment or anything."

Ben's dark eyes followed the path of her sweeping gaze. "This work has to be boring as hell for someone as intelligent as you obviously are."

"Thanks for the compliment." Cyndi shrugged. "It ain't brain surgery, that's for certain."

His lips quirked in an amused smile.

Cyndi's pulse rate fluttered. A little frightened by the disproportionate response of her senses to him, she went on the defensive. "I'm still waiting."

"Right." His quirky smile vanished, and he became all businesslike. "Here's the picture . . ."

Cyndi stood behind the counter, watching the play of expressions on his face, as Ben explained his current situation in brief, concise terms. His voice was steady, modulated, yet even with the lack of inflection or emotion, she could almost feel his worry and deep concern for his mother's health.

Not once during his recitation did so much as a hint of self-interest or pity taint his tone. Still, she clearly understood the pressure he had been under throughout the previous weeks. She understood because she had been there herself, knew the strain of responsibility, the weariness factor in attempting to crowd twenty-eight hours of work into sixteen-or eighteen-hour days.

One had to sleep on occasion.

"I'm not complaining you understand, but . . ." Ben sighed and shrugged. "That's why I didn't argue when my aunt ordered me out of the house for some R and R." He smiled. "I was just too damn tired to get into a hassle over it."

"But you'd rather be working," Cyndi stated, not needing to pose it as a question.

"Hell, yes." Ben grimaced. "This driving around aimlessly is driving me nuts."

"It would drive me nuts too." She paused, frowning. "But, what does all this have to do with me . . . and the proposition you have to make to me?"

His expression somber, Ben studied her for a moment. In an obvious ploy to play for time, he raised his mug, took a sip, and made a face. "It's cold," he said.

"I'll warm it up," she offered. The moment the task was completed, she gave him a hard stare and a stern suggestion. "Okay, suppose you stop hedging and get to the point."

"Right." He raked a hand through his hair, ruffling the smoothly brushed auburn strands. "I can deal with the pressure of looking after my mother and running my business, if that's all there is to it."

"There's more?"

"There's more." He smiled, wryly. "You see, the root cause of my problem isn't the result of mother's heart attack, although that was bad enough by itself." He shook his head. "It's the aftereffects that are making me crazy."

"Aftereffects?" Cyndi was gaining a new respect for dentistry; extracting was tough.

He gave a tired-looking nod. "When I turned thirty, my mother began dropping gentle hints about it being time for me to find a 'nice girl'—her words—get married, and settle down. At the time, and over the last couple of years, I just smiled and went my own way, doing my own thing."

"I presume you don't want to get married," Cyndi opined in a dry drawl.

"Correct." He nodded again, once, the move quick and final. "But, since her attack, and faced with the real prospect of her own mortality, she has launched a dedicated campaign. The gentle hints have become unsubtle nudges."

He paused, shook his head.

"Go on," she nudged.

He grimaced "She even got my aunt Louise into the act, which is, I'm sure, why I was practically run out of the house, *my* house, with instructions to rest, relax, and have fun, primarily with someone *female.*"

Cyndi was hard pressed to contain the laughter tickling the back of her throat, but she persevered. Ben looked so agitated, so put upon and frustrated, she didn't want to run the risk of insulting him with her laughter.

"Ah . . . mmm . . ." She cleared her throat. "I do see your predicament, but where do I come into it?"

"That's my proposition," he explained, speaking quickly. "I'm offering you a job, not sex for hire, but regular employment, with good pay and excellent fringe benefits."

Cyndi frowned, more than a little puzzled by his offer. "You want to hire me to be a companion to your mother for the duration of her convalescence?"

"No, of course not," he said, his tone impatient. "If I

wanted to hire a companion, I'd contact an employment agency close to home."

"My thought, exactly," she retorted, letting him know she had a patience limit, too. "So, then precisely what sort of employment do you have in mind?"

"I want you to go home with me as my wife."

Dead stop. Stunned by his blunt reply, Cyndi stared at him in utter disbelief.

"Well?"

"Well what?"

Ben heaved a sigh. "What do you think?"

"What do I think?" she repeated, torn between urges to laugh and curse at him. "I think you're not being driven crazy, because you're already crazy. That's what I think."

"But . . . why?"

"Why? Get serious." She laughed, only because she didn't like to curse. "You ask a complete stranger to marry you, then ask why when said stranger thinks you're crazy?"

"I did not ask you to marry me," he informed her in tones of cool reserve.

"You didn't ask . . . ?" Cyndi broke off, while attempting to hold on to her temper; she failed. "Then what in the hell are you suggesting?" she nearly shouted, slowly backing away from the counter.

"Cynthia, please." Standing, Ben reached across the counter to grasp her wrist, halting her retreat. "Let me explain my idea. I swear it's harmless and completely aboveboard."

"Let me go," she ordered, managing to keep her voice calm, determined. "I'll listen. But only if you let go of me."

His hand sprang back at once. "I'm sorry, I didn't intend intimidation."

"Accepted," she said, but she remained where she was, two steps removed from the counter. "Now, stop beating around the bush and get to the bottom line."

"Okay, here's the deal. I want to hire you to pretend to be my wife, live in my home and—"

She cut in. "Hold it right there. Live in your home. In Philadelphia. With *you?*"

"Yes, of course." The impatience was back in his voice. "My mother might find it odd otherwise, seeing as how she lives with me and couldn't help but notice."

"I'm finding this whole conversation more than odd," she snapped, flinging impatience back at him.

Ben chose to ignore her comment. "Naturally, we wouldn't be living together in an intimate way."

"Damn right," she inserted, thinking wryly that for a woman who didn't like to swear, she was doing a lot of it all of a sudden.

Again, he chose to ignore her. "It would be a pretense, somewhat like a theatrical performance," he explained. "A command performance, if you will, for my mother, until such time as her doctor declares her fit and healthy once more."

Men. Cyndi mentally rolled her eyes. "And when that time arrives, then what?"

"What do you mean, then what?"

"Elementary, my dear Ganster," she paraphrased, with silent apologies to Conan Doyle and evident sarcasm for Ben. "What happens when the doctor declares her sound? Do you then simply tell her it was all a play, enacted for her entertainment . . . if you will?" She arched a brow. "Somehow I can't imagine any mother appreciating that kind of deception."

"Elementary, my dear Cynthia," he threw her jibe back at her, with equal sarcasm. "When the time arrives, we simply get a pretend divorce to end our pretend marriage . . . and we'll be vocally grateful no children were born of the pretend union.''

"Geeze," Cyndi said. "And so-called experts claim that women are devious.''

"Drastic situations call for drastic solutions," he argued—actually sounding sincere. "My mother is fretting about my single state." Ben again ruffled his hair with raking fingers. "I'm afraid that her obsession to see me married will prolong the times of her recovery. I merely want to see her happy, relaxed . . . and well.''

"And yourself off the hook, of course," Cyndi said, none too kindly.

He nodded. "That too.''

Brought up short by his surprising honesty, she stared at him, for the moment perplexed.

"I don't get you," she finally admitted. "The way I see it, it would be a lot easier, not to mention honest and forthright, to simply get married—for real." She frowned. "Don't you know any nice, acceptable women?''

"Certainly." Ben bristled. "I know many nice, acceptable women." He hesitated, as if undecided about continuing. Then he went on, "In point of fact, I have been enjoying a mutually satisfying relationship with such a woman.''

Cyndi was stunned, not by his statement, she knew of several couples involved in, and to all appearances enjoying, similar relationships. And she didn't condemn them because she believed a relationship without commitment was worthless.

No, in truth, Cyndi was stunned by the searing sense of disappointment and near pain she experienced on hearing him admit to being involved in such an arrangement.

"I see," was all she could manage to reply.

His expression sharpened, as if he had just thought of something. "You're not involved in a relationship with someone, are you?"

"No." She shook her head, smiling wryly at the edge of concern in his tone. "There's no one special." She didn't deem it necessary to confess that there was no one at all. A woman was entitled to her pride.

"Good." He smiled and his expression eased. "So, will you consider my offer?"

For whatever perverse reason, Cyndi did not immediately reject his proposal, even though she knew she should. Instead, she countered flippantly, "I don't know. I haven't heard the particulars yet."

"Yes, of course. Sorry." He lifted his shoulders in a light shrug. "Okay, I'll lay it out for you. In exchange for your pretending to be my wife, no strings attached, for however long it takes my mother to attain a full recovery, I am willing to compensate you with a generous salary and college courses at the university of your choice . . . that is, a university close to my home, of which there are several."

College courses? Although she had been prepared to turn him down out of hand, this offer made her hesitate. The hesitation brought memories of the previous evening's family discussion, reinstating her feeling of being redundant and superfluous.

There was also one other element Cyndi couldn't deny; she was intrigued by the idea of pretending . . . it was so similar to reading, getting caught up in an interesting story.

She was tempted, sorely tempted. But, no, she couldn't, she told herself. Pretense, innocent pretense as in fiction was one thing. Deception was something else entirely.

Cyndi drew a breath to say no.

"In addition to salary and college courses," Ben said before she could speak. "Philly offers many and varied cultural advantages . . . museums, the theater, and so on . . ." He flicked a hand. "And, of course, there are many bookstores and libraries, lots of libraries."

Cyndi once again drew a breath to say no, while her mind whirled. *Libraries.*

"What do you say?"

Theaters.

"I think you'll love the city."

Bookstores.

"There's an energy there."

Museums.

"It can be very exciting."

Libraries.

"Are you game?" His voice held a hint of anxiety.

"Yes," she surprised herself as well as him with her quick response. "I accept."

Chapter Six

So that was why she was in an upscale shop in New York City with this particular man.

Three days had passed since Cyndi had shocked herself—and Ben—with her abrupt agreement to his proposal. Three days in which her life had taken a complete change. Days that now seemed more like weeks.

So much had happened.

To begin, Cyndi's father and her sister—after a natural skepticism at the outset, and after meeting Ben, who had not hesitated in producing his credentials, his home address and phone number, or in giving assurances that his mother would be on hand at all times—had encouraged her to go for it . . . so to speak.

Of course, Cyndi had not told her father or Jess the full details of Ben's idea. She hadn't lied to them, but had merely indicated that Ben had offered her the position of companion to his mother, as well as an opportunity to further her education with some college courses.

She had left out the sticky bit about deceiving his mother by posing as his wife.

Once having secured Cyndi's compliance, and her father's acceptance of the plan, Ben became all business-like and impatient. Claiming a need to get back to his mother, to his work, he literally whisked Cyndi away the very next morning, but not, as she had anticipated, to Philadelphia.

With a terse explanation that they had important preparations to make, Ben drove diagonally across the state, heading for New York City.

New York City. Cyndi had never been there, but then, she had never been to any big city. The very thought of going to New York was so exciting, she was hardly able to contain herself throughout the long drive, chafing at every stop he made along the way for a meal or just to stretch to get out the kinks.

They hit the Lincoln Tunnel at rush hour and joined the line of traffic inching its way into the city. Ben muttered more than a few colorful curses; Cyndi had been enthralled by it all.

The Marriott Marquis was located a relatively short drive from the tunnel; yet with the congested traffic, it took over a half-hour to reach the covered entranceway to the hotel.

Cyndi hadn't noticed. Wide-eyed with wonder, she stared at the tall spires of buildings, the pedestrians thronging the sidewalks and surging across the streets at intersections, the theater marquees.

She could barely stand it. It was all so thrilling.

By itself, the Marriott Marquis was a new and exciting experience. Cyndi had never been a guest in a hotel, and she savored every minute of it. Private cars, taxis, and limousines crowded the broad entrance drive, disgorging people of all colors, many speaking in exotic-sounding languages.

To Cyndi, it was almost like living an exciting story.

"This way, Cynthia."

The low sound of Ben's voice and his hand at her elbow drew Cyndi's attention away from her surroundings. Flashing a delighted smile at him, she allowed him to lead her into the building, trailing a bellman pushing a cart loaded with their luggage, one case hers, three belonging to Ben.

The elevators were a revelation. Constructed in the shape of rockets, with long panels of clear glass—plastic?—the cars carried the passengers up on the outside of a central column rising up through the middle of the hotel. Throughout the quick ascent, Cyndi stood, her nose not quite pressed to the panel, her gaze darting about, trying to take in everything at once.

The registration desk was on the eighth floor. There, they joined the line of guests waiting to check in.

From their position on line, Cyndi could see a large lounge area beyond the long registration desk. There were groupings of comfortable-looking chairs placed around low tables. A smattering of people were seated in them, drinks on the tables before them, chattering away in animated conversation with their companions.

Cyndi tugged at Ben's jacket sleeve. "Can we go in there and have a drink?" she asked in a hopeful tone, indicating the lounge area with a quick hand movement.

"Perhaps." A gentle smile curved his lips. "After we've settled in and freshened up for dinner. You can't see it from here, but there's a restaurant directly across from the lounge. I thought we might have room service deliver a meal to us, but"—he shrugged—"we can have dinner there if you prefer . . ."

"Yes, please," she cut in eagerly, before she was

tempted to change her mind. Having a meal delivered to her room was another never-before-experienced luxury she would have loved to sample.

"And then have a drink in the lounge," he finished on a soft chuckle.

When it came time for Ben to move up to one of the clerks at the desk, Cyndi stayed close to his side, listening and learning how to conduct oneself during this process. She was impressed by Ben's cool expectation of having his every desire fulfilled, and felt certain she would never be able to emulate his aura of self-confidence.

Upon hearing him refer to her as "Mrs. Ganster," Cyndi felt a zing of something—some emotion—ricochet through her. Shaken by the sensation, and reluctant to examine the cause of it, she firmly advised herself to grow up; as if a man like Ben, so self-assured, so aware of his place in his world, would ever consider a permanent alliance with a hick like her.

Slightly in awe of him, she meekly moved beside him as once again they followed a bellman pushing the luggage cart.

Cyndi's stomach seemed to drop as the elevator swept them up to the eighteenth floor. Upon exiting the lift, she immediately stepped to the inner barrier to peer down, down, down, to the floors below.

"Come along," Ben murmured, drawing her away from the barrier and back to his side. "You'll have time later to hang over the side and gawk."

"We'll be here longer than one night?" Cyndi asked, falling into step with him.

"Yes, three, possibly four nights." Smiling, he came to a halt behind the bellman, waiting until the door was unlocked and pushed open.

Wondering whose room it was, his or hers, Cyndi

hesitated about entering until he indicated with a flick of one hand that she should precede him.

A soft "Oh" escaped her lips as Cyndi walked into the room, which she immediately realized was the sitting room of a large suite. But it wasn't the realization that Ben had taken a suite for their accommodations that had snagged her attention and elicited surprise from her, it was the enormous window on the opposite wall. The drapes were open, revealing a panoramic view of the city beyond.

As if drawn by a magnet, Cyndi walked to the window, to gaze in wondrous delight at the city, bathed in the golden rays of the sinking sun.

So enchanted was Cyndi by the sight before her, she didn't hear the murmured exchanges between Ben and the bellman, or the door closing behind the latter.

"You like the view?" Ben's soft voice, so close to her ear, penetrated her bemusement, and sent a delicious quiver skipping down her spine. "I ordered it just for you."

"Oh, yes, it's wonderful." Feeling breathless, and taking him literally, she dragged her gaze from the view to offer him a smile of gratitude. "Thank you, Ben."

"Bennett." He'd shaken his head. "And you're welcome. Now, do you think you could tear yourself away to choose the bedroom you prefer?"

Cyndi was thrilled with the room; it was spacious— at least two and a half times bigger than her room at home, and she had shared that with Jess until her brothers left home. In addition to the bed, the room had a small table, a stuffed chair, a TV and a bathroom en suite. She was to have exclusive use of the bathroom.

Heavenly.

A quick shower, a change of clothes, and they were off again, to the restaurant for dinner.

The service was first rate, the server friendly and efficient, the meal excellent.

From the restaurant, she and Ben strolled into the lounge area and settled into the black leather chairs. While Ben ordered from the waitress, Cyndi sat and watched the elevators glide up and down the central column. Then the distinct sound of a cork popping snagged her attention.

"Champagne," Ben explained, pouring the sparkling golden liquid into tall slim flutes. "To celebrate your first visit to New York."

"Why, thank you," she responded, pleased by the thoughtfulness behind his gesture.

He then raised his glass.

Cyndi followed suit.

"Here's to a pleasant and profitable working relationship," he declared, toasting their association.

Cyndi had never tasted the stuff before, but one sip was all that was needed. She loved it.

"Good?" Ben asked.

"Yes." She laughed and wrinkled her nose at the tickling sensation from the bubbles. "Delicious."

They sipped their wine in companionable silence for a few moments, during which Cyndi wondered if she dared ask him for one more first. Perhaps the potent drink gave her courage, for suddenly, breathlessly, she'd blurted out her request.

"I was ... ahh ... wondering ... could we, maybe, have room service for breakfast tomorrow?"

Ben laughed, but he granted her request.

Breakfast at a table set before the window in the sitting room was wonderful. Life was wonderful. Ben was wonderful, considerate, and rather sweet.

While savoring the delicate flavor of a warm orange muffin, Cyndi deserted the spectacular view of the city to gaze upon the attractive man seated opposite her.

And, while relishing her breakfast, she secretly relished the realization of a little feeling of tenderness—well, perhaps more than a little—for this thoughtful and considerate man pretending to be her husband.

To her eyes, Ben was more, much more than merely good-looking; he was the embodiment of everything she had ever dreamed of, fantasized about, hoped for in a man . . . a man of her own. That Ben was not *her* man didn't matter—at least not too much. It was enough to know he existed on the same planet.

That he not only existed, but treated her as though she was important, was part of the wonder.

The wonder of it all endured throughout the leisurely meal. It was also the last quiet and relaxing period she enjoyed that day.

The moment Cyndi declared herself finished, Ben became brisk, telling her it was time to get moving, since they had a lot to accomplish that day.

Disoriented by his sudden change of demeanor, Cyndi allowed him to whisk her from the room, the hotel, and into a taxi. Bemused, she sat in the back of the cab, feeling she should hang on for dear life as the driver whipped in and out of traffic. She remained docile, amenable, until the cab came to a jarring stop in front of a swanky, expensive-looking salon, the name of which even she had heard of back in the hills of Pennsylvania.

Although Cyndi had stepped from the taxi at Ben's urging, she dug her heels in when he would have escorted her into the place with the elegant little gold-scrolled nameplate next to the door.

"No." Stopping dead in the middle of the sidewalk, she stared at him defiantly and held her ground.

"What do you mean, no?" Ben demanded, surprise evident in his tone and eyes.

"I mean, no," Cyndi retorted. "As in no, I am not going in there."

He frowned. "But . . . why not? I'm told there are women who would do just about anything for a visit to this salon."

"Well, I'm not one of them," she shot back. "And I am not going in."

"Cynthia . . ." He broke off, as if trying to hang on to his patience. He ground his teeth together; she knew he did, she could hear it.

"No," she repeated. "And it's Cyndi."

"Dammit, woman, I've made an appointment for you, and you will keep it."

"I won't."

But, in the end, she did.

The process took hours to complete.

She was subjected to a facial, a massage, a shampoo, a manicure, a haircut and styling, the works. To her dismay, though she felt out of place with the high-class clientele, and though she would never admit to it, she enjoyed the makeover and could hardly believe the results.

After her own critical examination, Cyndi was forced to conclude she looked a lot different, better . . . rather attractive.

Her complexion glowed with a healthy sheen. Her eyes, enhanced by the feather-light touch of makeup the specialist had instructed her on applying, appeared brighter, yet mysterious with feminine secrets.

And her hair . . . Though Cyndi had groaned at seeing her long tresses ruthlessly sheared, she loved the results of the style. Cut on a angle just below her ears, the ends were curved forward to swing against her face when she moved her head. She liked the silky look and feel of her hair.

"This had to have cost a bundle," she said, when Ben came to collect her.

He gave her a swift perusal, then nodded. "And worth every dollar." Grasping her elbow, he guided her into the taxi he'd left waiting at the curb. "Let's get going."

Wounded by his faint praise, and with her shoulders drooping, Cyndi blinked away the threatening tears and slid onto the cracked leather seat.

But she balked once again when the cab pulled up before a well-known department store.

"What now?" she muttered, tossing a narrow-eyed, fulminating look at Ben.

"What else?" he drawled, leading her into the store. "Clothing, Cynthia. From the skin out."

What could she have done? What could she have said? It was either submit, again, or cause a scene. And, although Cyndi was sorely tempted, she knew she simply couldn't do that ... besides, she knew Ben wouldn't tolerate it.

Other than the visit to the salon, the following days mirrored the first day.

Cyndi stared into the mirror, at yet another outfit she didn't want; this time a smooth wool long-skirted suit in a deep rich shade of amethyst.

The suit was gorgeous, sleek and chic. But, to Cyndi's eyes, it just wasn't her. She was jeans and sweatshirts, whereas this suit was—

"Cynthia."

Cyndi started at the soft but impatient sound of Ben's

low, rough-edged voice. Heaving a sigh, she gazed into the wide eyes of her reflection.

Might as well get it over with, she advised her image, a devil-may-care grin revealing her straight white teeth—she was rather proud of those teeth—before the man pretending to be her husband invaded the privacy of the changing room.

Squaring her shoulders, Cyndi turned and exited the cubicle, only to stop dead at the sight of Ben's direct regard.

Holy jumping hell!

His features frozen into an austere mask, Bennett stared in disbelief, transfixed by the vision standing cool and composed before him.

Could this . . . this enchanting creature actually be Cynthia Swoyer of the diner?

It was not the first time he had asked himself that very same question over the previous several days.

Who knew, who could ever have guessed that a four-hour visit to a beauty salon for the *works*—facial, manicure, haircut, and styling—plus a change of wardrobe could produce such radical results?

Maybe it was possible to make a silk purse out of a sow's ear, after all.

She tilted her head, peering at him. Her hair swung forward to brush her face.

A strange sensation unfurled in Bennett's stomach. He certainly did like the new hair style, the silkiness of it, the shimmer highlighting the honey brown color. But he wasn't at all sure he appreciated the way his fingers itched to touch the shiny strands.

"You don't like it?" Cynthia's voice was flat with acceptance.

Not like it? Bennett was hard-pressed not to laugh at the utter ridiculousness of her assessment. Lord save him. His mouth was dry, his palms were moist, and the recurring sensation too close to the stirring of sexual excitement to be borne was making itself felt in his mind and body.

"Ahheemmm ..." Bennett was forced to clear his throat which, fortunately, helped clear his mind. "It's a beautiful garment. Perfect, in fact."

"For what?" Cynthia glanced down at her form and frowned. "Wherever would I wear it?"

"Why, my dear, you could wear that suit almost anywhere, for almost any occasion."

The opinion came, not from Bennett, but the rather haughty-sounding middle-aged clerk, who looked like she needed a good meal, she was so thin.

Cynthia transferred her frown to the sticklike hovering woman, who had been effectively annoying Bennett from the beginning. "Like what?"

The clerk appeared nonplused by the question.

Even though he had long since grown weary of the woman's superior manner, Bennett took it upon himself to verbally spring to her rescue. "Like an evening at the theater," he explained, smiling benignly at the clerk, who gave a vigorous nod of agreement. "Or dinner in a fine restaurant."

"But—"

"We'll take it," Bennett interrupted his pretend wife, certain she was about to blurt out that she never went to fine restaurants. "The suit and all the others I've indicated."

"But, Ben—"

"Bennett." He again cut her off, scowling at her persistent use of the nickname and her resistance to his insistence on a new wardrobe for her. "I'd appreciate it if you'd change, Cynthia. I'm hungry, and if we don't leave soon, we'll be late for our luncheon reservation at Le Cirque." In a move of deliberate dismissal, he then turned to the clerk. "You will have everything delivered to the hotel this afternoon, won't you?"

To his relief—and the ease of his digestion—Cynthia held her peace throughout lunch, although she made her displeasure with him evident by simply remaining quiet for the most part while merely poking at the food on her beautifully presented cold poached salmon plate.

Silent, unapproachable, she made do with resentful glances at him until they returned to their suite in the hotel. The sight of the packages, set just inside the door of the sitting room, presumably by a bellman or someone from housekeeping, was all it took to set her off.

"I feel like a kept woman," Cynthia protested, glaring at the new and large pile of elegant store boxes and bags.

"And I think you must read too many lurid romance novels," Bennett countered, unwisely, as it happened. The light of battle flared in her eyes.

"Oh, do you?" Her arms flew out, and then her hands slammed to rest on her slender waist, her stance militant. "And would you like to hear what I think of what *you* think?"

"I don't think so." He drawled, keeping his voice bone dry. "It might injure my self-esteem."

"Oh, brother, give me a break." She rolled her eyes, visibly controlling an urge to laugh.

"I could counter with, 'Give me an arm,'" he rejoined. "But I won't, since I clearly recall your stated disdain for the obvious."

"You're real cute, you know that?" Try as she might to maintain her militancy, she was losing the battle.

"I do my best," he said, flashing her a teasing grin in the hope of vanquishing her anger.

"Your best is very good," she admitted, sighing.

"Thank you," he replied, both unsettled and astonished by the inordinate sense of pleasure he derived from her mild compliment.

"You're welcome."

Bennett could see the steam rapidly escaping from her boiling point, and he decided to seize the moment . . . before she thought up some other reason to attack.

"If you'll recall, we both have to shower and change," he said, still more amused than annoyed by her confrontational stance. "We wouldn't want to be late for the eight o'clock curtain at the theater, now, would we?"

If he had hoped his gentle reminder would effectively spike her guns, and he had entertained such a hope, she quickly disabused him of his wishful thinking.

"Why not?" she asked, much too reasonably. "Isn't being late the stylish thing to do?"

"Not for me," he said. "And not for this show, since they won't seat anyone after the curtain rises." He smiled; he couldn't help it, she looked so frustrated. "Besides, we wouldn't want to waste a minute of our last night in New York, would we?"

"We're leaving tomorrow?"

"Yes." Tender satisfaction curled through him as he watched her whirl and dash for her room.

Cynthia came to an abrupt halt at the bedroom door and turned a stricken face back to him.

"Which outfit should I wear?"

Controlling an urge to grin, Bennett strolled to the pile of packages, gathered them into his arms, and delivered them into her keeping. "That one dress you tried on, the green shot through with gold, would be perfect."

He paused, then went on in a dry drawl, "As I believe I pointed that out in the store when you tried it on."

"Oh, right." She looked chagrined, then came back at him in a chiding tone. "But then, you said that about several of the outfits I tried on."

Keeping the time in mind, Bennet decided to pass on that volley. Suppressing a smile, he opened the door for her. She stepped inside the room. "Green lingerie, black hose and shoes, Cynthia," he called after her.

Her muffled response came to him faintly through the closed wooden door.

"Thanks, Ben."

"Bennett," he shouted.

"Whatever," she yelled back.

Shaking his head, he started for his own room. Then it occurred that he would never have presumed to advise Denise on the proper attire for any occasion.

Denise. Bennett was struck by the realization that he hadn't given a thought to her in days. His brows knit, and then he shrugged and continued on into his room. He had to change. He didn't have time at the moment to think about his memory lapse regarding Denise . . . or her wardrobe choices.

There'd be time for that after he got home.

Chapter Seven

"We're almost home."

Home? Not her home. Her home was many miles and long driving hours away from this unfamiliar, traffic-congested area on the outskirts of Philadelphia.

The tightness of homesickness thickening her throat, Cyndi slanted a look at Ben. Her throat worsened, but that had nothing to do with homesickness.

Ben.

Cyndi resisted a need to sigh. Although she still felt uncomfortable about his having spent so lavishly on her clothing and makeover, she had buried her disquiet beneath a layer of gratitude, telling herself that to do otherwise would be not only childish but churlish. Besides, though she wouldn't admit it to him, didn't want to admit it to herself, she adored the clothes and the results of the makeover. Darn her contrariness.

He had been so kind, so patient, so very considerate of her . . .

Like last night, she reflected, a dreamy smile curving her lips and easing the painful tightness in her throat.

Last night had been wonderful, from the moment she had stepped out of her bedroom, feeling special, almost elegant in the ultrafeminine green dress.

And, Ben, bless him, had encouraged her feelings, gallantly bolstering her self-image.

"You look . . . lovely," he had murmured, the sincerity in his tone allowing her to overlook the brief and confusing hesitation in his voice.

For a moment, just an instant, Cyndi was caught, held breathless, fluttery by . . . something, an intensity in his dark eyes, a tautness around his mouth. And then it was gone. The light of amusement brightened his eyes, and a teasing smile softened his lips.

Ben had made the evening magical for her.

Dinner at Patsy's was delectable. Over the antipasto, his urbane, droll observations about some of their fellow diners was deliciously naughty and amusing. The show, a revival of a musical comedy hit, was delightful, with just enough risqué dialogue to jazz it up a bit.

After leaving the theater, humming one of the show tunes, he suggested they walk to Barrymore's, a famous bistro located just down the street from the Marriott, for drinks and a snack.

It was while they were strolling along—it would have been impossible to stride out, hemmed in as they were by throngs of tourists and theatergoers pouring out onto the sidewalks after performances—that an incident occurred which could have ruined the evening for her.

Terrified of being separated from him in the mass of humanity, Cyndi was hanging onto Ben's arm with both hands when she'd felt a slight tug on the narrow shoulder strap attached to the tiny evening bag he had insisted she carry. The next instant, she gave a soft cry on hearing the soft click of the catch being sprung on the purse.

"What the . . . !" Ben said in a near shout, reacting immediately.

She turned halfway around to glance down at her purse, and then, everything happened so fast it wasn't until afterward she realized what had happened.

A young man had flipped the catch on her purse with the intent to grab what he could and then run, merging into the pressing crowd of people.

Ben proved faster than the would-be thief. His arm shot out as he shoved Cyndi to one side, his long fingers encircling, like a manacle the young man's wrist.

"Let go!" the young man cried in a panicked voice, glancing around furitively. "I didn't do anything, I swear," he babbled, pulling on his arm.

Ben held him in place with what looked like effortless ease.

"Check your bag, Cynthia," he ordered. "Make certain there's nothing missing."

The checking process took mere seconds, and wouldn't have taken that long if she hadn't been so badly shaken, as all she'd been able to get into the tiny thing was a compact, a lipstick, a small comb, and a few tissues. But before she could report to Ben, the young man again yanked against Ben's grasp.

"You're not going any—" Ben had begun to snarl when a policewoman appeared.

"Trouble, sir?" The policewoman—young, attractive, and a veritable giant in height—asked Ben.

"Yeah, this bas—this jerk tried to snatch my . . . er. . . . my wife's purse," Ben explained, shifting his hard-eyed glittering gaze from the woman to Cyndi. "Is anything missing, Cynthia?"

Cyndi, her heart thumping from the adrenaline rush, her throat dried by the shock, shook her head in the negative, and croaked, "N-n-no."

"You want to press charges, sir?"

"No," Ben answered the policewoman wryly. "It would hardly be worth the effort . . . would it?"

"Afraid not, sir," she replied, her own tone wry with acceptance.

"That's what I thought," he muttered, releasing the man with obvious reluctance.

The would-be thief disappeared into the crowd, none of whom appeared aware of the small drama that had been played out before their eyes.

The incident was over. Cyndi sighed with relief, then stared at Ben, starry-eyed.

Not noticing the look in her eyes, Ben took her arm and urged her forward.

"Come along, Cynthia," he said, moving as fast as possible through the throng. "I think you could do with a drink." He slanted a grin at her. "Maybe two."

My hero, she thought, suppressing a nervous giggle as she quickstepped to keep up with him.

Later, after three glasses of wine and a snack of nachos, Cyndi felt as though she were gliding inches above the pavement as they walked back to the hotel.

She also felt like a woman falling in love.

At the time, bemused and beguiled by her charming companion and the events of the evening, basking in the afterglow of Ben's sincere-sounding compliments, his attendance on her, his physical protection of her, the feeling of falling in love added luster to the glitter of the evening.

The nasty incident that had occurred earlier washed away by the potent wine and her even more potent companion, she saw herself as a contemporary Cinderella . . . with a new look, new clothes, a prospective new home, and her own good-looking Prince Charming.

Now, drawing nearer—and too quickly—to Ben's home, the meeting with his mother, and the actual beginning of what was to be, in plain truth, nothing more than a blatant deception of the woman, Cyndi was scared silly.

What if his mother couldn't take to her?

What if she couldn't take to his mother?

What if his mother immediately saw through their pretense?

It was time for a reality check.

She was not Cinderella. Ben was not Prince Charming. They were not about to embark on a real-life fairy tale. Their pretense would not be innocent; it was based on deceit and lies.

Cyndi stole another glance at Ben.

How could he look so calm, so relaxed, so unaffected by the charade they were about to perform? she asked herself, tensing against the sting of conscience-induced panic.

As if aware of her furtive glances, Ben gave her a brief look and a quick smile.

"You've been very quiet since we left New York," he said, his voice calm, his grasp on the steering wheel almost casual. He spared another quick look at her. "Tired?"

"Yes," she said. No, she thought. Not tired, scared. Deception was so . . . so smarmy.

"Not used to the night life, hmmm?" Amusement ran lightly through his voice.

A flash of resentment sparked by his seeming uncon-cern sizzled through Cyndi—resentment and, surprisingly, a tinge of near dislike. She wanted to smack him. She didn't, of course. She contained the temptation to strike out . . . at least physically. Verbally, she let fly.

"You should have called your mother, prepared her," she chastised him, not for the first time. Cyndi had brought up the subject several times over the previous three days, but each time she had, Ben had quickly changed it.

Ben frowned. "Cynthia, we've been through this several times before." He sighed. "How many times do I have to explain that I want to surprise her?"

"But the shock, Ben. Her condition," she protested. "Aren't you afraid the shock might—"

"Bennett," he interrupted, impatiently. "The name's Bennett, Cyn-thi-a. And, no, I'm not afraid the shock might anything. Trust me. She will be thrilled."

Trust him. Cyndi swallowed a burst of nervous laughter. Trusting him had gotten her into this mess to begin with. Trusting him. Liking him. And, yes, wanting to prolong her association with him.

Either she really was falling in love with him—the conflicting resentment and near dislike notwithstanding—or she was seriously losing her mind.

Cyndi couldn't decide which condition would be worse.

Trust me.

Ben's fingers tightened imperceptibly around the steering wheel. He made a concentrated effort to relax his grip. Not for anything would he have Cynthia realize that her concern affected him in any way.

But she was right, he reluctantly conceded. He should have called his mother, prepared her to greet and welcome his supposed new "bride."

Why had he resisted, both Cynthia's advice to phone his mother and his own inner promptings to do so?

He knew that what he was about to do was disloyal and flat-out wrong.

There it was, glaring at him from the depths of his conscience. Bennett didn't like looking at it, acknowledging it, but he could no longer avoid it.

He slid a glance at Cynthia; there was a pinched look about her, uptight, nervous.

Not at all like last night, he thought, recalling how the sight of her had rocked him when she'd stepped out of the bedroom. Rocked him. Thrilled him. Turned him on. Her bobbed hair gleamed honey-gold in the glow of the table lamps. The gold-shot-through-green summer dress caressed her slender shape, tantalizing more by what it hinted at than what it revealed. The black hose and high heels enhanced the curves of her calves and her slim, delicate ankles.

Lord, who would have thought, believed, even dreamed that concealed within that frayed-aproned, ponytailed, scrubbed-faced young woman manning the counter of a run-down, out-of-date diner, there was a ravishing beauty?

And who would ever have thought that he could experience such intense fear and rage at one and the same time as he had at the sound of Cynthia's soft outcry when that bastard had tried to snatch her purse?

At the moment she had cried out, he had thought she had been hurt; the consideration had terrified him, damn near immoblized him.

Bennett felt a chilling tremor of remembered sensation, and a cold sweat beaded his brow. He also recalled the frightening thought that had flashed through his mind: *What if he should lose her?*

In taking action, Bennett had had to fight to contain

himself, his fury, because he had actually wanted to wreak serious damage on the slimy sneak thief, really serious damage . . . maybe even death.

Bennett contained a shudder.

But there was another reason why he had persisted in his determination to carry out his scheme. He didn't want to lose his connection to this butterfly emerging from her cocoon, however tenuous it might be.

When had he lost sight of his original purpose, that of keeping his mother content while she recuperated, while at the same time removing himself as her primary target of discontent?

More to the point, why had he thought for a moment that he could so blithely sidestep his conscience?

He couldn't go through with it.

Yet he didn't want to sever the connection with Cynthia. He didn't know, wasn't sure what, the attraction signified, other than the sexual draw and the fact that he was liking her more with each passing day. He had no idea if, in the end, there would turn out to be little if any significance to it. But he didn't want to lose touch at this stage of the game.

So there had to be another way.

There was. Bennett's fingers flexed on the steering wheel as a glimmer of an idea sprang into his mind. True, he would still be perpetuating a deception, but on a much smaller scale, minor in comparison, and less destructive in intent.

He'd do it.

The decision made, he swung the wheel, steering the car off the highway onto the graveled shoulder.

"Ben!" Cynthia exclaimed, startled.

He brought the car to a stop and pulled the hand brake before turning to face her.

"Is there something the matter with the car?"

"No." He shook his head. "Me." He drew a breath. "I can't go through with this, Cynthia. I'm sorry."

She exhaled a breath. "I'm not."

Her relief was palpable; Bennett felt he could actually feel it radiating from her.

"I'll pay you back, somehow, for the makeover," she said rapidly. "And, as for the clothes—"

"Cynthia, that won't—"

"Most of the stuff can be returned for a refund," she went on as if he hadn't spoken.

"Cynthia, no," he began again, sighing when she continued to rattle on.

"Of course, the dress, underwear, and accessories I wore last night can't be returned, but—"

"Cynthia," he inserted, raising his voice to override hers.

"But . . . but—"

"Will you shut up?" Bennett ordered, too loudly, evidently frustrated and out of patience with her.

She jerked erect in the seat, staring at him from surprise-widened eyes.

"That's better." He raked the fingers of one hand through his hair. "I . . . er . . . don't want to call off the whole plan," he said, formulating the idea as he spoke. "But I think we need to change the particulars."

She frowned. "The particulars? Such as?"

"The part about us being already married."

She let out another sigh of relief.

"We'll say we just got engaged instead." Feeling better about the plan and himself, Bennett relaxed against the soft leather seat, certain his new plan would work . . . and would alleviate the twinges of conscience.

Cynthia was shaking her head.

"What?" he asked, annoyance flaring. "What's wrong with it?"

She lifted one shoulder in a half-shrug. "I just don't see how telling your mother we're engaged will serve your purpose. I mean, wasn't the whole idea for me to be in the house, kind of looking out for her?"

"I'm afraid I don't see the problem," Bennett argued. "You can still do that."

She appeared shocked. "You'd still expect me to live in your home . . . with you . . . as merely your fiancée?"

"In my home, yes, but not with me," he was quick to assure her. "I have an apartment above my flagship store in Center City. I'll stay there most of the time," he shrugged. "Hell, I do now, or I did before Mother had the heart attack."

"I don't know," she said, her tone skeptical. "I can't imagine your mother accepting me into her home on the basis of an unexpected engagement." She frowned. "A wife is one thing, but a fiancée . . ." she shook her head and her voice faded.

"I can do as I like, as far as the house is concerned," he said. "It is mine, you know."

"You'd go against her wishes?" she asked, apparently appalled by the very idea. "Install me in the house whether or not she approves?"

"No, of course not," Bennett said. "I respect and love my mother." He had to smile as an image of her rose to mind. "I also know her. She's a pushover. I can almost guarantee that she will welcome you with a smile and open arms."

She was quiet for long seconds, gnawing on her bottom lip. Bennett had to suppress an urge to reach out a hand and place his fingers against her soft mouth to halt the ravishment.

"What do you say?" He finally broke her silence. "Will you agree to do it?"

She heaved a sigh.

He could have sworn he felt it.

Her features taut with tension and apprehension, she flicked a look at him.

He gave her a smile he hoped was reassuring. "Are you game, Cynthia? You agreed before. And now you're here. You might as well play along with me."

She sighed again; this one had the sound of defeat. "I . . . I'll give it a try," she murmured, then quickly added, "But I'm not making any promises."

"Good enough." Now he did extend a hand, his right hand. "Shake on it?"

She hesitated a moment, then slid her palm against his. Clasping her hand, Bennett found himself wondering how, after all the years of hard work in the home and the diner, her skin could be so silky smooth.

"Right." Releasing her hand, he turned back to the steering wheel. "Let's go home."

As he drove the car onto the highway, Bennett felt both depleted and elated, not unlike when he had run and won a long grueling race.

She should have said no.

Why hadn't she?

Ben . . . that's why.

She felt she owed him.

And, of course, she did.

Damn.

The thoughts flew fast and furious inside Cyndi's mind, making her head pound, her throat ache, and her stomach churn.

She was not a latter-day Cinderella. And Ben was certainly not Prince Charming.

Oh, Ben could be charming. Cyndi could testify to that. When it suited his purposes, he could turn it on

with the best of them—them being the users, the manip-
ulators.

And she, in her charmed stupidity, had allowed herself to be both used and manipulated.

Again the feelings of resentment and near dislike
reared their ugly little heads.

Damn.

She didn't want to do this. Marriage, an engagement,
either way it was nothing more than a scam. To her way
of thinking one was as deceitful as the other.

Yet she had agreed to his original plan, a fact she
now felt ashamed of.

If she had any guts, any grit, she would call a halt
here and now, Cyndi upbraided herself.

And then what? Logic asserted itself.

She felt an inner cringing. What could she do then,
if she did call a halt? She was hundreds of miles from
home, unemployed, and without prospects. She had
exactly two hundred and fifteen dollars and thirty-seven
cents in her wallet—hardly a princely or sustaining sum.

On the other hand, she chastened herself, if she possessed an iota of moral courage, she'd demand to be
taken to the nearest bus terminal to catch the first Capi-
tol Trailways bus heading to Western Pennsylvania.

But . . .

Cyndi's palm tingled.

Ridiculous, she thought, trying to dismiss the sensation. It was all in her head. A handshake, a mere touch
of skin on skin couldn't have such a searing effect.

Could it?

Of course not, she told herself. Imagination. That's
all it was, simple imagination.

Like she had imagined herself falling in love.

Lord, she wasn't a starry-eyed teenager, she was trudg-
ing right along toward thirty. And, by twenty-six, she

should know the difference between infatuation and love.

The very idea of falling in love, like one might fall into an unexpected hole in the ground, was ludicrous.

Wasn't it?

She stole a glance at him. Her churning stomach did an imitation of a triple flip on the trapeze.

So, okay, he was good to look at. So what?

So what? Stop kidding yourself, Cyndi Swoyer, you deep-sixed every one of your principles for a face with appeal and a charming manner, that's so what.

Dumb. Really dumb.

"Are you falling asleep?"

"No," she said, cringing at the word "falling." "I'm having a quiet nervous breakdown."

He laughed.

She glared at him. "It's not funny."

He laughed harder.

She made a rude noise.

"Come on, Cynthia, relax," Ben said in soothing tones. "There's nothing to be nervous about. I'm certain you'll like my mother, and just as certain she'll like you."

"That's what I'm afraid of," she muttered. "And the name's Cyndi."

Frowning over the former, he ignored the latter. "Why would you be afraid the two of you would not like each other?"

"Because I'll be living a lie!" Her voice crackled with exasperation. "We'll be lying to her from the get-go."

"But it's for her," Ben said with unruffled reason. "Our little white lie will make her happy, and being happy, she'll get well that much sooner."

Little white lie, Cyndi mused. Was there really such

a thing as a white lie? She doubted it. She had always believed that a lie was a lie was a lie. Period.

Which, she reflected, made her original surrender to his blandishments even more reprehensible.

"You're not thinking of backing out of our agreement, now, are you?" Ben was no longer laughing.

"I want to," she admitted.

"Jesus, Cynthia, we're almost there." Strain was evident in his voice; she liked the sound of it, thinking, why should she be the only one feeling stressed?

"You won't renege now, will you?"

She let him sweat for a few moments.

"No, I suppose not," she finally said, ending his mini panic attack. "And the name is Cyndi."

Ben ignored her reminder and addressed her compliance. "Thank you. You won't be sorry."

"I'm already sorry."

"Look, if it'll make you feel better about the thing, I'll make you a promise."

"What kind of promise?"

"When Mother's better, completely well, we'll tell her the truth, rather than just breaking our pretend engagement." He spared a glance at her. "Okay?"

Well, it wasn't a major relief to her conscience, Cyndi thought, but it was a concession. Unless she was prepared to get on a bus, she had little choice. And, weakling that she was proving to be, she didn't want to go, to leave him.

"Okay."

Soft as it was, Cyndi heard his sigh of relief.

Sure, she thought, nervously sliding her fingers through the shortened strands of her hair, only to have them swing forward again to brush against her chin. Of course he's relieved, he got his way . . . yet again.

She started when his hand touched hers. The contact

was so light, so gentle, and yet she experienced the same tingling sensation she'd felt when they shook hands. Speechless and wondering, she turned to stare at him.

"Calm down," he said. "Don't look like that."

"Li . . . like what?" She swallowed. "How do I look?"

"Scared, anxious." His smile was as gentle as his touch. "Your eyes reveal your feelings."

Oh, God, she hoped not.

"You have beautiful eyes, you know."

Cyndi blinked. "No, I—"

"Yes, you do. The gold-and brown-flecked green color reminds me of a small pond that was on the property of a friend of mine when I was a kid." His smile turned inward, became soft, reminiscent. "In the autumn, with sunlight dancing on the water and the leaves falling to float on the surface, the pond had that same sparkling green look."

Unused to compliments, especially poetic-sounding compliments, Cyndi sat numb for a moment, thrilling to the comparison Ben had made.

"Tha—" She had to pause to wet her lips. "Thank you, Ben, I don't—"

"Bennett."

Brought down to earth with a thud by the impatience that had chased the softness from his voice, Cyndi bit her lip and tore her gaze away from him to stare out the side window.

The sight that met her eyes confused her. They appeared to be driving along a back-country road. Wondering when he had left the highway, she turned back to face him.

"Where are we?"

"Almost home." Ben lifted a hand from the wheel to indicate the surroundings. "We're on the fringes of Bryn Mawr."

Cyndi had heard of it, at least she had heard of Bryn Mawr College—rather tony, wasn't it?

She didn't have time to ponder the question, for Ben turned off the road onto a short private drive. The house, set on rural-looking wooded land, and with a driveway that widened into a parking area before curving around one side of the structure, brought a soft appreciative "Oh" from her, then sent a shaft of trepidation quivering through her.

Chapter Eight

It was beautiful, the setting and the house. In dark red brick, with long windows and an arched, recessed door, the place reminded Cyndi somewhat of the Tudor design of homes she had seen depicted in glossy magazines or coffee-table books.

Brilliant red azalea bushes flanked the arched entranceway, and masses of white and pink impatiens bordered the house to either side.

Cyndi sighed, recalling the straggly bed of marigolds she and Jess had nurtured.

There was a feeling of serenity, solidity, and, to her, almost enchantment about the setting and this gem of the house, which was very large.

"What do you think?" Ben's quiet voice drew her from her bemused admiration.

"It's lovely."

"I like it."

"It's enormous."

"Nah." He laughed. "I'll admit the house is a good size, but it's certainly not a mansion."

She turned to give him an arch look before glancing back at the place. "How large is it . . . exactly?"

"Well . . . it is over five thousand square feet."

Cyndi shook her head. "Don't talk to me in square feet; that doesn't mean a thing to me." She smiled wryly. "Just tell me how many rooms, and about how big they are."

Ben's smile mirrored hers. "You know, you could see for yourself . . . if you'd get out of the car."

She gave another quick head shake. "I'm not getting out until you tell me."

He looked pained, but proceeded to describe the place. "There are five rooms on the first floor." A smile twitched at the corners of his lips, but he contained it. "I won't tell you the measurements. Suffice it to say, there's a large living room, a slightly smaller dining room, a good-sized kitchen, with a smaller adjacent room that was originally the pantry—a large pantry. When I had some remodeling work done a couple of years ago, it was sectioned into a small laundry room and an equally small bath. It has no bathtub, just a shower stall."

Oh, the deprivation of it, Cyndi thought wryly. "That's it for the first floor?"

"No." Ben shook his head. "There is one other good-sized room. It was formerly a den but is now a bedroom."

"For your mother?" she guessed.

"Yes. I had the change made while she was in the hospital," he explained. "I brought her straight here when she was released."

"Of course." Cyndi nodded approval. "There's an equal number of rooms on the second floor?"

"Yes . . . at least there were. There used to be four bedrooms and one bath. I had that rearranged when the remodeling was done, before I moved in. There are now three bedrooms—a large master suite with its own bath and two smaller rooms with a central bath."

"Hmmm," she murmured, her mind beginning to boggle, while her incredulous gaze climbed to the roof of the house. "And the third floor?"

Ben's gaze trailed hers. "It was a one-room attic. I had that changed as well. It now has a medium-sized bedroom, a small bath and a storage room."

Four bathrooms. *Four,* Cyndi thought, slightly stunned by the comparison of his home to the narrow, three-up, three-down house—with the later addition of a tiny bathroom—in which she had grown up.

Cinderella never had it so good.

"What, no garage?" she asked flippantly in an attempt to sound blasé and unaffected.

"Around back," he drawled, gesturing at the curved driveway. "Detached, three-car."

"What else," she muttered.

"Pardon?"

She shook her head. "And it's all yours."

"Yes. The house and"—he indicated the surrounding area with a sweep of his arm—"the land around it."

"Land?"

"Yeah, a little over three acres altogether, mostly trees, as you can see." He smiled. "My grandparents were determined not to be built in or bogged down with yard work. That's why they bought on the fringes of Bryn Mawr."

No wonder it has a rural look, Cyndi thought, while

being within a short distance of everything the city has to offer. Must be nice to have money.

"I can't even begin to imagine what a place like this must cost," she said without thinking. "Your grandparents must have been very rich."

Hearing what she had said, Cyndi was appalled at herself for her lack of tact. Flushing, she rushed to apologize. "I'm sorry, I—"

Ben silenced her with a flick of his hand. "Natural curiosity," he said, dismissing her apology. "But, no, they weren't. They were more than comfortably well off—a lot more, really. My grandfather owned his own business, my father took over when he retired. It was successful, profitable, though certainly not in the mega-million league."

Cyndi frowned in confusion.

"What?"

She hesitated.

"Cyndi, you may ask any question you like." He paused, then went on. "Actually, I think you should have a few facts, since I'll be introducing you to my mother as my fiancée, it would be normal for you to know the family history." He raised his dark brows. "So, what were you frowning about?"

She lifted one shoulder in a half-shrug. "I was just wondering why you struck out on your own, instead of going into your grandfather's business."

"My grandfather started his own small electronics business when the market was just really beginning to take off," he said, then grimaced. "I worked for the company while I was in high school and college. And, although I gave it my best, I couldn't get into the nuts and bolts of electronics."

"You were into books."

"Yes." He grinned. "Like you, I love books, all books,

but most especially old books, rare collectors' first editions.''

"You have some?" she asked, excited by the prospect of actually seeing a rare old book.

His grin widened, causing a twinge of response to ripple inside Cyndi.

"I have a room full, a few rather valuable ones, on the second floor of my flagship store in town."

"You're not rich . . . are you?" she yelped, growing even more nervous about getting entangled in his web of deceit.

Ben sighed and rolled his eyes, as if seeking help from a higher source. "No, I'm not rich. Not in the way I'm sure you mean. But, yes, I'm making a healthy profit. I'd say I'm about as comfortable as my grandfather was."

She shifted her gaze to his house and, without pausing to consider, asked, "What in the world is that place worth?"

"On today's market," he replied in a musing tone, "I'd say around a million and a quarter."

"Geeze!" she breathed on a note of awe.

"I didn't pay that for it, Cynthia," he said impatiently. "Come to that, neither did my grandparents."

"But you just said—"

"On today's market," he finished for her. "My grandparents bought the land and had the house built during the boom following World War II. I seem to recall hearing something about the total cost being somewhere in the neighborhood of fifty, sixty thousand . . . but I wouldn't swear to it.

"I inherited the house when my grandmother died," he reminded her. "Along with a few stocks, a little money, and her jewelry."

He went still for a moment, as if distracted. Watching

him, Cyndi thought she could actually see the wheels turning in his head. "What is it? What's wr—"

"Her jewelry," he murmured, as if he hadn't heard her. "Of course."

"Of course, what?" she asked, feeling she must have missed a clue or something.

"Her ring," he said, smiling, as though his two-word nonanswer explained everything.

"Huh?"

"Sorry." Ben laughed. "I was referring to one of my grandmother's rings, a particular one, and of course, that's the answer."

"Okay." Cyndi's eyebrows drew together in a frown of puzzlement. "What's the question?"

"A ring, Cynthia. We're about to go inside and announce our engagement—that is if I ever succeed in answering all your questions *and* prying you out of the car." There was a note of impatience in his voice, faint but there.

"So?" She didn't even try to conceal the combative tone in her voice. "And it's Cyndi."

He narrowed his eyes.

Refusing to be intimidated, she arched one eyebrow.

"So," he repeated grittily, "Mother will expect to see an engagement ring on your finger."

"Oh." Darn, she hadn't thought of that.

"Damn right."

"But—

"Fortunately, I thought of my grandmother's ring— her engagement ring—the most valuable piece in the small jewelry collection bequeathed to me."

"Which you wouldn't have thought of if I hadn't kept you in the car with my endless questions." She took great satisfaction in reminding him.

"Yeah, well, question-and-answer time is over," he

said, switching off the motor, thus the air conditioning, before releasing his door and swinging it open. "Out, Cynthia." His tone warned that he'd suffer no more arguments.

The nervous tension which had eased during the previous few minutes, coiled through Cyndi once again. Feeling more like a condemned person going to face a firing squad than a supposedly ecstatic, newly engaged woman about to meet the welcoming mother of her intended, she reluctantly exited the car.

Eyeing the house, which now appeared to have grown to massive proportions, Cyndi opened the door and stepped out, into the smothering heat of late July.

Ben was already pulling their bags, including the case he had bought for her new clothes, from the trunk. Joining him at the back of the car, she grabbed her own shabby case, which now contained nothing but shoes, the two pairs she had brought from home and the six pairs—three flat, three heeled—he had insisted on buying for her.

The trunk lid closed with a thunk; Cyndi imagined she felt the reverberation in her queasy stomach. A fine film of perspiration unrelated to the July heat sheened her forehead by the time they had traversed the short distance to the arched, recessed doorway.

Key in hand, and juggling the luggage, Ben unlocked the door, turned the patinaed-brass knob on the intricately carved wooden door and opened it with a nudge of the toe of one wing-tipped shoe.

Momentarily distracted by her irrelevant wonder at why this man didn't own so much as one scruffy pair of shoes, Cyndi was barely aware of the door swinging in noiselessly on obviously well-oiled hinges.

She stood in the shaded recess as if rooted to the

bricked walkway, peering into the rather dim interior, a spacious flag-stoned foyer.

"I'm trying to be a gentleman here, you know, waiting for you to precede me, but I'm not sure how long I can last." Ben's chiding jolted her into awareness. "These bags are getting heavy."

"Oh! I'm sorry, I—"

"Cynthia, will you just step inside . . . please?" He cut her off, heaving a sigh.

"Cyndi." Her response came automatically. But then, so did her reaction to the irritation in his voice. Sparing an instant to draw a deep breath, she straightened her spine, squared her shoulders, and took the fateful step.

The house was blessedly cool, and from what she could see of it from the foyer, even more impressive than the exterior. A stairway, one side open, ran up along one wall, widening at the base into the foyer. To the left of the staircase, Cyndi could glimpse a section of the living room through a wide, dark wood–framed doorway.

While retaining the classic elegance of a more formal period, the furniture and decorations she could see looked well used, lived in, welcoming, and homey.

Cyndi fell in love with the place on sight. To her instantly besotted gaze, the house appeared utterly enchanting.

"Mother? Aunt Louise?"

Ben's call wrenched Cyndi from the realm of enchantment and into the world of cold reality.

"Bennett . . . is that you?"

Cyndi's stomach muscles clenched as the modulated, cultured female voice wafted to them from the end of the central hallway.

"Of course, it's me, Aunt Louise," he responded,

lowering his voice as the woman came into full view. "Who else has a key to the door?"

The attractive woman could have been any age between thirty-five and fifty, Cyndi figured. Of average height, slender and sleek, she possessed an air of some consequence, as well as an off-putting look of haughtiness.

"We weren't expecting you." Smiling, her arms extended, the woman walked to Ben. "Why didn't you call to let us know you were on your way home?" she demanded, maintaining her smile for her nephew, while raking Cyndi with a narrow-eyed glance.

The suspicious glitter in the older woman's eyes sent a thrill of trepidation down Cyndi's spine.

"Because I wanted to surprise you and Mother," Ben drawled. Dropping the bags to the floor, he opened his arms just in time for the advancing woman to walk into them. "Where is Mother?" he asked, releasing her and stepping back.

"She's in the kitchen. We were—"

"I'm here, darling." Another feminine voice, lighter, friendlier sounding called from the depths of the hallway. "We were just getting a late lunch and . . ." Her voice trailed away as she appeared, her startled gaze shifting from Ben to Cyndi. "Hello. Who have we here?"

"Exactly what I was wondering," Louise said, a note of disdain marring the cultured smoothness of her voice.

Cyndi felt the fine hairs on her arms quiver, a feeling not unlike that caused by tiny bugs crawling over one's skin. She instinctively knew the woman was going to cause trouble, or at the very least would try to do so.

Hadn't she known this deception was doomed from the outset? Cyndi asked herself, fighting an urge to turn and run from the house. Ben inadvertently came to her rescue, helping her maintain control of her actions, if not her emotions, by taking her hand to draw her close to him.

"Mother, Aunt Louise, I'd like you to meet Cynthia Swoyer," he said, turning on her a gaze that was so soft, so tender, it stole Cyndi's breath away and opened a chasm of longing inside her. "Cynthia"—he turned to face and gesture to the two older women—"my mother and my aunt, Louise."

Forgoing her established reminder to him to call her Cyndi, she opened her mouth to say hello, nice to meet you, *something* intelligible, but was forestalled by his mother.

"Cynthia," she repeated, the light of interest brightening in her eyes. "The same Cynthia you mentioned during your telephone call the other day?"

"Yes, Mother, the very same." His fingers tightened around Cyndi's, as if in warning of what was to come. "She and I are engaged to be married."

His announcement was met with stunned silence for a few seconds, then the two women spoke simultaneously.

"How wonderful!" his mother exclaimed.

"Ridiculous!" his aunt cried, a bit shrilly.

Though Cyndi was inclined to agree with Louise on principle, she took exception to her tone of voice. Ben must have felt her stiffening, for his grip on her hand grew tighter still, almost to the point of pain.

"Indeed?" He leveled a drilling stare on his aunt.

"Ridiculous?" his mother repeated, her expression a mixture of shock and irritation. "Really, Louise, why would you make such an insulting statement?"

"Insulting?" Louise retorted, obviously aggrieved. "I beg your pardon, but I believe I was being practical."

"Practical!" his mother echoed in amazement. "I simply do not believe I'm hearing this from you."

Cyndi was beginning to wonder how long she and

Ben were to be held captive in the foyer when her erstwhile Prince Charming stepped into the fray to free them . . . at least for the moment.

"Ahh, look, ladies, could we hash this out later?" Though Ben had phrased it as a request, his question held the definite tone of a command. "Cynthia and I have had a long drive. We are tired. We want to freshen up, and since we skipped lunch, we are hungry and would appreciate something to eat."

Hungry. The magic word for a child to say to a parent, most especially a mother, Cyndi thought, amused by the electric effect the word had on Mrs. Ganster.

"Oh! Oh, of course!" the woman quickly agreed, tossing a look of extreme annoyance at her stern-faced sister. "Leave the luggage till later," she said when he bent over to pick up the bags. "While you and Cynthia"—she bestowed a warming smile on Cyndi—"freshen up, Louise and I will get lunch ready." She shot a challenging look at her sister. "Won't we, Louise?"

"Yes, certainly," the now cold-eyed woman acquiesced, turning her back to them to retrace her steps along the hallway. "I'll see to it."

Mrs. Ganster sighed.

Cyndi's soft heart went out to her.

Ben was frowning. "You and Aunt Louise will get lunch? Where's Ruth?"

"Ruth?" Cyndi gave him a puzzled look.

"My mother's housekeeper," Ben answered tersely. "Mother brought her along when she moved in with me." His tone gentled. "Didn't you, Mother?"

"I couldn't leave her behind and out of work." Mrs. Ganster looked to Cyndi, as if for female moral support. "Ruth is seventy-three, and she has been with me for ages. I'd be lost without her," she explained, giving Ben a look of chastisement. "Besides, who else would hire her?"

"Mother," Ben said, beginning to sound harassed. "I never said you shouldn't bring her with you. I like Ruth. I have always liked her. All I asked was, where is she?"

"Oh." Mrs. Ganster laughed. "Louise sent her off to visit her daughter in Arizona the day after you left."

"Uh-huh," Ben muttered. "Appears to me that Aunt Louise has acquired an inflated sense of her importance around here," he observed, glancing pointedly at Cyndi.

Obviously, his mother got the gist of his jibe, for she turned a stricken look on Cyndi. "I must apologize for my sister, Cynthia." Her hands moved, fluttered in a helpless gesture. "I can't imagine what has come over her."

"Please, that's not necessary, honestly, I . . ." Embarrassed by the situation and his mother's discomfort, Cyndi broke off.

Ben took a step forward. "You're not to worry—"

"We had prepared a chicken salad for lunch," Frances Ganster inserted, as if unaware of her son's having begun to reassure her. "But I can get something else for you, if you'd prefer."

"No, Mother." Ben gave a brief but definite shake of his head. "Chicken salad will be fine." He slanted a questioning glance at Cyndi. "Won't it, darling?"

Darling. Cyndi nearly choked at the unexpected endearment, the caressing sound of his voice.

"Ahhh . . . hmmm . . . Yes, of course," she got out. "I love chicken salad."

"Oh, good." The older woman beamed, almost as if Cyndi had absolutely made her day. "Lunch will be ready whenever you are, so you two run along now," she instructed, dismissing them with a wave of one soft, beautifully manicured hand.

At that instant Cyndi gave a silent thank you to Ben in gratitude for his insistence on her having a complete makeover, including a manicure.

She might even have given voice to her appreciation of his foresight and thoughtfulness, if she hadn't been distracted by keeping up with him as he strode across the foyer and started up the stairs.

"Wait, Ben," she pleaded, digging her heels into the stair as realization dawned. "I need my case, my makeup, my brush, my toothbrush."

Ben spun to scowl at her; nevertheless, he released his grip on her hand and started back down the stairs, grumbling to himself all the way.

Cyndi grinned as the one word, "Bennett", came through to her loud and clear. Attaining the foyer once more, he bent, grabbed her case, then hesitated a moment.

"Oh, hell," he said, tucking the case under one arm before reaching for the others. "I might as well take them all while I'm at it."

"Let me help you," Cyndi said, starting after him. The look he threw at her stopped her in her tracks.

"Just go on up, Cynthia," he ordered, quietly, if none too pleasantly. "I can handle it."

Whipping around, Cyndi stormed up the stairs, without a clue as to exactly where she was going, muttering mutinously, "Men! Strong like bull . . . dumb like ox."

"I beg your pardon?" he said, so close behind her she jerked in surprise. "I didn't hear you."

Good.

"What did you say?"

Damn.

"I . . . er . . . said, 'Those cases are full, they must feel heavy as rocks,' " she improvised.

Although Ben grunted and slanted a skeptical look at her, he made no verbal reply.

When Cyndi paused on the landing at the top of the stairs, he skirted around her to continue on along the second-floor hallway and came to a stop in front of a door, the first of two, on the left.

"I'll put you in here temporarily," he said, once again juggling the cases while turning the knob and swinging the door open. "Aunt Louise is in there." He indicated the second door with a quick head movement.

Thrown into confusion by his first remark, Cyndi barely heard the last part of it.

"Temporarily?" she repeated, wondering if he had changed his mind about her staying in the house.

"Hmmm," he murmured, motioning for her to precede him into the room.

Temporarily? Hung up on that one word, Cyndi was only marginally aware of the room she entered, though she did notice that it was as tastefully decorated as what she had thus far seen of the rest of the house.

"So don't bother to unpack," Ben advised her, following her into the room and depositing her cases at the foot of the bed. "I'll be moving you after we've finished lunch."

Cyndi felt as if the bottom had dropped out of her stomach. Had his aunt's attitude, her obvious rejection of her as Ben's fiancée, given him doubt about continuing on with his harebrained scheme?

"It'll only take me a minute to wash up," he said, heading for the door. "I'll meet you in the hall after we've made ourselves presentable. Okay?"

"Hmmm," Cyndi murmured vaguely, still pondering

his startling statement. Then, as he stepped into the hallway, her rattled senses came together.

"Wait, Ben!" she ordered, her tone sharp.

"Bennett," he said, heaving a sigh rife with despair. "And why should I wait?"

"I don't understand—" she began.

"What's not to understand about going down to lunch?" he asked, frowning.

Cyndi shook her head. "Not that, I—"

He threw her a puzzled look. "What, then?"

"You said you'd be moving me after lunch."

He nodded, still puzzled.

"Moving me where?"

"To my room, the master suite."

Chapter Nine

The chicken salad was delicious. The best Cyndi had ever tasted. It was even better than the salad her sister concocted, and Jess's chicken salad was excellent. Never before had Cyndi's taste buds experienced the combined flavors of chunks of chicken breast, salad dressing, celery, and some unidentifiable herbs tossed together with sweet white grapes and English walnuts; it didn't matter that the salad dressing was low fat, low cal.

She fervently longed to be able to relax and savor the beautifully prepared salad served on a bed of lettuce and garnished with wedges of tomatoes, slices of hard cooked eggs, and purple-hued Greek olives.

Unfortunately, it was not to be.

How could one appreciate food that kept getting stuck in a throat tight with tension? Cyndi reflected, gamely chewing each morsel into mush.

She took a deep swallow of iced mint tea to wash down the pulverized food, simmering with resentment against Ben for ruining her meal, and for other issues.

Cyndi had, of course, pounced on him immediately upon meeting him in the hallway after a quick trip to the bathroom to make herself more presentable, although how in the world she had become *un*presentable after doing nothing but sit in the car for a few hours, she couldn't imagine. As to Ben, she couldn't recall an instance when he didn't look presentable—damn his attractive male hide.

Nevertheless, Cyndi had pounced, firing questions, demanding answers. She had received not a one. Ben, in his often arrogant and frequently infuriating way, merely smiled and shrugged off her concerns.

"Later," he'd muttered, grasping her hand and descending the stairs. "We'll discuss it later."

Cyndi could have slugged him.

She was still tempted to do it, right there in the beautifully appointed dining room, in front of his lovely mother and miserable aunt.

Cyndi's heart warmed to Mrs. Ganster within moments of entering the dining room. The older woman welcomed her like a long-lost friend—or daughter—insisting at once that Cyndi call her Frances.

Ben's aunt, Louise, however, greeted Cyndi with a cool reserve bordering on suspicion. It quickly became clear that the woman considered her not nearly good enough for her precious nephew or the family. Pretentious and haughty, Louise displayed the tendencies of a first-rate witch.

Though uncomfortable in that woman's company, Cyndi really didn't mind for herself. She had had occasion to deal with her kind before, and she had held her own very well.

But she did mind for Ben's mother. The woman was still recovering from a heart attack, after all. The uneasy situation so obviously upset and embarrassed Frances, Cyndi considered adding Louise's name to her slug list.

"So, where did you say you went to college, Cynthia?" Louise asked with deadly sweetness.

The question was another—the tenth? the twelfth?—in as many minutes. She already had asked about her home, her family, their livelihood. The only thing Louise hadn't probed into was the state of the Swoyer finances.

Gritting her teeth to keep a discouraging word from passing her lips, Cyndi advised herself to stay calm, as she felt sure the financial query was about to be sprung on her.

"Honestly, Louise!" Frances scolded her younger sister. "You've kept Cynthia so busy answering questions she's barely had time to eat." She appeared seriously annoyed and, as if unaccustomed to it, distinctly uncomfortable with the feeling. "Must you pry?"

"Pry?" Louise looked affronted by the very idea. "I would hardly call an interest in my only nephew's *newly* acquired fiancée prying, Frances."

Seething at the emphasis the woman placed on the term "newly," Cyndi drew a deep breath in the hope of calming herself before attempting a response. Her pause to compose herself allowed Ben to dispel the moment of taut silence.

"Cynthia did not attend college, Aunt Louise," he said, abandoning his meal to insert himself into the inquisition for the first time. "Although she easily could have. She had earned a full scholarship, you know."

"Indeed?" Louise appeared stymied for a minute, but for only a minute. She speared Cyndi with a laser stare. "Then why didn't you matriculate, my dear?"

Matriculate!
Matriculate?

Oh, brother.

Cyndi almost strangled from the effort to keep from laughing in the pompous woman's face. She had cleared her throat to dispel the bubble of laughter, when another thought struck her, threatening to dislodge gales of the giggles and strangle her into the bargain.

In keeping with Cyndi's ongoing analogy of the fairy-tale scenario, her thoughts cast Louise in the role of stepmother rather than the wicked witch. To complete the characters in the improbable analogy, Cyndi whimsically inserted Frances into the role of fairy godmother.

Clamping a lid on her secret hilarity, Cyndi raised gleaming eyes to Louise.

If not the fabled wicked stepmother, the woman was certainly proving to be a dreadful snob.

What was wrong with "attend classes," anyway? She reflected. Or just plain "go to school," for pity's sake?

The giggles resurged.

Consequently, with the threat of yet another uneasy silence lengthening as Cyndi struggled to maintain a facade of control, Ben again took it upon himself to answer for her.

"Cynthia chose not to further her education at that time, Aunt Louise." Ben's expression was cold. His voice was hard. His eyes were down right steely. "You see, her mother passed away while she was in her senior year of high school. Being the eldest of four, Cynthia remained at home to help her father raise her siblings, as well as run the family business."

"How awful for you!" Frances cried, reaching out to grasp Cyndi's hand. "It must have been heart wrenching to lose your mother at such a vulnerable age."

The chill that had invaded Cyndi with Ben's stated intent to move her into his bedroom, except for that brief respite of humor, had intensified with each succes-

sive and too personal question from Louise. Now that
chill rapidly melted beneath the warmth of Frances's
genuine concern.

Cyndi's breathing, constricted ever since Ben had
dropped his verbal bomb, began to ease.

Frances's expression was so caring, her dark eyes, so
like Ben's, were so soft with concern, her handclasp was
so firm and supporting, that Cyndi was nearly undone.

The urge to laugh in Louise's face dissolved in a
sudden wash of warm tears. Lowering her head, she
swallowed several times, and blinked away the tears,
before attempting to respond.

"Yes . . . it was tough," she admitted, not bothering
to deny the truth of the matter. Glancing up at the
gentle woman, she tried a smile; it wavered just a bit.
"I . . ."—she swallowed again—"I adored my mother."

"My dear child," Frances murmured.

Cyndi bit down on her lip, hard.

Frances tightened her soft fingers around Cyndi's
hand.

Louise sat as if turned to stone, her eyes lowered.

Ben cleared his throat.

"I brought Cynthia with me to stay, Mother."

His abrupt statement of intent instantly thawed the
frozen tableau.

"Stay . . . here?" Frances's eyes grew bright with
expectation and enthusiasm.

Louise looked appalled.

"Yes, stay here." Purpose and absolute determination
glittered in Ben's eyes. "She is going to finally take some
college courses." The glitter softened as he directed his
gaze to Frances. "And keep you company, Mother."

"How wonderful," Frances exclaimed.

"But I'm keeping her company," Louise protested.

Ben scowled.

Frances turned to frown at her sister. "I simply do not understand you, Louise," she said. "You told me just this morning that you would be leaving soon after Bennett returned from his vacation."

Louise had the grace to appear embarrassed. "Well . . . I know, but—"

"But what?" Ben performed his one arched eyebrow routine, which by now was familiar to Cyndi. "You've changed your plans since this morning?"

Louise fidgeted, looking cornered. "No, I must get back. But, really"—she paused to glance at Frances—"think how it will look . . . I mean, I know there's a dearth of morals today, but even so, don't you think it will cause some talk, having Cynthia stay here in the house with Bennett?"

Cyndi wasn't surprised by the woman's suspicions; hadn't she voiced the same concern to Ben?

"Spare me, Aunt Louise," Ben snapped, apparently out of patience with her.

"They will not be alone together in the house," Frances reminded her.

"Come to that," Ben inserted, "I won't be here all that often."

"You won't?"

The two women spoke simultaneously; Frances with disappointment, Louise relief.

Ben shook his head. "Since I've got a lot of work to catch up on—thanks to my being away—I decided to stay in town at my apartment . . . at least for a while."

"Oh." Frances sighed. "Well, if you must."

Louise didn't say anything, but her expression of chagrin said plenty.

Checkmate, Aunty dearest, Cyndi thought, perked up considerably by Ben's explanation, as it sounded to her as if he wasn't expecting her to share the room—not to mention his bed—with him.

"Now, if all the questions are answered, and everyone is finished eating . . . ?" Without waiting for a reply, he reached across the table and took Cyndi's left hand. "I will make this engagement official."

Cyndi began to quiver inside as he opened his other hand to reveal a ring nestled in his palm.

"Oh, Bennett, your grandmother Ganster's engagement ring. How romantic!" Frances said, beaming at him in maternal approval. "I must confess I was wondering why Cynthia wasn't wearing a ring."

The quiver worked its way to the surface; Cyndi's hands trembled as Ben slowly, with great care, slid the ring onto her finger.

"A perfect fit!" Frances exclaimed. "I feel positive that's a good sign, Bennett. Your grandmother wore that ring with pride for over sixty years."

Her throat constricted, Cyndi stared down at her trembling hand as if at a foreign object.

Her lips parted on a silent gasp of appreciation. The ring was perfectly beautiful.

The delicate gold had been wrought into a setting in the shape of the larger outer petals of a rose, it cradled a large diamond with a blush of pink at its heart.

Cyndi felt terrible. She wanted to cry, but not for the traditional reasons of pride and joy felt by most young women at receiving the honor of such an exquisite token of loving affection. She wanted to weep with shame and remorse for the deception of Ben's lovely, kind, and wonderful mother.

A scalding tear escaped, and then another.

Frances smiled and handed her a tissue from the box she retrieved from the kitchen.

Louise wore a look of defeat.

* * *

Bennett heaved a sigh of relief as he closed his bedroom door behind him. It had seemed his mother would never get done hugging Cynthia and congratulating him. But finally, insisting he and Cynthia had to unpack, he had managed to extricate them from her arms, then the dining room.

However, his relief was short-lived.

"I feel like such a sneak." Cynthia stared at him, drenched hazel eyes filled with reproach. "A sneak and a fraud. Your mother is a lovely person, and I feel like I've betrayed her . . . her and your grandmother." She cast a guilt-ridden look at the ring on her finger.

"Betrayed? That's ridiculous, Cynthia." Infected by her sense of guilt, Bennett spoke with an edge of sharpness.

"Cyndi," she muttered. "And it's not ridiculous. Your mother is much too nice for this scam we're pulling on her, Ben."

"Bennett," he said, his voice harsh with frustration at his own uncomfortable sense of sneakiness.

"Whatever," she retorted. "Ben, Bennett, either way what we're doing is wrong."

"She's delighted." Bennett wasn't sure if he was trying to convince her or himself.

She rolled her eyes. "Yes, for now—because she believes this lie. But she's going to be hurt when she learns the truth."

"She need never learn the truth." Lord, he hoped she never did. Recalling his promise, he hastened to add, "At least, not the complete truth of the matter."

Cyndi hesitated. Her eyes shifted away from his. And then she raised her head, defiance in the angle of her chin. "I think we should confess, right now."

Every bit as uneasy in his mind as Cynthia, Bennett was tempted for a moment . . . but only for a moment. He knew that if he came clean, if he was totally honest with his mother, Cynthia would go, very likely to return home, definitely leaving her new finery behind.

Bennett didn't know why the idea of her returning home and leaving behind the things he had selected for her should bother him, he only knew that it did. And at the moment he wasn't inclined to delve into the whys and wherefores of his emotional confusion.

Whether in despair at his unusual lack of self-perception and incisiveness, or in response to her, he shook his head. "No, Cynthia, I don't agree. We made a deal. I expect you to stick to it."

Bennett could have sworn he could hear her grind her teeth. It made him feel like a jerk—but not enough like a jerk to change his mind.

"Well?"

"Well . . . what?" she muttered, glancing around the room for the first time since entering. "The room? It's beautiful, spartan, but beautiful."

"Not the room." He dismissed the suite with a casual flick of his hand. "Are you with me?"

She sighed.

"We made a deal, Cynthia."

"Cyndi, dammit," she flared. "I'm Cyndi. I'm not, never will be a Cynthia."

Ben couldn't help it; he laughed. "That doesn't make any kind of sense."

"It does to me," she insisted, her mulish expression somehow endearing.

Endearing?

Ben frowned, staring, fascinated, at her tightly compressed mouth. Mulish was endearing? You're losing it,

Ganster, he told himself, denying an inner prompting to soften her stiff lips with his own.

Kiss her?

Cynthia?

That was truly ridiculous.

He cleared his throat, and groped around in his mind to pick up the thread of their argument.

Oh. Yeah.

"Does keeping a bargain make sense to you?" he asked, his sarcastic tone betraying his impatience. But, was his impatience with her or with himself, his errant thoughts, and his surprisingly sensual reaction to them, to her?

Bennett didn't want to think about it. So, naturally, he applied more pressure to her.

"Well?"

"I hate it," she lashed out at him, her eyes shooting sparks, her breathing heavy.

"But you did agree."

"Your aunt doesn't like me."

"So what?" He shrugged. "You're not here to compete in a popularity contest."

"She thinks I'm not good enough for you," she went on. "I could tell, could almost feel her disapproval."

"I don't need her approval," he countered. "Neither do you."

"She's not a very nice person." A petulant note shaded her voice . . . petulance and a tinge of hurt.

To Bennett's sheer amazement, a strong and deep feeling of protectiveness swept over him. In fact, the feeling was so strong, he had to fight an impulse to go to her, draw her into his arms, reassure her.

The degree of protectiveness he had experienced in reaction to the purse snatcher was understandable; for all he had known at that instant, Cynthia might have been injured. But to feel that same intensity of protectiveness for her because she had been hurt by remarks made by his aunt . . .

Was he losing it or what?

He dragged in a quick breath. "Look, Cynthia, I know Aunt Louise was rude to you, but honestly, she's really not a . . . er, truly bad person."

She made a disgusted noise at his hesitation over the descriptive term. "Rude? The word witch sprang to my mind."

His lips twitched, but he suppressed the smile.

"She is neither bad, nor a witch," he intoned, exerting willpower over humor. "She is a little possessive . . . and rather full of her own importance and consequence."

"No kidding?" Cynthia drawled, sardonically.

"Perhaps I'd better explain the situation," he began. Then he sighed and motioned to the two comfortable wingback chairs facing each other in front of the fireplace. "Do you want to sit down?"

She started to shake her head. "I don't think tha—"

"Good," he cut her off, striding forward to take her arm and gently urging her to the chairs. "Don't think. Just, please, sit down, relax, and listen."

She gave him a "Don't push it, fella" look, but settled into the masculine-looking chair.

Seated opposite her, Bennett found himself pondering the wisdom of his suggestion. Leaning back in the well-padded chair, Cynthia crossed her legs, which hitched up her pencil-slim skirt, exposing not only her calves and knees but a glimpse of one thigh as well. All of which dried all the moisture in his throat and made his palms itch to touch, test the silky appearance of her smooth skin.

It *had* been too long since he'd been with Denise.

The thought drove every other consideration from Bennett's mind, shocking him with the realization of not having given a thought to Denise since he—they—had arrived home.

"You were saying?" Cynthia prompted him when the quiet between them lengthened.

"Oh ... uh ... yes, Aunt Louise." Bennett felt like a fool, then compounded the feeling by smiling like one. "She has always been a mite jealous of Mother—for no other reason than Mother is the firstborn."

"That's downright dumb." Cyndi declared. "As if your mother had anything to say about it."

Appreciating her blunt logic, Bennett had to smile, since he also considered his aunt's jealousy plain dumb.

"Perhaps," he conceded. "Nevertheless, every so often, Louise indulges in these little power plays, usually over minor, unimportant things and incidences. As a rule, Mother will tolerate her performance with patience and humor, at least for a time; then she will put a stop to it. There have never in my memory been any real hard feelings between them. They are good friends as well as sisters."

Cynthia's eyebrows shot up. "Are you suggesting your aunt considers the occasion of your engagement a minor thing or incident?"

"No." He shook his head, frowning. "Her behavior today has puzzled me—Aunt Louise is usually such a maddening Pollyanna. And I could tell it puzzled and upset Mother, too. I don't know why she . . ." He broke off as a possible explanation came to him. "Unless . . ." Bennett wasn't even aware of having spoken aloud.

"Unless?" she repeated.

He laughed without humor. "Unless she had someone else in mind and was hoping to play matchmaker."

"And would you have an idea of who that someone might be?" Cyndi asked, a little suspiciously.

"Not a glimmer." He gave another, sharper shake of his head, dismissing Denise from consideration, as his aunt had never met the woman.

"Then," she persisted, "why would Louise presume to take exception to your choice?"

"I haven't a clue," he admitted, shrugging. "But it doesn't matter, anyway. She'll be leaving to return home to California in a few days."

"Are you sure of that?"

"That was her intended plan."

"The best laid plans . . . and all that," she reminded him, her smile wry.

"Which reminds me," Bennett said, taking advantage of the opportunity afforded. "Do you intend to abide by the plan you agreed to with me?"

"I don't like it."

"You don't have to like it," he pointed out. "All you have to like are the benefits you will derive from it."

Cynthia winced.

It was a low blow, if not sheer blackmail, and he knew it, felt bad about it, but not bad enough to keep from hammering home his point.

"College courses, Cynthia," he reminded her. "Bookstores. Museums. Libraries."

She hesitated, gnawing on her bottom lip.

Without pausing to think, Bennett sprang from his chair to immediately drop to his knees in front of her. Raising a hand, he pressed his fingertips to her lips.

"Don't do that," he said.

"D-do what?" Her voice was scratchy. Her eyes were wide with surprise. Her mouth trembled.

Bennett groaned in silence and pressed his fingers more firmly to her lips.

"Don't savage your mouth like that," he murmured, leaning forward, as if drawn against his will. "If you want your lips savaged, let me do the biting."

Her eyes grew huge; their clear hazel depths became cloudy.

"Cynthia?"

"Cyndi."

"Whatever." His murmur echoed her earlier response. "I think I'm going to kiss you." He was homing in on her mouth as he whispered the warning.

"Why?" Her voice was dry, and barely there.

"Damned if I know."

He brushed her mouth with his. Her lips were dry. He felt a duty, and a desire, to moisten them. Tentatively, he stroked her bottom lip with the very tip of his tongue.

Cynthia drew in a quick gasp of breath.

So did he. She tasted like . . . more.

"B-B-Ben?"

Bennett didn't think to correct her; he didn't think period. He couldn't think beyond the need to crush her soft lips with his and to delve into the honeyed depths of her mouth with his suddenly voracious tongue.

It was crazy. It was improper. It was wrong.

It was like tasting erotica.

And merely tasting was not nearly enough.

Bennett's body went sensually ballistic.

Never had one kiss made him so very hot, so very hard, so very fast.

Molding her lips to his, he deepened the kiss, scouring the inner recesses of her mouth with his hungry tongue. Close to his ear, he could hear her soft, rapid breaths. The sound set fire to his senses.

He had to touch her, feel her soft body curved and yielding to his own hard angles. Clasping her around the waist, he drew her forward in the chair until her breasts were flattened against his chest.

Cynthia made garbled sounds.

Since they didn't seem to be a protest, Bennett accepted them as encouragement. Not that he needed any. What he needed at that moment was to feel his hand curling around her small, firm breast. Insinuating one hand between their melded bodies, he captured one, teasing the nipple through the material of her cotton blouse and lacy bra.

Excitement shot from his fingertip to his groin as the nipple sprang to life, hardening at his touch.

The necessity for breath broke the kiss.

Good Lord! Who would have believed . . . Bennett thought, dragging deep breaths into his starving lungs. Staring into Cynthia's bewildered eyes, hearing her own labored breaths, he ordered himself to back off and give her space.

His gaze swept down over her trembling form, the sight that met his eyes stealing his hard-fought breaths . . . and his resolve.

Pulling her forward on the chair had inched the skirt up to her lap, revealing her summer-bare thighs . . . and the junction concealed by a swath of pink silk.

Disobeying his self-imposed order, Bennett greedily took her lips again, devouring her mouth with his lips and tongue, while he nudged her knees apart with his hips, then moved his taut body into the cradle of her thighs. Curling his free arm around her slender bottom, he drew her unresisting body over the edge of the seat cushion.

Startled, Cynthia yelped into his clinging mouth, and flung her arms around his neck, plastering her soft, pliable form to his hard body.

Bennett shuddered in near-painful delight at the sensations streaking like flowing fire through his loins, now pressed tightly against her feminine mound.

He had to have her.

Making a low growling sound deep in his throat, Bennett bore her down to the carpeted floor.

Chapter Ten

The feel of the carpet fibers through the thin cotton material of her blouse broke into the bemusement blanketing Cyndi's mind.

What was Ben doing?

Ben was thoroughly kissing her, among other things.

She was kissing him back.

That much was evident.

The part that threw Cyndi was how very much she was enjoying his kisses, his probing tongue, his touch, the feel of him between her thighs, his manhood straining against her femininity.

If she didn't stop him, at once, Cyndi knew it would be too late to do so.

But, did she really want to stop him?

Ben had somehow loosened her blouse, opened the buttons, and unclasped her bra. His hand captured her breast. Cyndi arched her back in automatic response to the electrifying touch of his warm palm, the flick of his finger against her nipple. A soft moan was wrenched from her throat when the electrical current tingled into the core of her femininity.

Who would ever have thought it could be like this, so exciting and pleasurable?

Certainly not Cyndi. But then, she had had little experience with which to make a comparison. Other than that inept Bruce Harte, when she was seventeen . . .

"Oh!" Cyndi cried, the curl of his tongue around her taut nipple scattering her thoughts.

"You like that?" Ben's voice had a deep, smoky quality that heightened her excitement.

"Y-Yes!" Cyndi gasped, beyond the point of denial, or refusal.

"So do I," Ben purred, performing the sensuous curl of his tongue once more. "But, it's not enough," he said, his voice muffled against her skin, his warm breath bathing the wetness there, drawing a shiver from her. "I must feed on you."

Feed on her? Cyndi blinked, confused by his terminology. Whatever could he . . . ?

"Ohmygod, ohmygod, ohmygod!" she breathed, gasping when his lips closed around her nipple and he began to suckle her.

Reacting instinctively, she arched her back higher, striving for more of the new and unfamiliar and thrilling sensations created by his hungry mouth.

At that instant, Ben thrust his hard body into her arching form. The ache there unfurled into a throbbing demand for . . . something, a something Cyndi couldn't imagine, but which she needed desperately.

"Ben." She could barely breathe, never mind speak, articulate the desire clawing inside her. "I feel . . . I must . . . I . . ."

"I know," he muttered. "I feel it too—and I must," he said in a sexy growl.

He shifted to one side. Cyndi felt his hand tug on her panties. Without a thought—she couldn't think!—she raised her hips, allowing him to whisk the filmy briefs from her. Not even the clinking sound of the unfastening of his belt buckle or the whirr of the zipper being lowered alarmed her.

But alarm and a chilling sense of fear raced to the fore at the alien feel of his erection pressing into her, against the barrier of her innocence.

His lips took hers at the instant his shaft broke through the membrane.

Cyndi's cry of pain was muffled inside his mouth.

Ben went stone-still, and then he tore his mouth from hers, rearing back to stare at her in astonished disbelief.

"You're a virgin." Sheer amazement lent his raspy voice an element of awe. "Cynthia . . . I . . . I . . ." He sputtered to a halt, his eyes stark as he started to withdraw from her.

"No," she shook her head; strands of her hair tangled in the carpet fibers. "It's all right, now. The pain is gone," she assured him, not bothering to add that the driving desire was gone as well.

"You're sure?" His voice held uncertainty and concern. But, even as he asked, his hips moved, pushing his body deeper into her own.

Thinking that it made no difference, now, with his penetration complete, Cyndi nodded in response and gritted her teeth to endure the ordeal.

Stiff as she was, unable to relax her tensed muscles, his deep thrusts into her untested body still hurt her. Curling her fingers and her toes into the carpet, Cyndi clenched her teeth to keep from crying out, determined to bear with him to the bitter end.

But that didn't mean she had to look at him. She closed her eyes to blot out his face, the tautness sharpening his features, the flush of passion staining his cheeks, the tendons cabling his arched and straining neck.

Fortunately for her rigid body and her abused teeth, the end came quickly.

Ben gave one final thrust, made a grunting sound low in his throat, then shuddered, his long body shaking with the force of his release. He knocked the pent-up breath from her when he collapsed onto her tension-tightened body.

It was the absolute last straw for Cyndi. Releasing her grip on the carpet, she raised her hands to shove against his shoulders.

"Get off me . . . please," she said in a choked and grating voice. "I can't breathe."

Ben heaved a sigh, flattened his hands on the floor to either side of her, and pushed himself back, then off her still stiff form.

Cyndi immediately tugged down her skirt, then grasped the edges of her blouse, drawing them together to cover her breasts, wincing as the material brushed over her tender, sensitive nipples.

Seeing the brief flash of pain in her expression, Ben muttered a shockingly obscene expletive. "I'm sorry," he muttered, flopping onto his back beside her.

Cyndi felt more than saw his hands drop to his crotch, fumbling for an instant; then she heard the whirr of the zipper being raised.

"About what?" she retorted in a voice perilously close to breaking. "Your actions or your language?"

"About your . . . about everything," he said, wincing.

"What's done is done," she said, her tone reflecting her sense of weariness. "Sorry doesn't change it. The dirty deed is done, so to speak."

"I know." He sighed. "But I'm still sorry."

She moved her shoulders in a weak shrug.

"I . . . uh . . ." He frowned. "I should have stopped. As soon as I felt the resistance, I should have stopped, I know that, but . . ."

Cyndi turned her head to stare at him with dull eyes, and duller senses. "Why didn't you?"

"I . . ." Ben's eyes shifted away, but almost immediately came back to gaze directly into hers. "I lost control. I don't understand it." He frowned again. "I can't recall the last time that happened."

Cyndi stared at him pensively, wondering if his admission was supposed to be a compliment to her, to her compelling and irresistible sensual appeal.

Sure, she told herself. Right. You bet. And, if she believed strongly enough, and applauded hard enough, Tinker Bell would live. Get real.

"Cynthia?"

"Yeah?" She blinked, unknowingly chasing the faraway look from her eyes.

"I . . . am . . . sorry." He rubbed a hand over his eyes, so he didn't see the face she made at him.

"It . . . is . . . a . . . little . . . late . . . for . . . that," she returned in the same measured tempo.

Another flush, but of shame, not passion, brushed his high cheekbones. "I'll make it up to you."

"How?" she demanded. "Once it's gone, it's gone." She refrained from admitting that she wasn't particularly sorry it was gone. Hell, she had to lose it sometime, she ruminated with a flash of fatalistic, if slightly hysterical humor. She was twenty-six, almost twenty-seven. Who ever heard of a twenty-seven-year-old virgin these days? In truth, she was sorry she hadn't been able to enjoy it.

Ben winced again. "You're taking this well." His tone gave evidence of his surprise.

"What had you expected? Tears? Recriminations?" Cyndi felt a humorless smile tug at the corners of her lips. "Maybe you expect emotional histrionics." The tug on her lips grew stronger. "Do you imagine me the ruined Victorian innocent, running from you in a flood of tears, seeking protection from your mother, sobbing about being compromised?"

"You read too much," Ben accused, his chastised expression changing to incredulous consternation. "How can you make cracks at a time like this?"

Cyndi raised her brows into an exaggerated arch, in the hope of concealing any evidence of the despair she was suffering. "You'd prefer the histrionics?"

"No, of course not." He moved his head back and forth, the friction of his hair causing a faint crackle of electricity in the carpet fibers. "But—"

"But, nothing," she interrupted with finality. "Look, I haven't been traumatized by the experience. In fact, in the beginning, I wanted it just as much as you." God, she was being so rational and adult about the incident, she was making herself sick.

He shook his head, as if confused and off balance, not unlike a boxer who has just received a brain-jarring blow to the temple.

"If you wanted it, and believe me, I could have sworn you did, why did you freeze up on me?"

"Shock," she admitted. "Understand, I knew it would hurt, I just never realized it would hurt that badly."

Ben's expression became at once strangely embarrassed and masculinely egotistical. "I am rather large."

Tell me about it. Cyndi didn't voice her wry thought, but she did give him an I've-been-there look. "And rather proud of it, as well," she retaliated.

He felt the sting of her barb. "I should have stopped as soon as I felt you freeze."

"Yes," she agreed. "And you should stop agonizing

over it now. I'm tired, so if you don't mind, I'd like to get up off this damn floor."

"Oh." He jolted upright. "Of course." He scrambled to his feet, then extended a hand to help her up. "I'm sor—"

"Do not say you're sorry again," Cyndi ordered. "Or I just might throw up."

A frown puckering her brow, she glanced around the room, really taking note of it for the first time, quickly deciding it was well worth a second look.

It was huge, decorated in shades of hunter green and wine-dark red. The furnishings were spartan, as she had noticed before. In addition to the two wingbacked chairs they had so briefly occupied, the spacious room contained a large double dresser, a compact computer desk, and two bedside tables. The bed itself looked enormous in comparison to the single bed Cyndi had slept in for over twenty years at home.

The sweeping movement of Ben's arm caught her eye.

"Do you think you will be comfortable in here?" His question caught her attention.

"Comfortable? Me? In here?" Cyndi blurted out, the suspicion stirring again that he would ask her to share it with him, especially now, after their intimacy, however unsatisfactory. "With you?"

He sighed. "No, Cynthia."

"Cyndi," she said, distraction making her reminder sound rather vague. "I don't understand."

"Obviously," he returned, a tad sardonically. "I never intended you to share the room with me."

"But . . . where will you sleep?"

"In the room where your things are now," he explained. "That is when I'm here. If you'll recall, I did tell you all at lunch that I'd be spending most of my nights in my apartment.''

That was true, Cyndi conceded with a quick nod. What was also true was that he would probably be spending those nights with the ''friend'' he had told her about. Why had she feared for an instant that Ben might entertain the idea of having her share his bed, when he had another woman, a sexually experienced woman, ready and willing to share it with him?

Cyndi's spirits, already battered, took a dive.

''I can clear out the things I'll need fairly quickly,'' he went on, supremely unaware of her inner agonizing. ''There is plenty of closet space.'' He repeated the sweeping arm movement, indicating one complete wall of mirrored sliding doors. His arm moved again, a finger pointing to yet another door. ''The bathroom.''

Her own bathroom? A reluctant smile broke Cyndi's somber expression. Her very own bathroom!

''Well?''

She blinked. ''Well, what?''

''Does the arrangement suit you?'' Up until that point, Ben had shown infinite patience, but it was starting to slip. ''Do you think you will be comfortable in here?''

Will autumn follow summer? Cyndi thought, suppressing a bubble of laughter, which was somewhat scary, considering the quiver escalating into a quake inside her.

Perhaps her mind was starting to slip along with Ben's patience, she mused, dismayed by the sudden sting of threatening tears. It was either get a grip or lose it altogether.

Composing herself to respond with some degree of control—which wasn't easy as her trembling hands were still holding the edges of her blouse together, and her throat felt blocked by a load of rocks—Cyndi nodded her head.

"Yes," she replied, managing to hold her voice steady. "I believe I can be comfortable here."

"Good." Blatant relief came through in Ben's firm voice. "I'll get to work moving my stuff."

He turned away.

"I need a shower." Her statement, not a plea, not even a request, brought him swinging around again.

"Yes, of course." Ben ran a glance over her, noting her fingers clutching the blouse together, the crumpled look of her skirt; then his glance shifted to his own body. His lips twisted in distaste. "So do I."

Cyndi didn't move. Should she stay where she was, or go to the room he'd taken her to earlier? She stared at him, waiting for directions.

"You may as well stay here." Turning abruptly, he strode to where he'd set down his cases by the door. "I'll grab a quick shower," he said, scooping up the case that contained the clothes he'd had cleaned and laundered in the hotel, "Then I'll bring you your cases." He opened the door, glanced over his shoulder at her. "I'll clear the rest of my things out later." He raised his eyebrows. "Okay?"

"Yes."

His gut churning, Bennett practically ran to the guest bedroom, as though trying to escape the expression of reproach in Cynthia's eyes.

What in hell had possessed him? he asked himself, slamming into the room to collect her cases.

Standing stock-still, he scoured his mind and emotions for an explanation of his precipitous and disastrous action against her.

He had known her barely a week, for God's sake.

Simply by agreeing to his proposal and coming home with him, Cynthia had placed her trust in him—her trust and her innocence.

Her innocence.

Oh, shit.

A virgin, no less.

A thrill, atavistic, instinctive by nature, yet disturbingly pleasurable, tore through him.

I have been the first with her.

Fast on the heels of the thought came another, a demeaning realization: He had stolen from her something that was not his to take, something precious, and irreplaceable.

What had happened to that strong sense of protection he had felt for her?

Bennett scraped a hand through his hair.

But, how the hell could he have known? Cynthia was . . . what? Twenty-five? Twenty-six, maybe? Other than women who had taken a vow of celibacy, he wouldn't have believed there was a virgin alive over the age of nineteen or so.

What was wrong with the men in Cynthia's neck of the woods, anyway? Were they dumb and blind or just plain stupid? Bennett asked himself in genuine puzzlement.

How could any normal male miss Cynthia's many attributes? She was not only very attractive, good to look at, but intelligent, amusing, if in a dry way, hard working, and loyal as the day was long.

If he was honest, Bennett had to admit that he had felt the pull of her attraction from the beginning, the first time he'd entered the diner.

And the pull had increased during their stay in New

York, growing stronger with the enhancement of her appearance, her feminine qualities.

Where he had thought her pleasing to look at in the beginning, Bennett now thought her beautiful, beautiful and sexually alluring.

Back there, in his bedroom, he had had to taste her, and the taste of her had shut down his reasoning process, turning him from protector to predator.

But . . . Good Lord! How could he have known her skin was so very soft, like satin? Who could have guessed her long legs were so silky, her breasts so smooth? Why had he not realized her full lips would taste so sweet, her mouth would be so enticing?

The mere touch and taste of her had sent his sense and his senses into orbit.

A flimsy excuse for his behavior, Bennett ruefully acknowledged, but there it was, not pleasant, not pretty but factual.

The lustful demands of his body had superseded the cooler cautioning voice of his mind.

In all fairness to himself, he acknowledged Cynthia's role in her own initiation. She had not attempted to stop his admittedly clumsy seduction of her. After the fact, she had even confessed to wanting him.

The recollection reactivated Bennett's senses, which in turn stirred his body to renewed arousal.

He wanted her again.

Damn his hide, he wanted her again.

But he couldn't . . . he shouldn't.

Bennett's thoughts swirled, searching for plausible reasons for his apparent aberrations.

He was overtired due to the weeks of worrying over and caring for his mother while continuing to run his business with his usual dedication.

He had been tempted by his close proximity to Cynthia during their stay in New York.

He had been without a woman for some months.

Denise had been away too often.

Denise.

"Damn." Bennett swore aloud.

He hadn't given a thought to Denise since he had arrived home hours ago. Hell, he hadn't given any serious thought to her since he'd left home.

Despite the no-strings, open relationship he had been sharing with Denise, he could not help the uneasy feeling of having been unfaithful to her.

However ludicrous, considering their situation, or more accurately, lack of one, the feeling caused a cramping sensation in Bennett's stomach muscles.

It didn't matter that he and Denise had made no vows, legally or otherwise, to one another. It didn't matter that he had suspected her of having indulged herself on several occasions when she had been away on business trips; they were only suspicions, after all.

Still, Bennett had known and accepted from the beginning that Denise was not above using her body to advance her career. He had known because she had made no secret of her position, stating up front that she would do whatever it took to reach the top. He had even given her a grudging respect for being so forthright and honest with him about it.

Not wanting commitment himself, and complacent within their loose and unfettered arrangement, he had listened, completely understood, and kept his peace.

Denise was an adult. She had made no promises to him. He had no claim on her, nor would he have allowed her any claim on him.

And yet, he had never been with another woman since they'd begun sleeping together.

His sense of honor would not allow it.

A feeling of shame, intense and deep, washed over him. He squirmed within his mind and conscience, his stirring arousal deflated now.

Bennett had always considered himself a decent person, not perfect, but as good as most and better than some. He was a loving son, a kind and generous employer. He was honest, he paid his employees a decent wage, and he didn't cheat on his taxes. He regularly contributed to several charities. He even occasionally went to church with his mother. He worked hard and lived quietly.

Still, the shame burned him.

He had traded his honor for a moment's testosterone appeasement.

Cynthia deserved better, a hell of a lot better than a quick roll on the floor.

She deserved better than him.

Bennett accepted his own verdict. He might still want her—might, hell, he *did* still want her—but what he wanted was beside the point.

He had used her, misused her, and she had not complained, raised a fuss, or made threats of any kind. She had exonerated him of all the blame by taking some of it on herself, admitting that she had at least initially wanted him too.

But Bennett knew full well where the blame lay, and he'd have to live with it.

He didn't have to live with it in this house, however.

His ploy to keep his mother happy and content was in place, and he was determined to continue on with it, until such time as the doctor declared his mother as well and fit as could reasonably be expected.

As for Cynthia . . .

Bennett grimaced. Cynthia could have anything,

everything, her heart desired—college courses, books, clothes, whatever. He would gladly foot the bills without complaint.

And, more important than any monetary consideration, Bennett made a silent vow that Cynthia would have freedom from any more advances from him.

He would make his visits to his mother as brief as would be possible without causing her to speculate. He'd be as charming, as pleasant and amenable and, yes, even affectionate to Cynthia as he could, without actually touching her.

God . . . Bennett prayed, don't let me touch her. Because he knew if he did, however innocently . . . well, it wouldn't remain innocent very long.

He could do it.

He had to do it.

But damn! It wouldn't be easy.

Chapter Eleven

Cyndi spent a long time in the shower, the warm spray cascading over her, mingling with and washing away the tears flowing down her cheeks.

She should have stopped him when he'd pulled back, shocked by the realization of having pierced her innocence, she told herself.

No, she shook her head, flinging water against the walls of the shower stall. She should have stopped him long before that, because by then, it was too late, too late to save her virginity, too late for him to withdraw . . . too late, much too late.

A sob ripped from her throat, and she shuddered.

She felt shamed, abased. She wished she could blame Ben, exonerate herself by placing responsibility, all of it, on his shoulders.

Those shoulders were so much broader, stronger, than hers.

But Cyndi's conscience wouldn't stand for it, wouldn't

allow her to play at mental dodgeball to avoid shouldering her share of the blame.

What she had said to him was true; she had wanted him, in the beginning. And she was positive that, had she protested before Ben had reached the point of no return, he would have backed off.

Too late . . . too late.

What must he think of her now? Did he believe she had deliberately led him on, only to humiliate him?

But she hadn't. She couldn't. She . . .

Cyndi didn't turn off the taps until the bout of weeping subsided.

She longed to go home, to crawl into her father's arms as she had when she was little, whenever she had had an arm, or knee, or her feelings scraped. She wanted to pour out her emotions to that gentle man with the crooked back, the eyes bright with humor, and the loving, fiercely protective heart of a lion.

Her father would listen, understand, and offer sage advice.

A wry smile feathered Cyndi's lips as she patted dry her tender, sensitized inner thighs.

Knowing her father, she felt sure his advice would be for her to get back on the next bus heading east and fight for what she wanted.

But what did she want?

Cyndi sighed.

She wanted everything, she admitted to herself with innate honesty. And to her, everything was all rolled up into the person of Bennett Ganster, even though he wasn't Prince Charming.

But wanting something and getting it were two different things. She knew, better than a lot of others, the truth of that.

The hurt inside far exceeding the twinges of soreness

between her legs, Cyndi sadly faced the brutal fact that Bennett did not want her, at least not in any meaningful way.

Oh, for certain, he wanted her compliance in his scheme to keep his mother happy and content, while sabotaging that kind woman's campaign to get him to marry and produce a grandchild.

The proof of Bennett's intent weighed heavily on the third finger of Cyndi's left hand.

And, yes, he wanted her physically for the moment, had willingly, and probably would again willingly, use her to assuage his sexual tension until such time as his "friend" returned—if she allowed it.

Cyndi's soft mouth set into a grim hard line of determination. She would not—could not—allow it to happen again. Her pride would not admit it, nor would her sense of self-protection.

Reason warned her that though the first time was painful and uncomfortable, a second engagement would be infinitely more exciting and pleasurable ... and devastating to her mental as well as emotional well-being. Because, though Bennett might want her physically, his emotions were not involved.

She was there, available, no longer virginal. And Ben being all male, obviously didn't need to feel emotionally connected to become physically connected.

Whereas, the opposite applied for Cyndi. The idea of making love—no, having sex unhindered by emotional involvement—was the biggest of all turnoffs.

The simple truth was, she was in love with him.

Cyndi mused on that not so simple fact as she peeked around the bathroom door to see if the coast was clear. Relief washed through her as she noted her cases set by the enormous bed ... and the absence of the rightful inhabitant of the room.

Her introspection continued as she dressed.

What to do?

The wry smile returned to tug at her lips. What could she do, other than have herself committed? Falling in love hadn't been part of the bargain. But a bargain made was a bargain, darn the luck.

So, she couldn't go home, run away from her feelings, the upheaval of her emotions. She had given her word, and barring sudden disaster, she never went back on her word.

Besides, running away wouldn't solve anything. Her feelings and emotions and diminished pride would run right long with her.

Of course, that didn't mean she had to play out Bennett's game according to his arbitrary rules of conduct.

Consigning his attire dictates to the devil, Cyndi rummaged through the cases jam-packed with the new finery he had purchased for her and pulled out a pair of soft, faded jeans, a shocking pink cotton camp shirt and sneakers that had seen better days.

Feeling more herself in her own clothes, she was standing before the wide dresser mirror, brushing her shower-dampened hair into place, when a soft knock sounded on the door, immediately followed by Bennett's voice.

"May I come in, Cynthia?"

"Cyndi," she muttered, steeling herself for whatever he had to say before raising her voice a notch to reply, "Yes. It is your room, after all."

The door opened. Ben stepped inside and quietly shut the door behind him.

One look at him and Cyndi had to stifle a laugh. He was attired in jeans, a soft cotton pullover, and running shoes—not sneakers, running shoes.

So much for her attire defiance.

One look at his face killed her urge to laugh. His features were locked into an unrelieved expression of steely determination and purpose.

What purpose? Cyndi wondered, telling herself she couldn't care less.

Uh-huh.

She didn't have too long to wait for an answer to her silent query. It merely seemed like forever.

Standing tall, his bearing militaristic, Ben faced her with the proud detachment of a brave man facing a firing squad.

Was he expecting her to shoot him? Or just shoot off her mouth at him? Cyndi was taking refuge in humor.

"Cynthia, I won't say I'm sorry again—" he began in a soft but strong tone.

"Oh, good." She didn't hesitate to interrupt him, certain she'd freak out if he once again offered her an apology, regardless of how sincere it was. That she didn't bother to correct him about her name was a telling indication of her less than stable emotional state, an indication he evidently missed.

"Of course, I am sorry, but—"

"Cheese-and-rice, Ben!" she exploded. "Will you give it a rest?"

"Cheese and rice?" he repeated, frowning. "What's that supposed to mean?"

Cyndi gave him a dry look. "Even though I slip now and then, I really don't like to swear." She smiled . . . almost. "You figure it out."

He still looked puzzled.

She rolled her eyes, as if in supplication to a higher, wiser authority. "Repeat cheese and rice to yourself, real fast," she instructed.

It only took an instant, then his expression cleared.

"Yes, I see," he said, making an obvious attempt not to smile. "Clever."

Cyndi shrugged. "I didn't originate it."

"Uh-huh." His face assumed its former grim look.

That made her uneasy. Enough chitchat, she decided, beginning to feel awkward facing him across the room like a duelist confronting an adversary.

Take the bull by the horns, she silently advised herself, and either throw the sucker or be gored and have done with this verbal waltz of evasion.

"You came for your things?"

"No."

"You came for my things?"

His eyebrows met in confused consternation. "No . . . I just brought them to you a little while ago."

"I know," she said, heartened somewhat by his baffled expression.

"Then why did you think I had come for your things?" he demanded, losing a bit of his cool.

"To toss me out on my . . . er, rump, and send me on my way," she answered with hard-worn composure.

Apparently, he felt it was his turn to explode . . . so he did.

"For God's sake, Cynthia, do you see me now as some sort of monster or something?"

"Cyndi," she said, but vaguely, her mind latching on to the one word "monster." It fit—kind of—with her silly on-going analogy, although, in this fairy tale, the word "beast" would fit better.

"Answer me," Ben snapped at her, jolting her out of her fantasy into the here and now.

Truth be told, Cyndi liked the fantasy, at least that world held out the hopeful promise of happily ever after; reality didn't come close.

"No, Ben," she finally replied, sounding extremely

weary, even to her own ears. "I don't think you're a monster—or something." A cynical smile curved her lips. "I do think that you are a pragmatic, opportunistic, sometimes ruthless man—all qualities necessary to survive in this less than gentle world," she hastened to add before he could interrupt in response.

Ben winced, as if she had actually struck him. "I've hurt you very badly," he said in tones of remorse. "Haven't I?"

Somehow, from somewhere inside, Cyndi dredged up a smile and a response of bravado. "I'll live."

"Yes, you will." Ben's jaw tightened. "And without harassment, of any kind, from me," he went on, his voice flat, steady.

"You want me to leave, don't you?" Cyndi asked, voicing her deepest fear.

"No." He gave a sharp shake of his head. "I don't want you to leave." His lips twisted in self-derision. "In fact, I came in here fully prepared to beg you to stay on and keep to our agreement." He drew a quick and harsh-sounding breath. "Although, should you decide to leave, I'll understand."

"Ben . . . I . . ." Cyndi's voice failed, silenced by the conflicting emotions of relief and regret.

"Bennett," he said, not forgetting to remind her. "Before you say anything else, let me assure you that, if you stay, I give you my word—for all that's worth to you now—that I will not pressure you in any way. You may do as you wish. Come and go as you like. Have anything you want within reason. I will support you without complaint."

"Penance, Ben?" she murmured, disliking him intensely at that moment for casting her into the undesireable role of the woman wronged.

"Yes, I suppose so," he answered candidly, this time forgetting to remind her of his name.

"Or expediency?" she suggested, angry with him, and with herself for her own weakness for him.

"That, too," he admitted with blunt and fantasy-killing honesty.

"Of course." Cyndi suddenly felt beaten, crushed by the truth. She longed to sit down, lie down, die. Pride and the last shreds of her inner strength kept her upright, her composure intact.

"Understand," Ben's soft voice broke into her reverie, "if you decide to stay, I won't be able to leave for a while, a few days or so, at any rate. And we will have to play out the farce of the engaged couple, for appearance's sake."

Cyndi nodded, then stilled, holding herself together with sheer willpower.

"Naturally," he continued, his voice beginning to show strain, "I will have to make periodic visits, weekends and such, during which a display of affection will be on order."

"Naturally." Cyndi managed the one drawling word in response when he paused and arched a brow.

"But," he went on, doggedly, "I swear, I will not touch you in any personal way."

The cut direct, Cyndi reflected, recalling evey Regency romance novel she had ever read.

"Not that I won't want to."

That got her attention. She raised her brows.

"You're a very lovely woman, Cynthia, inside and out." His voice was now hoarse and ragged. "Very lovely . . . and very desirable."

The thought of dying lost its appeal. If he found her desirable . . . well . . . Proving the adage that hope

springs eternal, Cyndi felt revived, reinvigorated; her
faith now restored in the possibility of ever after.

"Will you stay?"

How could she go now? Could the dreamer deny the
allure of the dream? So, odds were, she didn't have a
hope in hades of seeing her dream come true, but where
would the world be without its dreamers?

"Yes," she answered, steeling herself for whatever the
future held in store for her, be it Ben or utter rejection.
"I'll stay."

He didn't even try to suppress his deep sigh and slight
smile of relief.

"Bennett. Cynthia?" The call from Frances ended
their strange interlude.

"You'd better answer," Cyndi said, mentally shaking
herself into a semblance of animation. "Or," she went
on in a voice dry as dust, "she might wonder what in
the world we could be up to."

Ben's eyes narrowed at her unsubtle barb, and his
lips thinned; but he didn't return her fire. He turned
instead to open the door.

"We'll be down shortly, Mother," he called out.
"We're just about finished up here."

We're just about finished . . . Well, that said it all, didn't
it? Cyndi thought, crossing from the dresser to the open
suitcase on the bed.

"Where should I put my things?" she asked, not looking up when she heard the door close.

"All of the drawers are empty on the right side of
the dresser, so are the spaces on the right sides of the
closets—take your pick."

Still refusing to look at him, Cyndi nodded numbly,
chilled by the remoteness of his tone.

Ignoring Ben, his attitude and his actions, as he

moved about collecting his stuff, she went to work unpacking her cases.

She barely filled two of the six dresser drawers allotted her and only a small section of the closet space, which she deemed roomy enough to hold most of the inventory of a small boutique.

The entire process required less than ten minutes of her time. Her unpacking complete, she stood, irresolute, staring at the empty cases.

"I'll take care of those," Ben said, startling her with his sudden appearance beside her.

Already on edge, and unnerved, Cyndi was jolted and instinctively stepped back, eliciting a muttered curse from Ben.

"Dammit, I gave you my word, Cynthia," he said impatiently. "I wasn't going to touch you."

"Cyndi," she reminded him, just as impatiently. "And I didn't think you were going to touch me. I didn't hear you, that's all—you startled me."

"Oh." He grimaced. "I didn't mean to sneak up on you or anything." He offered her a faint, conciliatory smile. "Look, while I realize too well that you have every reason to resent me, avoid me, this won't work if you're going to flinch away from me every time I come near you."

"I'm sorry." Cyndi groaned in silent despair at her response. Why should she apologize to him?

Ben was shaking his head. "No apologies necessary." He sighed. "While I know you might find this hard to believe . . . I do understand the strain you're under, due entirely to my . . . shall we say . . . less than gentlemanly behavior?"

"Yeah, we can say that," Cyndi replied, trying to lighten the heavy atmosphere with flippancy. Then, she went one step further, and grinned. "But only because we're both book people."

Ben's remote expression shattered from the force of the burst of laughter that erupted from his throat.

The delightfully masculine sound of his laughter eased the bands of constraint in Cyndi's chest, the stranglehold of tension in her throat, freeing her to laugh with him.

The sound of her unrestrained laughter sobered him, but just for a moment. Then, a teasing smile tilting the corners of his mouth, he hesitantly extended his right hand to her.

"In that case, do you suppose we could have peace in our time?" His tone was shaded by whimsy.

The shading held appeal for Cyndi. A spur-of-the-moment response springing to mind, she smiled and placed her hand in his. "And go boldly forth where no man—or woman—has gone before?" she asked, managing to keep a straight face.

Ben grasped her hand, laughing again; it sounded even better, more attractive, this time. The warmth of his hand, curling around hers, chased the last lingering chill of despair from her.

She might be the world's biggest fool, Cyndi mused, her smile wobbling only a little, but, at least, basking in the warmth of Ben's laughter, the brief touch of his hand, she was no longer a frost-bitten fool.

Which, she reflected with wry humor, curling her fingers into her palm to hold on to the warmth when he released her hand, proved her earlier assertion to him. She would survive.

Chapter Twelve

The weeks had flown by.

Summer was almost over.

Louise was gone—finally.

Ben was gone most of the time.

By and large, Cyndi was glad for that . . . except at night, when she lay alone and awake in *his* bed, his huge, empty bed.

It was during those nighttime hours that she suffered pangs of regret for what he'd done—for what she had allowed him to do—and remorse, for many reasons, not the least of which was her weakness, emotional and physical for him; her continued compliance, however reluctant, in his scheme to free himself by deceiving his mother about their relationship.

Other than those mostly dark-time mental demons, Cyndi was reasonably content, or at least content enough to convince her father of her well-being whenever she spoke to him on the phone.

Carl Swoyer had not sounded convinced when she

had rung him late in the afternoon on the day she and Ben had arrived at the house.

Of course, Cyndi had been rather upset at the time, and so was not completely successful in concealing her tense and confusing emotional state.

But she had managed better on subsequent calls home, which she made twice a week. On those occasions, sometimes her father answered, and he sounded different, more chipper than he had in years.

Curious, Cyndi mused on the cause of her father's suddenly lighter and brighter outlook.

At other times, when Jess answered the phone, she also evinced a new lightheartedness.

If Cyndi hadn't known better, she might have concluded that her absence had caused their more positive, upbeat attitude. But she suspected what was going on, the mysterious changes intrigued rather than injured her.

The mystery, or part of it, was solved the second time Cyndi spoke with Jess.

"Cyndi, you won't believe it!" her sister exclaimed.

Laughing at the vibrancy and excitement in Jess's voice, Cyndi responded, "How can I believe it, when I haven't a clue as to what you're talking about."

"Mr. Adams . . . Jeffrey . . ."—Jess rushed breathlessly—"He . . . Cyndi, he asked me out to dinner!"

Cyndi laughed again, delighted to hear the note of sheer happiness in her sister's voice. "I suppose I don't need to ask if you accepted?"

"Are you kidding?" Jess's laughter echoed back at her. "I couldn't get the yes out fast enough!"

"Go for it, Jess," Cyndi advised before asking to speak to their father.

She was happy for Jess, she told herself later when she was alone, curled into a ball in Ben's big bed. Of course, she was happy for Jess. It was just . . . She sighed. It was tough being the oldest and the one without romantic prospects.

Once, Cyndi had been surprised to hear the voice of Emily Davidson.

Hmmm. And her father had been sounding bright as a newly minted coin. Were her father and Emily engaging in some extracurricular activities? The amusement she derived from the thought gave evidence of how well Cyndi was settling into her new environment.

Still, the brief stab of envy she experienced told her more than she wanted to know about the arid landscape of her own emotional terrain.

Cyndi quickly plugged the self-pity leak in her mental outlook. She had plenty to be thankful for, she reminded herself, mentally ticking off her blessings. She was living in a lovely home, within striking distance of a cultural banquet—libraries, museums, bookstores, and theaters. And she would soon be attending college classes.

What more could any reasonably intelligent woman want? she chided herself.

Ben, her self chided back.

She banished the thought with an impatient shake of the head and advice to lose the tendency to introspection and get on with her life.

She had spent the waning weeks of summer trying to follow her own advice.

To her pleased surprise, Cyndi and Frances quickly developed a deep and mutual affection for one another, after the once unpleasant and disapproving Louise had made her protracted exit from the scene.

Yet, in all fairness to Frances's sister, Cyndi had to acknowledge the effort Louise had eventually put forth

to correct her initial reaction to Ben's sudden and unexpected announcement of his engagement.

"It was simply such a shock," Louise had said, a few
days after Cyndi's arrival, not actually apologizing, but
unbending enough to soften her tone and offer a conciliatory smile to her nephew and Cyndi.

Although secretly Cyndi was less than impressed by
the older woman's halfhearted attempt at damage control, Ben, at least, was relieved, since his aunt's softening
seemed to bear out his claim to Cyndi that Louise had
always been a blazing Pollyanna.

At the time, Cyndi had decided that this particular
Pollyanna must have lost her illusions with encroaching
age, but she had prudently kept her admittedly biased
opinion to herself.

Frances glowed with approval for her sister.

Ben was happy in his restored faith in his aunt.

Cyndi wasn't about to burst any balloons. She had
more than enough on her plate, without causing conflict over Louise.

Dealing with Ben, playing the role of the loving new
fiancée, required every ounce of Cyndi's strength and
fortitude.

Whenever he touched her hand, whenever his voice
deepened with a note of caring, whenever his eyes darkened with emotion, Cyndi, knowing full well that he
was putting on a benefit performance for his mother
and aunt, still experienced a melting sensation.

Though Ben scrupulously adhered to his word and
did not touch her in any personal way, having him touch
her at all, hearing him call her his darling in soft and
low tones of affection, tore at the very fabric of Cyndi's
emotional endurance.

Her resolve and reserves were rapidly diminishing by

the time Ben, to her heartfelt gratitude, finally took himself—and his performance—off.

Afraid Louise would revert to her earlier sniping once Ben's imperious presence was no longer evident to keep her in check, Cyndi had steeled herself for a renewed assault that fortunately never occurred.

Frances made sure of that. In her gentle, yet determined way, she made it abuntantly clear to her sister how delighted she was with her son's choice of a future bride.

To her credit, Louise appeared to know when she was beaten. Putting a good face on the situation, she left to return to California the day after Ruth, Frances's friend and housekeeper, returned from Arizona.

From their first meeting, Cyndi had decided that Ruth was worth her weight in gold.

Small, thin, wiry, her hair white as fresh snow, her brown eyes bright with the joy of life, Ruth was a veritable fountain of energy and friendliness.

Quite like Frances had, from day one Ruth accepted Cyndi into her life with smiling eyes, embracing arms, and an open heart.

Cyndi had volunteered to do the cooking, prepare all the meals, the day after she and Ben had arrived at the house. Both Frances and Louise were happy to relinquish the chore. But Frances was quick to forewarn Cyndi against continuing the practice after Ruth returned from her vacation, since the housekeeper had always been adamant about another woman in her kitchen.

Nonetheless, Cyndi had dared to invade the older woman's domain, first to chat, then to offer help. She knew Ruth's acceptance of her was complete when the woman gave her free rein at the stove.

So Cyndi was content—or as content as she possibly could be under the circumstances.

Other than a few quick overnight visits, during which he said little of substance, and intermittent phone calls, during which he merely inquired about how she was getting on before asking to speak to his mother, she had had no meaningful contact with Ben. And yet, for some inexplicable reason, she continued to sink ever deeper in love with him.

Still, her conscience remained on active duty, jabbing her when least expected with twinges of guilt for her part of the deception of his mother.

Cyndi hated the charade more with each passing week, simply because she'd come to love Frances almost as much as she loved her son.

However, by keeping busy, Cyndi managed to be reasonably happy.

And she certainly was busy, busy making all kinds of new and wonderful discoveries.

One of the first of these was made in the master bathroom—her bathroom for the duration.

Until Ben's and then Louise's departures, Cyndi had made do with quick showers in the separate shower stall. But, on the evening of the day of Louise's leave-taking, she'd decided to treat herself to a long, soaking wallow in the huge tub, which to Cyndi looked more like a small swimming pool.

It did occur to her that two could wallow quite comfortably in the tub. Growing warm all over, she had quickly derailed that particular train of thought.

Her discovery came after she had eased herself into the steamy, scented water. Curious, and wondering what the purpose could be for the small chrome disc set into the broad rim of the tub, Cyndi had reached out and touched it, simply lightly touched it.

Then, jolted, she'd pulled her hand back at the noise, like that of a motor kicking in, and the sudden appearance of bubbles in the churning water. Although she had never seen one before, she knew what it was.

A spa!

"I love it!" Cyndi cried aloud, her laughter bouncing off the tiled walls. "Keep your prince's palace, Cinderella. I'll take the frog's spa!"

The frog, otherwise known as Ben, made the first of his quick-stop visits on Thursday of the following week.

"Bennett, how lovely!" Frances exclaimed when he strode into the dining room just as she and Cyndi were setting the table for lunch.

"I'm afraid I can't stay long," he warned, going directly to his mother to give her a hug. "I'm on my way to the Bucks County store, and stopped by to visit." He'd stepped back to grin at her. "I was hoping you'd offer me lunch."

"Yes, of course," Frances said, frowning. "But when are you coming for a long visit?"

"Don't know, pretty busy," he said, evasively, turning to embrace Cyndi. "Hello, darling," he'd murmured, but loud enough for Frances to hear. "Is Mother treating you well?"

"Bennett, really!" Frances exclaimed.

Cyndi could barely respond due to the tightness in her throat, the sudden warmth and weakness in her body. Captive within his embrace, she could feel the taut strength of him, could smell his distinctive scent, and she shivered from the hair-stirring breath of him.

It was only when he released her and moved away that Cyndi found her unsteady voice.

"Y-Yes," she assured him, smiling at the older woman. "Your mother has been wonderful."

"And Ruth?"

"Don't you worry about Ruth, young man," the housekeeper said, bustling into the room to give him a stern look. "I know how to behave."

A smile twitched Ben's lips. "No kidding? When did you learn to do that?" he asked, laughing as he swept her into an embrace.

Ben was charming, amusing them throughout their lunch with an embellished account of the trials and tribulations he endured at the hands—and dry wit—of his aggravating but indispensable secretary.

And then he was gone.

And Cyndi could breathe freely . . . again.

Cyndi's second discovery actually was two discoveries in one—the combined treasures of Ben's book and classical music collections, both of which were extensive. She found the books in a wide, floor-to-ceiling closet, the CDs in the long credenza next to the stereo CD system, the day Ruth allowed her to dust the living room.

"May I read some of these books and play some of the CDs sometime?" Cyndi asked Frances, excited by her discovery of the two treasure troves.

Frances smiled at the thrilled expression on Cyndi's face.

"My, dear, you may read and play all of them, anytime," she answered. "And the music as loud as you like." Frances laughed at Cyndi's surprise. "It will be almost like attending concerts again."

Cyndi's look of surprise changed to one of puzzlement. "Why don't you attend concerts anymore?"

Before replying, Frances glanced around, rather furtively, Cyndi thought, as if to make certain Ruth wasn't within hearing range.

"Although I didn't tell Bennett or Ruth, I really wasn't feeling too well toward the end of the concert season last year," she softly confessed. "And I missed the few summer concerts offered because my mind was . . . ah . . . otherwise occupied."

Frances didn't elaborate, but then Cyndi didn't need clarification. She knew Ben's single state to be the cause of Frances's preoccupation.

Cyndi's conscience tweaked her.

Promising herself a closer inspection of the book titles later, she slipped a disc into the machine.

The opening strains of a Mendelssohn violin concerto performed by Isaac Stern swept away the twinge of conscience, and Cyndi entered another realm.

During those final weeks of summer, the stereo system's volume turned on high so she could hear it anywhere in the house, Cyndi feasted on the selection of musical delicacies on display in the credenza.

She saved the books for quiet Sunday afternoons, and the even more quiet nights, any night, every night, after she had retired to the emptiness of Ben's bed.

On the Friday of the week of Cyndi's book and music discovery, Ben arrived, announcing he would be staying the entire weekend.

Frances was thrilled.

Cyndi was cast into a near panic from fretting over what in the world they would talk about.

As it turned out, it wasn't half as bad as she had feared.

"So, what have you been doing with yourself?" he asked, after the obligatory embrace.

Shaken once more by being held so closely, if imper-
sonally, to his arousing body, Cyndi slipped her hair
behind her ears with trembling fingers, then smiled
before attempting to respond.

"I . . . er . . . I've been reading a few of your books
and playing some of your CDs," she answered in a
breathless rush. "I hope you don't mind?"

"Not at all. Not at all," he said expansively, if rather
tritely. "Be my guest."

And that encapsulated the tone of the weekend, for
both of them. Trite.

If it hadn't been for the opportunity to escape into
the stirring music, Cyndi didn't know how she would
have endured it.

Fortunately, Frances appeared not to notice anything
was out of sync.

Cyndi heaved a sigh of relief when Sunday evening
came and Ben departed.

Her third discovery was found in the exhilaration of
driving Frances's small Mercedes, having only before
driven her father's old truck, the black bomb.

Ruth instigated that singular experience.

"We need groceries," she announced, her voice
pitched high to be heard over the blasting stereo.
"We're running low on fresh vegetables."

Cyndi immediately turned down the volume on the
New York Philharmonic recording of Rimsky-Korsakov's
Scheherazade, Leonard Bernstein conducting.

"So go to the supermarket," Frances advised Ruth;
waving her away. "They're just getting to my favorite
passage of the music."

"Can't," Ruth said, shaking her head. "I'm in the

middle of cleaning out the fridge. I was hoping Cyndi would be a sweetheart and do the shopping."

By this point in their association, both Frances and Ruth were calling her Cyndi, much to Ben's obvious disgruntlement the first time he heard them do so.

"I would gladly go, but ..." Cyndi began, then paused, hesitant to remind Ruth of her lack of transport.

"Good," Ruth said into the minisilence. "You can take Frances's car." She arched a brow at her employer. "Can't she?"

Frances agreed at once, smiling at Cyndi. "Well, of course she can."

"And she can take you with her," Ruth decreed, as if she were the one in charge, which, as Cyndi had swiftly ascertained, she was.

Frances's serene expression dissolved into uncertain concern. "I'd love to go, but—"

"But nothing," Ruth cut in adamantly. "You've hardly been out of this house in months. You just ride along with Cyndi." She dismissed Frances's protest with a wave of her hand. "Get the dust blown from your mind."

Quiet while she had been observing the interaction between the two women, Cyndi covered her mouth with a hand to muffle an impending laugh at Ruth's bluntly voiced suggestion to her employer.

Frances was not displeased; in fact, she laughed in response to the gibe. "You fear I've been growing cobwebs in my mind, do you?"

"Don't you?" Ruth retorted, planting bony hands on equally bony hips.

"I'll get myself ready to go," Frances said by way of an answer. "Come along, Cyndi, it would appear we're in charge of replenishing the larder."

Cyndi was an excellent driver, and except for a few

nervous moments at the outset, due to her unfamiliarity
with the vehicle and to her awareness of how expensive
it was, she loved being at the wheel of the car.

After the success of her first outing with Frances,
Cyndi was soon assigned the responsibility of doing all
the necessary running and fetching, usually with Frances
ensconced in the passenger seat beside her.

Which, in turn, resulted in the very best of Cyndi's
discoveries.

She and Frances quickly became more than friendly
companions. They became fast and close friends. So
close were they, in fact, Cyndi succeeded in talking not
only Frances but Ruth into accompanying her on jaunts
to investigate the available cultural facilities.

On a twice-a-week basis, the threesome, seemingly
so mismatched and yet completely in tune, haunted
libraries, museums, The Avenue of the Arts.

It was great fun, exploring together, laughing
together, lunching together, learning together, and
proving the old adage: one is never to old to learn . . .
or even have fun.

Frances even accompanied Cyndi to check out the
campus of Penn, the university she had chosen to attend
on a part-time basis.

The size of the campus, the sheer numbers of students, both terrified and excited Cyndi. While she was
eager to get started, she also was anxious about doing
so.

Later in the afternoon of the day they explored the
Penn campus, Ben made another of his hello-goodbye-
see-you-later visits.

This time he came as they were getting ready to sit
down to dinner.

"Do I detect the aroma of broiled flounder and baked potatoes?"

All three of the women started at the sudden and unexpected sound of his voice.

"Bennett, you surprised us!" Frances scolded, laughing as she walked into his open arms. "Why didn't you let us know you were coming?"

"Because I wanted to surprise you," he said, gently setting her aside to turn to Cyndi.

She steeled herself against the effects of his embrace, her steel quickly melting in the warmth of his encircling arms.

Ruth saved Cyndi from betraying her feelings for him.

"Have you had dinner?" the always practical housekeeper asked.

Laughing, Ben brushed a kiss over Cyndi's cheek; then, dropping his arms, he turned to Ruth.

"No." He shook his head. "I was planning on begging a scrap from Mother's table."

"'Begging a scrap'?" Ruth retorted. "You are a scrap—and a tardy one at that." Heaving a phony sigh of long suffering, she swung around and headed for the kitchen to get him a place setting.

Over dinner, adhering to the precedent he had set from the beginning, Ben went into his charming, amusing, affectionate mode. He laughed, he teased, he explained his laxity in visits and calls.

"It's been a hellish month," he told his mother, flashing a smile around the table to include Cyndi and Ruth in his explanation. "What with several publishing houses changing shipping schedules, replacing employees changing positions, and then updating the computer–cash register hookup—not to mention Connie's penchant for driving me to the edge—I've been up to my . . . er, armpits in alligators this past month."

"Oh, Bennett," Frances said in tones of concerned commiseration. "Are you working too hard?"

On your *friend*? Cyndi thought cynically, dismayed by the sudden shaft of pain in her chest.

With each passing day—and night—the mind-curdling memory of Ben's casual divulgence of his involvement with his "friend" loomed bigger and darker in Cyndi's mind. She cringed at the visions her imagination conjured, tormenting scenes of him kissing, caressing, making love, performing that most intimate act with the faceless woman.

Though Cyndi repeatedly told herself she had no right to resent his "friend"—to despise her—in her heart, she continued to do both.

"No, Mother, I'm not working too hard," Ben assured Frances in a gentle tone, with a gentle smile. "I can handle the work and the pressure. It's just, I miss seeing you and . . ." His voice trailing away, he softly sighed, then cast a longing look to Cyndi.

This coming so swiftly on the heels of her rumination about his relationship with his friend, Cyndi was hard pressed not to smack him on his lying mouth. Instead, she forced herself to return the yearning look, but took her revenge by fluttering her eyelashes at him dramatically.

His lips flattened into a straight line.

Hers curved into a sweet smile.

"You know," Ruth observed, evidently as oblivious as Frances to the tension shimmering between their two companions at the table, "for an engaged couple, you two don't see a heck of a lot of each other."

Uh-oh. Now what? How to respond? Cyndi blinked—and went blank. So, naturally, she looked to Ben, her eyes telling him she had no answer to give.

He suffered no such lack of mental agility . . .

Or was his flexibility due to sheer deviousness?

With a deep, heartfelt sigh, he turned to Ruth, the hard line of his mouth smoothing into a smile of rueful regret. "I know," he said, sighing yet again. "But that's why I'm working so very hard. I want to get my desk as clear as possible . . . so I can then afford some time exclusively for Cynthia." He turned his head to give her a look of besotted adoration.

Frances and Ruth sighed in unison, apparently touched by the depth and breadth of his conflict between devotion to his love and to his livlihood.

Stunned by his outrageousness, his duplicity, Cyndi even forgot to correct him about her name.

"I can't wait for that day," he dared to go on in a deep, soft voice filled with an anguished longing.

Too much. Cyndi exerted all of her willpower to control an impulse to rise from her seat, appauding wildly as she cried, "Bravo" for his perfectly executed performance.

To her everlasting relief, Ben excused himself soon after dinner, again citing his by now down-pat alibi of work, this time a meeting of the managers of his bookstores.

But she didn't get off scot-free. Ben actually had the nerve to kiss her, really kiss her, a soul-deep and emotion-shattering experience.

Cyndi felt the imprint of his mouth long after he had released her with a show of reluctance.

That night, his bed seemed even bigger, colder, emptier than before.

Cyndi despaired of her weakness.

Where was her pride? she demanded of herself. How could she allow herself to yearn for him, want him, knowing he was sharing another bed—and himself—with some woman?

It was demeaning, demoralizing, soul destroying.

And yet . . .

Cyndi loved him.

Then, the week before the first semester's classes were to begin, and at Frances's urging, Cyndi packed suitcases, Frances, and Ruth into the car and drove to Cape May, New Jersey, where she made another most delightful discovery . . . that being the Atlantic Ocean.

Cyndi immediately fell in love with the quaint charm of Cape May, with its tree-lined streets and old, beautiful Victorian houses, most of which had been converted into bed and breakfast establishments. Though Cyndi would have loved to stay in one of the Victorians, it was not to be. Frances inquired, but was informed that every one of them was booked through until the end of September.

"Perhaps next time," Frances said, obviously as disappointed as Cyndi. "But the hotel is nice, too. I've stayed there on previous visits. The view is magnificent, as you'll see."

Cyndi did and she was awestruck by the panoramic view of the ocean.

Though she felt diminished by the enormity of it, she was also fascinated by it's scope.

Having only seen the ocean in movies and TV shows and news coverage, which due to the limited scope of these media couldn't convey its full impact, Cyndi was both thrilled and enthralled by the Atlantic.

It drew her like a magnet.

Whether she was at the wide window of the room Frances had told her about in the large old hotel located directly across the road from the beach, or was standing entranced at the end of the pier that extended from the promenade paralleling the beach front, the great waters drew her like a legendary siren.

The constant motion, the slow buildup of the rollers, the swish as the waves receded, fired Cyndi's imagination.

After dinner, just before dusk, Cyndi left the two older women to their comfort in the white wicker rocking chairs on the hotel's beach-facing veranda, and made her way to the pier.

Oblivious to the laughing, chattering tourists strolling about her, Cyndi stood, her arms braced on the guard-rail, staring out at the undulating water.

Attuned to every nuance of sound, she imagined she could hear the sea whispering secrets into the shifting sands as foaming waves broke onto the beach and then withdrew.

If the sea could talk, what stories it could tell, she mused, recalling the phrase, while unable to remember who originated it or what it was from.

And the stories would be wonderful, she decided, losing herself, her heartache, her worries and daily concerns in a soft haze of fantasy.

In the fertile plains of her mind, she heard and understood the whispered tales of adventure, of lives lost, and trade routes discovered. There were detailed accounts of fierce pirates who sported black eye-patches and had golden rings in their ears; of audacious privateers, sacking other vessels for loot in the names of their countries; of intrepid merchant seaman, bravely battling the inhospitable North Atlantic; and of terrible battles fought over countless centuries by warring countries.

And there would be tales of love—of man's love of the sea conflicting with man's love for women.

A mist crawled in off the ocean, gray wraithlike tendrils creeping onto the beach, stealthily curling around Cyndi's stilled form.

She liked the mist; it concealed her from the world within its amorphous embrace, cloaked her aching loneliness from prying eyes, muffled the reality of the anguished cry that fought to make itself heard deep within her.

Why couldn't Ben love her?

Chapter Thirteen

"The king lives! Long live the king!"

Not in the best of all possible moods, Bennett came to a halt just inside the office, scowling with fierce disapproval at his secretary.

If her devil-may-care grin was any indication at all, Connie was less than impressed.

"You know, employees have been fired for less provocation," he said in a near growl, knowing the threat was empty and fully aware that Connie knew it, too.

Where would he ever find anyone smart enough— or dumb enough—to replace her, as she had taken pains to point out to him on numerous occasions.

"Rough night, huh, Gangster?" Connie favored him with a patently false smile of commiseration.

"Yeah." Bennett didn't bother blistering her about the name. What's the use? he thought sourly. Connie didn't pay any more attention than Cynthia did to his repeated strictures against nicknames.

"So shut up and lay off," he snarled, ignoring the giggles stifled by her hand as he strode past her and into his own small office.

Connie's giggles followed him.

Slamming the door shut, he stomped to his desk and dropped tiredly into his chair.

The scent of freshly brewed coffee tickled his nose, drew his eyes to the small table in the corner of the room. The table held an automatic coffeemaker and a tray with four cups turned upside down, indicating that they were clean. An old apartment-sized refrigerator stood next to the table.

The coffee carafe was full, steam still rising from its indented lip, evidence that Connie had very recently prepared the brew.

Pushing himself out of the chair, Bennett walked to the table and poured a cup, grateful for his secretary's thoughtfulness.

What would he do without her?

He smiled at the thought. Even though he threatened to replace her on an average of once or twice a week, he knew he'd be lost without her . . . at least for a long while.

Connie knew it, too.

His smile wry, Bennett raised the cup and took a tentative sip of the brew. Unsurprisingly, it was strong and delicious, as usual.

He had lost count of the times he had thanked whatever fate had directed Connie to him at the very beginning, when he'd been setting up his business. He also had patted himself on the back for having had the sense to hire her on the spot.

Connie was decidedly not the run-of-the-mill secretary or one of the newer kind who, firmly entrenched in the principle of equality, refused to do unrelated work for their employers—like making coffee in the morning.

And yet, Bennett knew Connie was a feminist, she made sure he knew that she considered herself his equal in every sense, except physical strength.

Early on in their relationship, when Bennett had dared to tease her about her willingness to make the coffee, Connie had responded with coolly thought out, unquestionable logic.

"I make the coffee, and do other little favors, because I choose to do so." She had arched her eyebrows. "Isn't that what equality is all about ... the right to make one's own choices?"

And so, Connie babied him and bullied him, and kept his office running like clockwork.

If he had any sense at all, Bennett mused, returning to his desk and settling into his chair, he'd ask her to marry him.

A brief flash of amusement lightened his dark expression.

Connie wouldn't have him on a bet. Not that she didn't like him; she freely admitted that she both liked and respected him. But she had also admitted that she was holding out for her own Mister Right, and Bennett didn't fit the description.

Sipping the hot liquid, Bennett mused on the similarities between his intrepid secretary and the equally intrepid young woman he had convinced to play the role of his fiancée.

The realization struck that, if or when the two eventually met, he would likely find himself in real serious trouble.

By herself, Cynthia represented about as much trouble as Bennett could handle.

The coffee was good, but it wasn't good enough to

soothe the sudden shaft of mixed emotions he experienced at the thought of Cynthia.

Cynthia.

Hell.

Bennett gritted his teeth until his jaw ached.

After over a month of playing hide-and-seek with Cynthia, his jaw wasn't the only thing aching. His entire
body ached. His mind, as well, added to his feeling of
misery.

Cynthia.

Contained within that one name, that lovely name,
lay the root cause of Bennett's bruised feelings and
black mood. The sad truth of it was, he had no one to
blame for it but himself.

He had started the farce in the first place.

Morose, Bennett told himself he had been better off
before he'd had that brainstorm, when his only problems had been dealing with his work, the aftereffects of
his mother's heart attack, and her concentrated efforts
to see him married and settled.

Settled? Hah! Bennett had never felt less settled—or
more churned up.

At least before that damnable vacation he'd been
getting sex on a fairly regular basis.

Still a little uneasy in his mind, he raked a hand
through his hair, then seared his throat with a deep
swallow of coffee. He had cause to be uneasy, he
reflected, shifting in his chair.

A man, any man, would naturally grow uneasy upon
suddenly discovering he could't perform or, to put it
crudely, couldn't get it up.

"Jesus," he muttered, recalling too clearly the first
time he had been to bed with Denise after she had
returned from her business trip.

Could it possibly be over three weeks ago since that

disappointing, embarrassing night? It had happened on the very day of her return from the West Coast.

Grimacing, Bennett opened his mind to the other memories of events of the previous month.

Denise returned from her trip three days after Bennett had taken up partial-permanent residence in the apartment above the center-city bookstore, three days that had seemed to be the longest he'd ever lived, existed, struggled through.

"Hello, Bennett, I'm back at last," she said, sounding too upbeat to his disgruntled mind. "And I had a very positive trip," she'd continued, offering the information in a self-satisfied tone.

"Good," he responded, trying to sound as though he meant it. "We'll have to get together and celebrate. How about tonight?"

"Oh, I was so hoping you'd suggest it," she murmured in a seductive purr. "What did you have in mind?" Her voice went even lower.

"Dinner and . . ." his voice trailed away, the fading not from excitement, but from confusion and concern over his lack of excitement.

"Yes," she breathed the word into the phone, into his ear, apparently assuming his voice had been a victim to eager anticipation. "I like the "and" part best."

"Are you at home?" Bennett asked, striving for a note of enthusiasm.

"No. My plane just landed a little while ago," she answered. "I'm calling from my cell phone, hoping to get you. Right now, I'm in a cab heading for town." She paused for half a heartbeat, then suggested, "Why don't you meet me at my place?"

Although he agreed to meeting her, Bennett was

assailed by misgivings as he drove across town to her condo, located in one of the new complexes overlooking the Schuylkill River.

He fervently hoped that seeing Denise again, being with her, holding her, kissing her, making love with her, would put an end to the ambiguity of his feelings.

Denise looked the same: chic, smart, vivacious, and eager to resume their former relationship.

Bennett tried to accommodate her—Lord, how he tried.

But nothing worked. Nothing. From the minute he arrived at her door.

"Bennett, hello!" Denise practically sang the greeting. "Come in, come in."

She was in fine spirits, obviously still on the high from a successful business trip.

Unwilling to shoot her down with his own deepening sense of depression, Bennett put forth an effort to share her euphoria.

"This calls for a special dinner," he said, smiling into her glowing eyes and reminding himself that she was a stunning woman. "Where would you like to go to eat?"

"The dining room," she answered at once, her eyes sparkling.

Bennett felt like sighing; he smiled instead. "Yes, but which one?"

"That one." She turned to point to the small dining alcove off the kitchen.

He wasn't surprised, he was relieved. But, playing along with her, he pretended surprise. "You prefer to stay in this evening?"

"Yes. It was a long flight—two stopovers—and I don't feel like changing to go out."

A genuine smile curved his lips as he ran a slow glance

over her. Denise, always, looked as if she had just stepped off the cover of a fashion magazine.

"And so," she went on, "I called our favorite restaurant from the cab, right after I talked to you. Our dinner should be arriving in about," she glanced at the exquisite watch encircling her wrist, "fifteen minutes."

She laughed at his stunned expression; their favorite restaurant didn't do take-out dinners.

"You amaze me," was all he was able to say. In fact, it was true; Denise did amaze him; she simply didn't excite him anymore.

Still laughing, and indicating the elegant living room with a flick of one hand, she turned to walk along the short hallway leading into the kitchen. "Make yourself comfortable," she invited. "I put a bottle of wine in to chill. I'll be back in a moment with a drink for you."

Releasing the sigh he hadn't even realized he'd kept pent up, Bennett strolled into the living room. A frown drew his brows together as he gingerly settled into a chair. He had never felt comfortable in that room; it was too perfect to allow for comfort.

Denise floated back into the room, a dark bottle of very expensive champagne in one hand, two slender wine flutes in the other.

"I've been saving this for a special occasion," she said. Pouring out the wine, she handed a glass to him, then raised her own. "Here's to successful, and very profitable, business ventures."

"Hear, hear," Bennett agreed, startled by the sudden realization that their toasts were always the same, never to health or happiness, or even peace on earth at New Year's Eve, but always centered on business and profit. And he was just as guilty as she of the same single-minded ambition.

Nevertheless, he sipped the wine, and he continued

to sip it liberally throughout the excellent dinner he barely tasted. The conversation he engaged in he didn't retain.

The wine didn't work, not at the table or later, in her bedroom.

Try as Bennett might—and he certainly did try— nothing worked; not the feel of her body melting into his when he drew her into his arms, not the taste of her mouth when he kissed her.

Nothing worked.

The sight of her pale, naked body, the wine-scented taste of her mouth, the touch of her smooth skin against his hands—her flesh left him cool, unaffected and unaroused.

She went still when her hands slid down his torso and cradled him.

"Bennett?" A mixture of confusion and anxiousness had laced her passion-thickened voice. "What's wrong?" Her fingers probed his flaccid flesh. "Why . . . ?"

"I must be . . . ahh . . . too tired," he muttered, feeling sick and embarrassed. "I've been putting in long hours, working hard, especially this past week, after being away from the office for so long."

"Too bad," she murmured, stroking him, then sighing when her efforts proved fruitless. "I know these past months have been rough." She redoubled her efforts, her fingers gentle but firm. Still, his flesh did not respond. She sighed, either in defeat or disappointment.

Bennett's neck and face grew warm, his forehead became damp with perspiration from his deepening sense of humiliation.

"Denise . . . I . . ."

"It's all right," she quickly assured him. "I do understand. I know that stress, emotional or physical, can effect a man's potency."

Impotency? A searing slash of pure terror sliced through Bennett, intensifying his embarrassment and humiliation.

"I'm sorry," he apologized, cringing inside as an echo of another apology, made so recently to another woman and for an altogether different reason, whispered through his mind. But then common sense reasserted itself at the recollection of why he'd had to apologize to that other woman.

Breath shuddered from his throat; he definitely had not been impotent on that occasion.

"It's all right, Bennett," Denise repeated. "Really."

She reiterated her assurance again before he left her that night, opining her belief that he would be back in fighting form once the stress induced by his mother's heart attack, added to the burden of his normally heavy schedule, had normalized.

Despite her assessment of his condition, Bennett had returned to his own apartment convinced his problem had more to do with guilt over his misuse of Cynthia than the stress of overwork.

But, irrational as he knew it was, deep down in the dark places of his mind where fear and insecurity lurked, waiting to ambush the unwary, Bennett knew a growing fear for his sexual life.

What if his loss of control, his surrender to passion that precipitated his near ravishment of Cynthia's virginal body, had rendered him impotent?

That terror was dispatched on his first visit home, the day he stopped by on his way to his store in Bucks County.

Cradling the cup of cooling coffee in his hands, Bennett shivered, reliving the contrasting sensations of cha-

grin and joy he had experienced when he'd taken
Cynthia into his arms. Although he had suffered chagrin
on feeling her stiffening rejection, sheer joy had surged
through him with the immediate and strong flare of
physical desire rising to torment his body.

His potency reestablished, Bennett felt better able to
cope on subsequent meetings with Denise, though he
still could not respond to her.

He puzzled over the weirdness of the situation for
several weeks, trying to make sense of it all.

His deepening moodiness and expanding irritability
gave proof of his failure to figure things out. And his
condition was not improved when, at their last meeting,
Denise told him, gently and kindly, that she would not
be seeing him again.

"It's time to call it a day, Bennett," she said, soothing
his wounded ego with a sigh of regret. "It's apparent
to me, and by now it should be to you, that whatever
we had together is now gone."

He didn't argue or try to change her mind. How
could he, when what she said was true? Sure, his ego
was dented—no man enjoyed being dumped. But, in
all honesty, he had to admit that what she said was true;
what they had had was gone, over and done with.

He was now free of romantic entanglements, free to
pursue his business with single-minded intent . . . so why
did he feel so lousy?

Cynthia.

Bennett tossed back the last swallows of the coffee
without noticing that it had gone stone cold.

Still caught in the grip of memories, he relived each
successive visit home.

On the occasion of his second visit, intending to spend
the weekend for appearance's sake, Bennett had
opened the door and stepped into a wall of sound. The

unmistakable strains of the music from *Romeo and Juliet* hit him with the force of a physical blow.

Catching sight of him, standing stunned in the foyer, Frances hurried to him from the living room. An amused smile tilted her lips.

"Your fiancée has discovered Tchaikovsky," she said, in a voice pitched to be heard over the music. "She's been playing it all week."

"The *Romeo and Juliet* Overture?" Bennett asked in amazement, craning his neck to peer into the room, yet unable to spot the woman in question. "Where is she, by the way?"

"No, of course not the same piece. She's just about run through the Tchaikovsky selections." Frances laughed. "And she's curled up on the floor, centered between the stereo speakers."

"Good Lord, she'll go deaf."

Bennett's prediction went unfulfilled, as Cynthia gave evidence of excellent hearing when, to his relief, the music reached conclusion.

But, by Sunday evening, after two days of solid Tchaikovsky, he feared for his own hearing . . . never mind his sanity.

The jarring ring of the phone jolted Bennett from his path on memory lane. Knowing Connie would answer it, he eyed the instrument with displeasure, which in itself was telling, since it was so out character for him. After all, along with the fax machine and E-mail, the phone was an important tool in his business.

"Ed Podestry from Lehigh Distributors on line one, Bennett." Connie's voice crackled through the intercom next to the phone.

Sighing, Bennett depressed the call button, said, "Thanks," and lifted the receiver.

"Hi, Ed, what new and exciting distribution problems have you got for me today?"

That first call kicked Bennett's working day into high gear, allowing him to escape the disaster of his personal life while dealing with the on-going necessities of his business life.

Yet, at every pause in the action, however brief in duration, his mind persisted in reviewing the events of his visits home.

It became obvious to Bennett early on that not only his mother but Ruth as well had figuratively and literally embraced Cynthia.

Within a very short period of time, the two older women were treating Cynthia as if she had been a part of their lives for years.

Wonder of wonders, Cynthia had even managed the seemingly impossible feat of coaxing his mother out and about again. And Ruth went too. It was damn near amazing.

Bennett found it amusing yet difficult to imagine his mother and Ruth trekking along in Cynthia's wake as she fed her spiritual hunger on the cultural fruits offered in the city.

Contrarily, while Bennett was glad of his mother's and Ruth's unqualified acceptance of and affection for Cynthia, even grateful for her almost magical effect on his mother's rapidly improving condition, he also felt twinges of envy and guilt . . . envy for the affection she evinced for them and not for him . . . guilt for having placed all of them, himself included, into this deceitful and thus untenable position.

How could it end, he wondered on particularly glum and moody days, other than in pain and disappointment for everyone concerned?

But, if nothing else, and if only for a brief amount of time, Cynthia appeared to be having a wonderful time, thoroughly enjoying herself, driving his mother's car, listening to his music, reading his books.

A smile flitted across Bennett's compressed lips as he recalled another of his quick visits home.

In that instance, instead of walking into a wall of sound, he had stepped into a pool of silence.

Ambling into the living room, he had quickly observed the reason for the unusual quiet.

Ensconced in the recliner chair, his mother was napping. Curled in the corner of the sofa opposite the recliner, Cynthia appeared engrossed in the hardcover book in her hands.

"What are you reading?" he'd softly asked.

Startled, she'd glanced up, closed the book; then raising a finger to her lips to caution him to be quiet, she rose and crossed to him.

"Who is Scaramouche?" she had asked in a teasing murmur as she walked past him into the foyer.

Laughing to himself, Bennett hadn't needed his mother to inform him that Cynthia had discovered the volume by Rafael Sabatini—one of his own favorites.

But he did not laugh during a later visit when, on addressing her as Cynthia, his mother and Ruth had firmly corrected him before she herself had a chance to do so.

"Cyndi," they had declared, in unison.

He had had a sinking feeling of being outnumbered, outflanked, and thus was out of sorts.

*   *   *

Bennett's memory machine switched off, and he sat staring morosely at his office wall.

Throughout the previous weeks, during each and every one of his visits home, while Cynthia had been discovering the joys of exquisite music, good literature, and dashing about in a Mercedes, he had been discovering new and interesting facets of her character.

Of course, from day one Bennett had judged Cynthia to be nice, decent, hardworking, and friendly, as well as the possessor of a well-developed, if slightly quirky, sense of humor. Later, when she had told him a little about herself, her situation, he had learned of the depths of her love and devotion to her father and family.

Then, during their brief sojourn in New York City, he had realized that she could be independent, but was willing to bend . . . and she cleaned up pretty well, too.

Still, she slowly revealed new facets; the intensity of her thirst for knowledge about life as well as for that to be found in the works of intellectuals and artists—writers, musicians, poets, and artisans. His mother had made it her business to inform him that Cynthia was unfailingly kind and pleasant to every person she came into contact with, from the haughty manager of an upscale art gallery to the homeless person she had slipped money to on the street.

Cynthia appeared to possess an abundance of genuine affection, a capacity for caring, a love for people, life, and learning.

While expressing her own inner joy, she received more joy in return.

Ruth loved her.

His mother loved her.

From all accounts, everybody loved her.

Blooming in the warmth of the love freely expressed

by Frances and Ruth, Cynthia apparently couldn't do enough for them.

By her efforts, she had halved Ruth's workload. And with her encouragement, she had succeeded in coaxing Frances out of her fears and out of the house and back into the throbbing beat of life.

At that moment, even as Bennett stared at his office wall, he knew the three companions now friends, were in the town of Cape May, in the state of New Jersey.

As for him, after all these long weeks of self-denial and repression, he was merely in the state of mental and physical frustration.

Something had to give; Bennett had a sneaky suspicion that that something would be him.

Chapter Fourteen

Bennett appeared, without warning as usual, late in the afternoon of the day Cyndi, Frances, and Ruth returned from Cape May.

Cyndi was in the laundry room, washing the crumpled clothing the three of them had worn at the shore. Ruth had left minutes before to go to the supermarket. Frances was in her room, resting.

"Hey, where is everybody?" Bennett called from the kitchen. "Mother? Ruth? Cynthia?"

"Quiet," Cyndi ordered, stepping out of the laundry room to confront him—none too pleased to be relegated to last on his query list. "Keep your voice down." She indicated Frances's bedroom with a sharp head movement. "Your mother is taking a nap."

Instant alarm flickered across his face. "Isn't she feeling well? Did you call the doctor? Was the trip too much for—"

"Hold it," she cut in, softly but forcefully. "She's fine,

but the drive home tired her, and she decided to have a nap.''

He didn't appeared convinced. "Are you sure?" He made a half-turn toward the doorway. "Maybe I'd better check on her, just to make sure," he said, spinning around to stride to the hallway.

"Ben, really." Cyndi quickly intercepted him in the doorway. "She's fine, as I said, just a little tired. She took the mail that had piled up while we were away and went to her room. I peeked in on her a few minutes ago, and she was sleeping. Why disturb her rest?"

He hesitated.

She held her position in the doorway.

"Well . . . if you're certain—"

"I am." Cyndi sighed. Then, rattled by the sight of him, so close, so darned appealing, she demanded, "What are you doing here, anyway?"

"I own the place," he snapped. "Remember?"

"Yes, of course," she snapped right back. "Although it would be easy to forget . . . we see so little of you."

His demeanor changed at once; guilty color tinged his smooth cheeks. "I know, but I've been so busy catching up," he said, excusing his tardiness for about the hundredth time.

"Mmmm," Cyndi murmured, afraid that if she made a comment, any comment, it wouldn't be kind.

"But things have leveled off now," he went on in a tone of appeasement. "And so—"

"So you came for dinner," Cyndi cut in on him without compunction.

"No." Ben gave her a stern look.

"No?" She gave him a skeptical look in return. "There's a first."

He drew a slow breath, as if in an effort to hang on

to his patience. His features taut, his eyes narrowing, he drilled her with an intimidating stare.

Quashing a tiny inner quiver of trepidation, Cyndi met his narrowed gaze with enforced composure.

"I came to invite you out to dinner." His statement was as terse as his features were taut.

Startled, Cyndi could only stare at him in surprise. As it had been gritted through his teeth, his invitation could certainly not be construed as romantic or even complimentary. Therefore, she concluded, he wanted something from her.

Was his "friend" on another business trip and thus unavailable to him once again? she wondered, hurt and anger compressing her chest.

Dammit! She would not play substitute again—never, ever again.

"Why?" she asked with blunt directness, not in the mood to go traipsing around any conversational bushes, metaphorically or otherwise.

"Why?" He frowned—scowled would be a better description. "For a meal, of course."

"Uh-huh."

"What's that supposed to mean?"

Cyndi could see that he was losing his hold on his temper, but that didn't bother her; her short fuse was about gone too . . . long since.

"Come on, Ben," she said, moving around him to put some distance between them—like the width of the room—and the kitchen table. "You barely acknowledge that I'm alive for almost two months, and now, out of the blue, you stop by to invite me to dinner?"

"But—"

She laughed; it hurt her throat, and her heart. "I know you believe I'm boringly naive, and maybe I am, but I'm not stupid."

"I never said—or thought—that you were," he inserted in protest.

"Whatever." She shrugged; the small movement seeming to take a monumental effort. "Even so, I would have to be both naive and stupid not to suspect that you've probably got an ulterior motive for inviting me out." She paused to draw a breath, but not long enough for him to get in a word of denial. "So then, why not do us both a favor and simply tell me what's on your mind—get it over with?"

He regarded her with steady contemplation for long seconds, as if mentally shuffling through his options. Then, he apparently decided to go with the truth and let the pain stab where it may.

"Mother and Ruth are growing suspicious about the validity of our engagement," he said with blunt and crushing candor. "I think we need to start seeing more of each other, on a social basis."

Cyndi cringed inwardly, recalling their stay in New York, the sensation of living a fairy tale, of walking on air, their last night there.

The heady feeling of falling in love.

Fiction, Cyndi chided herself. A fool's paradise. Fantasy land for the realistically impaired.

He has a "friend," so grow up.

"Well?" Ben's tightly controlled voice sliced through her moment of self-ridicule. "Will you have dinner with me?"

"Ahhh . . ." Cyndi raked her mind for an excuse, any excuse to decline. She didn't want to have dinner with him, didn't want to be alone with him; didn't even want to be in the same county with him. Not because she didn't trust him, but simply because she didn't trust herself, not with her seemingly idiotic ability to forget his "friend"—i.e. lover.

"I . . . I can't." She blurted out the first lame excuse that came to her equally lame brain. "I've got to finish doing the laundry."

"Of course, you don't."

The contradiction didn't come from Ben, who was looking at Cyndi warily, as if she had possibly been out in the sun too long while at the shore, but from Frances, whose bemused expression was a precise reflection of her son's.

"Ruth and I are capable of doing that," the older woman went on as she entered the room. She bestowed a satisfied smile on Ben, as though he had made her day complete with his invitation.

"But . . . but . . ."—Cyndi sputtered, "what about dinner for you and Ruth?"

"I believe Ruth and I can manage the laundry and one meal." Frances's lips twitched in amusement. "Although, I must admit you have spoiled us by taking over the preparation of most meals."

"Cynthia has been doing the cooking?" Ben sent a frown to both women.

"Not all of it," Cyndi inserted.

"But most of it," Frances corrected.

Ben's frown gave way to a complacent smile. "Then you deserve a night out." He arched a brow at Frances. "Wouldn't you say so, Mother?"

"Certainly," she agreed. "In fact, in a vague way I believe I just did." She dismissed them with a wave of one hand, in which she held an envelope. "You two just run along and spend some quality time together."

Outflanked, Cyndi scoured her mind for a reasonable-sounding escape.

The light of challenge gleaming in his dark eyes, Ben gave her one of his phony, nerve-scraping smiles of besotted adoration.

She glared at him.

He chuckled, then turned to his mother.

"What do you have there?" He motioned to the envelope in her hand. "A bill for me to pay?"

"This?" She held up the envelope and shook her head. "No, it's not a bill. It's a letter from Louise."

Oh, goody, the wicked stepmother of the piece, Cyndi thought, masking a grimace with a hastily contrived expression of mild interest.

"How is she?" Ben asked, not even bothering to appear very interested.

"Apparently suffering pangs of conscience," Frances answered, sighing.

Louise? Cyndi's mind boggled.

"Aunt Louise?" Ben frowned. "Why?"

"Well, it seems my misguided sister envisioned herself a matchmaker. She even flew east last month in the hope of pairing you up with the lovely, recently divorced daughter of a dear friend of hers."

Uh-huh, that explains quite a lot, Cyndi thought, vividly recalling Louise's near hostile reaction to Ben's sudden announcement of his engagement to her.

"She . . . what?" Ben asked, his tone and expression registering astonishment, most likely because he himself had theorized just such a probability.

"Yes, incredible, isn't it?" Frances murmured, giving the letter a shake. "Louise writes that the young woman is currently living in Baltimore, that she met her in early June when she was visiting her parents in California."

Ben looked annoyed, extremely annoyed.

Cyndi felt hard pressed not to laugh—it was all so . . . so . . . aging Pollyannaish.

"Why in hell would Louise entertain the idea that I required her assistance in finding a woman?" Ben angrily demanded.

Frances made a helpless gesture and again shook the letter. "She confesses in here of thinking you and this young woman would be perfect for one another."

Ben snorted.

His mother continued. "Louise had planned to invite the woman to the house to meet us ... after you returned, rested and relaxed from your vacation."

Nearly choking on the grim laughter crowding her throat, Cyndi headed for the door. "I ... er ... need to shower and change if we're going out," she muttered, beating a hasty retreat from the kitchen.

She looked radiant standing in the living-room doorway, Bennett thought, bemused, a perfect summer flower in full blossom.

Cynthia was dressed in the mauve and pink chiffon dress he had insisted on purchasing for her. Her skin glowed a pale gold from the kiss of sunshine on her days at the beach. Her honey brown hair shimmered with a healthy sheen.

Her hazel eyes were stormy.

She didn't want to go out with him, and she didn't care if he knew it.

Didn't care *if* he knew it? Her stance, the tilt of her chin said she *wanted* him to know it.

Bennett suppressed a sigh and an impulse to spring from his chair, cross the room, and literally sweep her off her feet, into his arms.

He didn't make any of those tempting moves. Instead, mindful of his mother's presence, he slowly rose and sauntered to her.

"You look lovely," he murmured, taking her left hand; it was cold to his touch. Was she afraid of him? His stomach muscles clenched at the thought. Finding his voice, keeping it steady, was hard. "I'll have to take you someplace special for dinner."

Chagrin banked the rebellious fire in her eyes. "Am I overdressed?" she asked, her voice cracking with anxiety. "Should I change?"

"No, of course not," he was quick to reassure her. "You look—"

"You look beautiful," his mother's gentle voice broke in. "Exactly like an ecstatic young bride-to-be, out for an evening with her fiancé."

Oh, hell. Bennett groaned in silent dismay, certain his mother's compliment was the last thing Cynthia wanted to hear.

"Thank you, Frances." A flush of color tinging her cheeks, she smiled and lowered her eyes.

But not before Bennett caught sight of the strain in them and at the corners of her mouth.

"Shall we go?" he asked, his thumb brushing over the ring on her third finger as he gave a light tug on her hand—her now nerve-damp hand. Was it his imagination, or had he felt her flinch, a tremor run through her?

"Yes, run along, children," his mother ordered, dismissing them with a smile. "Have fun."

Fun? Where had he heard that dictum before? he asked himself with wry cynicism. What was it with his mother, anyway? She was continually chasing him off with the command to have fun.

Fun—with a woman who couldn't bear his touch? Nor, obviously, did she want to be reminded of the ring, his ring, gracing her slim finger.

God, what am I doing? Bennett dredged up a smile and motioned for Cynthia to precede him into the foyer, to the door, and then out of the house.

His thoughts got sidetracked as he followed her to his car.

He liked the way she looked, the way she smelled. Most particularly, he liked the way the full, filmy skirt of the dress swirled around her long, slender legs when she walked.

What was he doing—other than beginning to sweat, that is? Bennett ruminated, attempting to corral his fractured thoughts.

Damned if he knew.

Mere moments ago, he had felt he knew precisely what he was doing. With his invitation for her to have dinner alone with him, he had intended, had hoped, to dispel the tension that had coiled around them, and in him, throughout every day of these past weeks.

By spending time alone with Cynthia, he had wanted to, had cherished the possibility of, recapturing the congenial relationship they had briefly cultivated during their stay in New York City.

Bennett's thoughts rambled on as he handed Cynthia into his car. No, he was lying to himself, he acknowledged, sliding behind the wheel and pulling the door shut with a resounding thunk. After weeks of frustration and of suppressing his needs and desires, he hoped for more, much more than congeniality.

"Where are we going?" Her voice was low, soft, riddled with uncertainty.

Bennett shifted around to look at her; it was a mistake. Looking wasn't enough. He ached to reach out, let his fingers glide down her soft cheek, press them to her softer mouth.

Recalling what had occurred, that soul-damning but thrilling incident he had precipitated the last time he had felt compelled to press his fingertips to her mouth, he curled them into his palm.

"I must confess," he said, in a voice rendered husky and uneven by his thoughts. "In anticipation of your acceptance, I made a reservation in a recently opened restaurant in town that I've been hearing good reports about."

Her eyes flickered . . . with anger or dismay? he pondered. But he wasn't left long in the throes of speculation. Cynthia glanced down at herself, a frown puckereing her brows.

"Are you positive I'm not overdressed?" she asked in a timid, gut-wrenching tone.

"Yes, Cynthia, I'm positive," he answered with solid conviction. "I have been informed that this place is very upscale."

"Oh, God!" she muttered. "I'll probably embarrass you and humiliate myself by using the wrong fork."

"Stop it." Bennett was suddenly angry in her defense, fiercely protective of her sensibilities and uncertainties. "You did fine in every restaurant we dined in in New York."

"I . . . I did?" she asked tremulously, slanting what he felt sure was an unconsciously flirtatious sidelong glance at him.

He smiled and tempered his tone. "You know damn well you did." His voice softened of its own accord. "I was proud to be your escort."

"Thank you," she said meekly. Then a smile teased her lips. "And the name's Cyndi."

Bennett could no more contain his laughter than he could control the yearning ache deep inside him—although he had certainly tried.

"So I've been told," he murmured, shaking his head as he switched on the motor. The big car growled to life, then subsided into a purr. "Repeatedly," he tacked on, in exaggerated disgust.

She gave a small, reluctant laugh.

He set the car in motion and threw a taunting glance at her. "Nevertheless, you will remain Cynthia," he cautioned. "Forever and ever, amen. But, most especially this evening, since we'll be dining in a very tony restaurant."

The cuisine, the decor, the general ambience of the restaurant far exceeded the word-of-mouth praise Bennett had been given.

As he had requested, they were seated at a small table in a semisecluded corner.

Fat lot of good it had done him, Bennet thought, midway through his entrée of perfectly prepared filet of sole. Cynthia was about as talkative as the potted plants forming a crescent of privacy around them.

Watching her lift a morsel of romaine lettuce from her salad plate and pop it into her mouth, Bennett sensed his nerves pop beneath his skin.

Feeling somewhat like a lecher, he watched her chew, then swallow. Against his better judgment, he allowed his gaze to trail down her throat. Then of their own volition, his eyes drifted lower.

The manner in which the chiffon draped over her breasts, revealing while concealing, was playing pure hell with his libido.

Get it together, Ganster, Bennett chastised himself, dragging his gaze to her face.

"Er . . . what do you think?" he asked, cringing inside at the inanity of the query.

Cynthia raised her eyebrows. Rightly so, Bennett told himself.

"About what?" Her brows lowered, came together in a frown. "The food or the restaurant?"

"Both," he replied, groping for brilliance, and coming up short, way short.

"Excellent," she said. "To both. I like the elegance of the decor," she continued. "And the food"—she glanced down at her plate—"my salmon—everything—is delicious."

It was a start. Not a great start, he allowed. But at least she had responded. Now, he had to find a way to keep her talking.

"I was just wondering . . ." he began, as if musing.

"Yes?" she prompted when he fell silent.

Inspiration hit a fly ball; Bennett plucked it out of his gray matter. He knew for a fact, because his own mother had told him, that since she'd been given the use of the Mercedes, Cynthia had been haunting bookstores, primarily those of the big chains. The imparted information had been a blow to his ego, but not even the Inquisition could have extracted from him the truth of how hurt he had been by the knowledge.

"The store is open late tonight, and I was wondering if you'd care to stop in before I drive you back to the house?"

She didn't try to hide her surprise. "Your store?" she asked in stark disbelief.

Man, if this admittedly late-coming invitation to visit his store amazed her, he reflected, she really did think he was some kind of a jerk.

With good reason, he conceded, honestly if reluctantly. The very fact that she felt she needed a personal invitation was telling. He was a jerk.

"Well, of course, my store." Bennett managed a smile; it wasn't easy, but he produced one. "You really don't think I'd invite you to check out one of my competitor's stores, do you?"

Cynthia laughed.

Progress.

Encouraged, Bennett forged ahead. "Let's see." He shot a quick glance at his wristwatch. "It's now eight-ten, the store is open until nine. That leaves us plenty of time to finish here and get to it." He shrugged. "I can help close up." He smiled again; it was easier this time. "What do you say? Want to see it?"

"Yes," she said, with a flattering degree of eagerness. "I've been hoping you'd suggest I stop by sometime."

"No time like the present," he said, his voice a purr of satisfaction.

That satisfaction doubled when she opted to skip dessert, telling him she would much rather see his store than increase her calorie intake. Her eagerness to finish and leave was pure balm to his ego.

Bennett was in an expansive and mellow frame of mind when they exited the restaurant. He barely noted the exorbitant total when he handed his credit card over to the server.

After adding on a more than generous tip he signed the receipt with a flourish.

Chapter Fifteen

The building that housed his store was larger than Cyndi had anticipated.

Old, the structure was three stories tall, quite wide, and long, very long.

While she found the building interesting, it was the store itself, its very uniqueness, that captured Cyndi's imagination.

And it definitely was unique.

Although her experience of bookstores admittedly was limited, Cyndi had been running wild through those in the environs since arriving at Bennett's home, and she had never run across any other quite like this one.

To begin with, the interior was brightly painted and brightly lighted, lending a friendly, welcoming look. And the only merchandise on offer was books, books, and more books; hardcover books, mass-market paper-back books, audio books. There were no videos, no cute Post-it note pads, no greeting cards, not even any magazines. Just books, which, naturally, explained the name Bennett had given his stores—Just Books.

Shelves and shelves and shelves of books.

Cyndi felt as though she had died and gone to book heaven.

Interspersed among the shelves, both lining the walls and arranged at angles down through the center of the store were low, padded benches and chairs; a silent invitation to shoppers to sit, rest, relax while perusing a volume of interest.

Then, in addition to the benches and chairs, the center shelves had been relinquished in a large section in one corner at the back of the store, to accommodate a scattering of small tables surrounded by chairs, and a small coffee bar, inviting the browser to sit, get comfortable, indulge in an American coffee or a cappuccino and some quiet conversation, if desired.

Overall, the atmosphere was an inducement to scholarly pursuits or sheer reading pleasure.

To Cyndi's way of thinking, the planning behind the layout of the establishment made a definite statement about Ben's character.

So, also, did the attitude of his employees in regard to him.

The three clerks working in the store hailed Ben, in turn, the minute he ushered Cyndi through the wide entranceway.

"Hi, Bennett," the young man behind the register called upon spying his employer. "You stop by to help or harass the peons?"

Startled by the young man's seemingly disrespectful remark, Cyndi stared at him in disbelief.

He was tall, very thin, with a shy, bookish look about him curiously at odds with the rakish grin he flashed at Ben.

More startling still to Cyndi was the grin Ben flashed back at the man.

"Cynthia," Ben drawled, urging her forward to the counter. "I feel duty bound to introduce you to the store manager, Rashid Quinn . . ."

He shook his head at the look of surprise Cyndi wasn't quick enough to conceal.

"Don't ask," he advised dryly, shifting a wry glance to the man. "But, around here, he's known as the professor . . . for obvious reasons."

Well, yes, Cyndi mused, stepping closer to extend her right hand. Despite his youth, the clerk looked like a professor.

"Rashid, my . . ."—Ben paused for a heartbeat, then went on,—"fiancée, Cynthia Swoyer."

As she looked at Rashid, Cyndi wasn't sure who was more surprised by the announcement. There was an instant of hesitation; then he laughed and grasped her hand.

"It's a genuine pleasure to meet you, Ms. Swoyer," Rashid said earnestly, squeezing her hand with more vigorous enthusiasm than she might have wished.

"Nice to meet you, Rashid," she murmured, relieved when he released her abused fingers.

"When did all this happen?" Rashid was quizzing Ben, sounding more the close friend than an employee. "And why are we the last to know?"

We being Rashid and the two women who had converged unnoticed on the corner of the counter.

"You're not the last to know," Ben said, including the two women with a sweeping glance. "In fact, other than family, you three are the first, as we have not to date made a formal announcement."

Cyndi was so shocked by his presumptive declaration she didn't know whether to be angry or dismayed. At the same time, she was rather amazed that he had bothered to explain at all.

Yet another insight into his character?

The thought was fleeting, because, first and foremost, there was anger. However, she was wise enough not to embarrass them both by tearing into Ben in front of his employees.

So she held her peace; but it wasn't easy.

The two women offered their congratulations to Ben, thus reminding him of his failure to introduce them to the fiancée under discussion.

"Cynthia, say hello to, Pat Holden," he said, indicating the smaller of the two women. "And Lynn Leonard, our senior staff member."

"Hello, Pat, Lynn," Cyndi responded politely, shaking hands with the women in turn. "I'm happy to meet you."

"And we're delighted to meet you," Lynn said, as if she meant it. "Aren't we, Pat?"

"I'll say." Pat laughed. "It's about time some woman brought Bennett to heel." She tossed a taunting look at Ben. "But, I'm afraid you've got a tough row to hoe with him. He works too hard, you know?"

So he's been telling me, Cyndi thought. Aloud, she phrased it a bit differently.

"He has mentioned it . . . on occasion."

Ben sliced an arch look at her.

She offered him an innocent smile.

The three clerks laughed.

"Okay, boys and girls," Ben said briskly. "Let's get it done." He glanced at his watch. "It's already past closing time." He moved to walk around the counter. "I'll close the register while you three tidy up the place."

"Ah . . . Bennett," Pat said, laying a hand on his arm

to halt his progress. "Mr. Blumenthal is still back in the coffee area."

"Sid?" Ben frowned, then he smiled.

Cyndi's breath caught in her throat. Lord, it seemed unfair for any one man to possess such a soft, yet sexy smile.

"Rashid, you close the register," he directed. "Ladies, you take the tidying patrol. I'll talk to Sid. Come along, Cynthia." He grabbed her hand and headed for the coffee area in back. "I want you to meet Sid—you're gonna love him."

How could she have missed seeing the man when Ben was giving her the grand tour of the store? Cyndi mused as they approached the coffee area.

Drawing closer, she realized why she had overlooked him. He appeared to be an elderly gentleman, and he was seated, hunched over an open hardcover book on a table partially hidden by the coffee bar. His absorption in the book, whatever it was, was so complete, apparently he didn't even notice when she and Ben came to a stop beside him.

"Sorry to disturb you, Sid, but I'm afraid I must. It's closing time."

The man started.

So did Cyndi, surprised by the low, respectful, very gentle sound of Ben's voice.

"Oh, it's you, Bennett." Mr. Blumenthal blinked, then straightened to peer up at Ben. His dark brown eyes were bright, gleaming with humor and intelligence. "Closing time did you say?"

"Yes . . . sorry."

"Should be, too," Sid grumbled, in a good-natured way. He tapped a frail-looking finger on a page of the book. "I was just getting to the good part; Sherman is on the march south." He cocked a bushy, gray-speckled brow. "Now I'll have to buy the book."

Ben gave a quick head shake. "Not tonight, Sid. The register's closed."

Sid heaved a sigh, disappointment etching his tired features.

"Tell you what," Ben said, amusement twitching the corners of his lips, "you take the book with you. If you decide you like it enough to buy it, you can pay for it tomorrow." He shrugged. "If not, just return it when you've finished reading it."

Cyndi was more than surprised by Ben's suggestion; she was stunned. The twinkle that sprang to life in Sid's eyes gave a clear indication that this was far from the first time this scene had been enacted.

Bemused by this latest, and deepest, glimpse into Ben's personality, Cyndi responded automatically to his formal introduction of her to Sid. But she was keenly aware of the penetrating look on the old man's face, the probing of his eyes as he studied her.

Nodding, he picked up the book, cradling it like a priceless treasure in his arms, then turned that piercing look on Ben.

"This one," he said, nodding again. "Marry her quick, Bennett." He angled his head to again peer at Cyndi. "This one is a precious jewel, more valuable than any of those old volumes you have upstairs."

"I know, Sid," Ben murmured, so softly she could barely hear him. "You go on home now, have your glass of tea, and enjoy the book."

"Thank you, Bennett." Sid took one hand from the book to pat Ben on the arm. "You're a good man."

"Good night, Sid."

Deeply affected by the exchange, Cyndi stood mute, watching as the man shuffled away.

"Let's go, gang," Ben called, and his voice, raised to carry throughout the store, dispelled the lingering bemusement clouding Cyndi's mind.

"Rashid, lock up after Mr. Blumenthal," he went on. "Pat, Lynn, get out of here."

The three clerks didn't hesitate in carrying out his orders. Rashid handed a rectangular money bag to Ben on his way to the rear door.

"Register prove out?" he asked the younger man.

"To the penny." Rashid grinned, waved, and echoed Pat's and Lynn's calls of good night.

Ben followed them through the receiving room in back to secure the locks for the night.

"Aren't we leaving, too?" Cyndi asked when he returned to where she waited, still standing in the coffee area.

"In a little while," he said, coming to a stop beside her. "But I thought ... maybe, you'd like to see the rest of the place?"

"Including that room upstairs Mr. Blumenthal mentioned?" Cyndi asked, recalling his telling her about his collection of rare books.

"Yes, if you like."

"He's not going to buy that book, is he?" she asked, moving as he directed her to a door, cleverly concealed behind the coffee bar.

"No." Ben slanted a smile at her as he inserted a key into the lock and disengaged it.

"Who is he?"

"A learned man. He was a teacher for some thirty-odd years ... before fringe benefits," he answered, pushing the door open and motioning her to precede him into the lighted hallway beyond.

He paused at the doorway, his other hand moving, first to punch in a code on a panel of buttons, activating the security system, then to a row of switches on the wall.

Even expecting it, Cyndi started when the store was plunged into darkness.

He went on with his explanation. "Sid is a historian, he knows more about our Civil War than any other person I have ever met . . . including my college professors. And yet, he continues to study."

"At your expense?" Cyndi softly suggested, stepping back as he followed her into the hallway.

"Doesn't cost me a dime, Cynthia," he said, taking her arm to lead her to another door almost directly opposite on the other side of the hallway. "Sid will take better care of that book than some parents do their children; it will be returned in perfect condition."

He shrugged and smiled, unknowingly setting her pulses racing. "Eventually, somebody will buy it; someone who can better afford it."

"But . . ." She fell silent in surprise when, upon unlocking the door, he opened it to reveal the sliding metal grate of a small elevator.

Ben smiled at her expression and slid the grate back. "After you," he said.

Cyndi eyed the cubicle, which appeared approximately four feet square. Then, shrugging, she stepped in and moved to the side, allowing room for him.

Ben entered and pulled the solid door shut; the lock snicked into position.

Cyndi raised her brows.

"It's automatic," Ben explained. "And it is locked at all times . . . wouldn't want anyone taking a dive down the shaft," he drawled. "Inconvenient."

"A bit," she agreed, laughing.

Laughing with her, he closed the grate and activated the lift; it ascended slowly, creaking and groaning all the way. Cyndi's stomach lurched along with the car when it came to a halt.

"Third floor," Ben informed her in tones reminiscent of department-store elevator operators of yore, sliding back the grate and then fitting the key into the lock in yet another door. "Offices and storage room."

Cyndi stepped out of the lift and into another long hallway. As on the first level, there was a door opposite the elevator.

Exiting the lift, Ben strode past her to unlock the door, push it open, and motion her forward.

Upon entering, Cyndi could see the area was large, but not quite as spacious as the store, and sectioned off into separate rooms.

"Storage room and a small rest room," Ben said, indicating two doors toward the back. Taking her arm, he steered her to a door near the front, which stood partially ajar.

"And that door, down there?" Cyndi pointed to a door located along the hallway toward the front, several yards beyond on the same side as the elevator.

"Stairway to the front entrance, separate from the store entrance."

"So there are stairs," she said, smiling. "I was beginning to wonder."

Ben raised his eyes. "Of course there are; the staircases were in place before the elevator was installed."

"By you?"

"No, Cynthia," he said patiently. "That elevator is a lot older than I am." He arched a brow. "Any more questions?" He flicked a hand at the door before which they were standing. "Or are you ready to see where I work?"

"No, no more questions," she said, drawing a smile from him with her meek tone.

He pushed the door open. "Connie's office," he said, striding into the room, and beckoning her to follow. "And this is my hideout," he went on, striding across the room and opening the door to an office at the front, giving her a glimpse of long windows overlooking the street three floors below.

Both rooms were neat, utilitarian, with everything in its place. Connie's office contained a desk, on which rested a computer, a telephone console, a fax machine, and in one corner a plant with shiny green leaves. A low table next to the desk held a laser printer, as well as a compact copy machine. A bank of filing cabinets ran along one wall. Two plastic-seated waiting-room chairs sat side by side along the wall opposite the desk just inside the door.

Ben's office wasn't a lot more elaborate. In it were a large desk, a high-backed chair behind it, two padded chairs in front of it. To one side, a table bearing a coffee pot and a tray of cups was placed against the wall. Next to that was a small refrigerator. A large, old-fashioned safe sat against the wall inside the door. Miniblinds were the window's only covering. That was the extent of the furnishings. There were no frills, not even one live plant.

Immediately upon entering, Ben went to the safe, clicked in the code to open the lock, and stashed the money bag.

"I'll deposit it tomorrow," he said, setting her pulses racing once more with a melting smile.

Unsettled by the effect of his smile on her, Cyndi made a show of glancing around the room.

The very spareness of his working space revealed yet another aspect of his character; here was a man who took his work seriously.

"Well, what do you think?"

Cyndi shifted her gaze from the empty, spotlessly clean coffee pot, to his watchful eyes.

"Very businesslike," she answered candidly.

"I'm serious about my business."

My thought exactly, she mused, smiling.

"Are you ready?"

Her smiling lips curved down into a frown. "Ready? For what?"

"My rare book room."

"The one Mr. Blumenthal mentioned," she said. "Yes, please, I'd love to see it."

They retraced their steps, back to the elevator, then down to the second floor. Cyndi noted the difference the minute she stepped from the lift. The hallway was much shorter, and although there were four that she could see, the doors were located differently. There was one directly across from the lift, one toward the front, and two at the back.

With a hand motion, Ben pointed out another door, on the same side as the elevator. "The stairs," he said, unnecessarily, as Cyndi had figured that out for herself. He indicated the door opposite and the one to the front. "My apartment."

"Ummm," Cyndi murmured, curious to see where he had been staying, yet uncertain about the prudence of being alone with him in there, possibly to see unmistakable evidence left by his lady friend.

Though Ben arched a brow at her, he didn't comment. Taking her hand he started toward the back. "The fire escape," he said, as they passed the first door. He moved on to the second door, key in hand.

Light flooded the room as Cyndi crossed the threshold. This was a book lover's haven. It was not very large, and there were no windows. A couple of overstuffed chairs were placed at random around a low round table in the center of the carpeted floor. The lighting was indirect, yet bright enough for comfortable reading. Every inch of available wall space contained shelves stocked with books.

"Oh . . . Ben . . ." She breathed out the words, staring in wonder at the display. "Are all of these books rare collector's editions?"

"No." His voice was soft, and close, too close for Cyndi's equilibrium. "And the name's Bennett."

Unnerved, barely aware of his murmured reminder, she took a step, and then another, ostensibly to examine the spines of the books.

"These volumes have value, certainly, because they are old—and in good condition," he explained in that same hushed tone, too close again, as he had moved in tandem with her steps. "But there are no old first editions in here. The few I own are kept in a vault."

"I . . . ah . . . see." Cyndi sounded breathless, because she was, breathless and suddenly weak and irritated at herself for her fluttery, excited reaction to his nearness.

"Do you?"

A quiver rippled through Cyndi at the now whispery sound of his voice. He stood so close to her, she could feel the warmth of his breath ruffle her hair, could inhale the scent of the wine he'd drunk with dinner and the even more potent combined scents of spicy cologne and healthy male.

"Yes . . . yes . . . I . . ." She paused to take a quick breath, and probe her mind for the thread of the conversation. What had they been discussing? Oh, yes, the books . . .

"Cynthia." Ben's voice was nearly nonexistent, just a shimmer of sound teasing her ear.

She felt more than heard him, vibrated to the note of hunger and passion on that shimmer of sound.

"There are no windows in here," she babbled, saying the first thing that got by her saturated senses. "Why are there no windows in here?"

"Climate control," he murmured, grasping her shoulders and turning her to face him. "Air temp, humidity, etcetera."

"Oh, yes, of course, I . . ." She stared straight at his chest, afraid to look at him.

"I'm going to kiss you, Cynthia."

Her head jerked up and she stared into his eyes . . . only to discover herself reflected in their smoldering depths.

"No," she said, pushing the raspy-sounding refusal from her parched throat.

"Yes," he said, lowering his head.

Cyndi jolted, as if electrified, when, before his mouth touched hers, the tip of his tongue laved her lips, moistening them.

"Ben don't—"

He swallowed her protest when his mouth covered hers. His kiss was no tentative foray, no hesitant test, but a commanding possession of her mouth.

Cyndi's starved senses went wild in response to the sheer boldness of his sudden display of unleashed passion. She could no more resist the audacity of his ravaging mouth than she could cease breathing.

Elation singing through her, she parted her lips to the demanding probe of his tongue. With his first thrust into her mouth, she grabbed his shoulders and hung on to him to keep from collapsing onto the floor.

Deepening the kiss, Ben released his grip on her shoulders to gather her trembling body into his arms, crushing her softness to his hardening form.

Cyndi was lost, her sense, her reason vanquished by

the physical contact, the perfect fit of hard angles to soft curves.

His tactile fingers skimmed the length of her spine; his palm flattened against the hollow at the base, drawing her into the solid evidence of his need.

Cyndi wanted him, ached for him, craved the thrill of once again experiencing the fullness of him filling the emptiness inside her.

She loved him. Right or wrong, she loved him, desperately, and he . . .

Has a friend.

Cold reality restored balance.

She had to breathe; she had to think. Tearing her mouth from his, Cyndi pushed against his shoulders in a silent demand for freedom.

"Cynthia . . . what . . . ?"

She silenced him with a shake of her head, near frantic with the sudden recall.

She had promised herself earier, when Ben had so unexpectedly arrived at the house, that she would not play substitute again.

Yet, here she stood, nearly undone by the desire he had so effortlessly aroused with one kiss, like a dumb sleeping beauty awakened by passion.

The damned frog.

Hurt and anger vying for supremacy, Cyndi backed away from him.

Looking not at all pleased by her withdrawal, Ben frowned. "Cynthia, what's wrong?" Narrowing his eyes, he went on before she could respond, "And don't say you weren't enjoying the kiss, because I could feel your response, from your lips, your body."

Betrayed by her surrender of her love for him, Cyndi felt trapped, and like an animal hurt and cornered, she attacked.

"I'm already playing one deceitful role," she lashed out at him. "I refuse to take on the even more distasteful role of substitute lover."

Ben, who had started toward her, stopped dead, as if he had hit a stone wall. "Substitute lover," he repeated, looking baffled. "Cynthia, I haven't a clue as to what you're talking about."

"Your *friend,*" she said, her voice scraping over the second word. "You know, the one you told me about that day in the diner. The one you have a mutually satisfying arrangement with . . . that *friend.* Is she away on business—and unavailable?"

"No, Cynthia," he answered, his tone rife with annoyance. "She is not away, at least not so far as I know. Weeks ago, my friend and I mutually agreed to go our separate ways."

"And now you're looking for another friend, another arrangement?" she asked, her tone heavy with sarcasm. "And you've decided I'd do, since I'm already involved in one less than honorable arrangement with you?"

Ben had gone still while she was ripping into him, concern darkening his eyes.

Concern for her? Cyndi wondered. Or for himself, the man who had concocted the scheme to appease his mother while he applied himself to his business— whatever form that might take.

It was nearly impossible for her to equate that man with the character traits revealed by the man—the very same man—in the store below, or was Ben's drive, his self-determination to the point of self-absorption the one flawed facet of that otherwise seemingly sterling character?

"No, Cynthia, I am not looking for another friend." His voice firm and steady, intruded into her groping thoughts. "Not a friend of that type, at any rate," he amended. "I desire ño more arrangements of that kind." He took one careful step toward her. "But, I had hoped—"

She interrupted him, not wanting to hear, afraid to hear, what he had hoped. "Please, I would like to go back to the house now."

"Cynthia," he began again.

"I mean it Ben," she said, striding to the door and swinging it open. "I want to go back."

Rushing to the elevator, she left him little choice but to follow.

Chapter Sixteen

Frustration was a living thing eating at Bennett, and it was feeding on his nervous system.

Although he had attempted to explain to Cynthia, to reassure her that she was wrong in her assessment of his intentions, she had curtly aborted his attempt, refusing to discuss it.

She had maintained a frigid silence throughout the subsequent drive back to his house.

Relief mingled with regret as Bennett brought the car to a stop in the driveway.

Cynthia immediately groped for the door handle, obviously desiring to get away from him as quickly as possible.

"Wait," Bennett ordered, wincing at the harsh note of command in his voice.

Her hand stilled, but she didn't turn to look at him. "Why?" Her tone was flat, cold.

"It's Friday, isn't it?" he asked, withdrawing an envelope from the inside pocket of his jacket. "Here's your salary.'' He offered it to her, as he had every week since bringing her home with him.

She eyed the envelope warily, as if afraid it might suddenly morph into something deadly.

''As you'll be starting your classes next week,'' he went on, when she finally took the envelope, ''I added a little extra for expenses.''

That got her attention.

Cynthia turned to face him, her expression cold and closed. ''I don't need it,'' she said, in tones colder than her expression. ''You've already paid the tuition for my classes.''

Bennett cursed himself, for as remote as she appeared, he wanted to drag her into his arms and kiss her senseless, rendering her into the same condition he was in.

He heaved a sigh instead. ''You'll be needing books and probably other supplies, and—'' She ruthlessly cut him off. ''I have enough, more than enough for my expenses,'' she said, again turning to the door.

''Cynthia.'' He halted her with his sharpened voice. ''What I said earlier still stands; we must spend more time together . . . for Mother's sake.''

She remained still, and silent.

''Do you understand?'' he demanded.

''Yes.'' A bare whisper.

''And you will comply?''

''Yes,'' she fairly hissed.

''Then, good night, Cynthia.''

''Good night . . . Bennett.''

Alarm held him in thrall as he watched her jump from the car. Clutching the envelope in her hand, as if she had forgotten its existence, she ran along the walkway, and entered the house without a backward glance.

Bennett. Bennett. Bennett.

How often had he chided her about his preference for his full name? Bennett asked himself, staring at the now darkened house.

More times than he could remember, he reflected, frowning. How could he have known—guessed—that hearing her at last obey his request—pronounce his name in tones of utter detachment—would have an effect on him similar to that of a chasm splitting open inside him?

Damn. Damn!

Had he insulted her, not once but twice this evening, first with a kiss, and them with money? Had Cynthia felt cheapened in some way by both of his offerings?

But, God knew, he had meant no insult or disrespect; he liked her too much to risk hurting her.

Still, he had hurt her before, and badly; for although Cynthia had not repelled him, in relinquishing his control to passion, he had taken from her the precious innocence of youth.

And less than an hour ago, he had tried to repeat his performance.

But, it was different now, Bennett assured himself, still staring at the house, yet no longer seeing it. For he was no longer looking out, but in, examining the difference in his feelings and emotions.

He had liked her almost at once, Bennett recalled, a smile of remembrance shadowing his lips. From the outset, when he had stepped inside that diner, Cynthia had revealed to him a pleasant personality, a sharp intelligence and a keen wit.

Over time, as he had gotten to know her better, she had proven genuine, confirming his first impression of her. Cynthia was loving and giving, willing to sacrifice her own needs for her beliefs, her love of family.

While Bennett had felt confident that his mother would accept Cynthia, simply because he proclaimed her his choice, he had never dreamed his mother would not only open her arms to the girl, but her heart as well, and even an insensitive fool could see that Frances had quickly come to love Cynthia.

Bennett didn't even want to think about the effect on his mother, the ramifications, should she discover the truth of the situation.

He didn't want to hurt his mother.

He didn't want to hurt Cynthia, either.

But . . .

He did want Cynthia.

No. Bennett frowned and shook his head. What he was feeling, had been feeling for some time, was more then mere sexual impulse.

Alarm expanded in Bennet as enlightment struck with the force of an illuminating bolt of self-knowledge.

Damned if he wasn't in love with her.

The smothering heat of summer still blanketed the land. The trees and grass, though still green, had a limp, tired look. Autumn would not officially begin for almost three weeks, yet already classes at the University of Pennsylvania had begun.

After an initial seizure of nervousness, Cyndi calmed down enough to grope her way around the campus to the designated sites of her classes.

Unfortunately, her nervousness was not entirely due to the natural trepidation anyone might be subject to upon embarking on a new venture.

Eventually, one grew accustomed to new beginnings. Cyndi's problem stemmed primarily from her inability to accustom herself to the suddenly new and unnerving situation in which she found herself with Ben.

Following the night she had come so close to surrendering herself, and the last fragments of her tattered pride, to him, Ben had been a frequent and persistent presence in her life.

She could not fault him for his behavior; he was unfailingly pleasant, polite, and considerate—except when, and always in front of his mother, he drew her into his arms. During those instances, his mouth devoured hers with voracious disregard, testing her strength of will, her emotional stability, her determination to appear aloof and uneffected by him.

There were moments—increasing in number with alarming speed—when Cyndi was sorely tempted to consign pride, will, and determination to the devil, to just give in to her physical need for him.

Those moments were intensified with each successive phone call home. While Cyndi was both pleased and relieved to hear reports on the ever-growing closeness of the relationship between her father and Emily, her ego took a hit every time she spoke with her sister.

Jess was ecstatically in love, and from all indications, Jeffrey Adams was afflicted with the same besotting malady.

Cyndi could not deny the twinges of envy she felt for her sister; Jess was not yet nineteen, Cyndi was twenty-six . . . and in love with a man who, while giving ample evidence of physically wanting her, gave no such evidence of suffering the symptoms of the malady that had struck Jeffrey Adams.

Why shouldn't she accept what Bennett was offering? she asked herself, with increasing regularity. Aside from the natural, and very real, health concerns, the sharing of sex seemed to have become a casual indulgence, almost blasé.

So why shouldn't she indulge herself, drench her senses with the heady essence of Ben?

Cyndi was playing mind games, and she knew it. She couldn't throw principle to the wind for a few moments of physical gratification with Ben.

She loved Ben, yes, but making love with him, knowing he didn't return her love, would destroy not just her dreams but a vital element of her self.

And she knew herself well enough to realize that she couldn't face losing a part of herself; it was hard enough facing the reality of no happily ever afters.

Nevertheless, despite her inner turmoil, before mid-September, Cyndi had managed to settle in, and had even made a few tentative friendships.

The first was a woman, a few years older than Cyndi but every bit as nervous.

Her name was Gwena, a name Cyndi had never heard before, but liked at once. She was tall, skinny, seemingly all flailing arms and long legs.

Other than the fact that they both were part-time students, Gwena and Cyndi had little in common.

In contrast to the rural setting and close-knit family life Cyndi had known, the other woman had grown up—or fought her way up—in the inner city, with little family support, both of her parents having to work long hours to keep the family together. Having grandparents and other relatives who were scattered around the country, she and her brothers and sisters were mostly on their own.

Gwena was street-smart and savvy. She was all flashing eyes and hard angles, and she had a sharp mind and a sharper tongue.

Being opposites, they gravitated to one another, and

began the ritual of having a cup of coffee together after their first morning class.

Then there was Andy, medium height, lanky, and scruffy around the edges. At thirty-two, and living alone in a two-room flat, Andy had finally managed to save enough money to scrap his uninspiring job and return to college to complete his postgraduate work.

Cyndi's maternal instincts had kicked in the first time Andy had hesitantly sidled up to her to awkwardly introduce himself.

The cerebral type, shy and uncertain, he projected a little-boy-lost look. She figuratively took him under her wing. Loping along beside the two women, he made it a threesome for the morning coffee break.

And then, soon after Andy had latched onto Cyndi and Gwena, another man—older, mature, polite, and well mannered—approached them.

"I couldn't help but notice that we all"—he encompassed the three of them with a sweeping glance—"appear to attend most of the same classes."

"And?" Gwena prodded, suspiciously, arching her brows.

Rather than taking offense at her off-putting tone, he gave her a benign smile. "I also couldn't help noticing that you three usually go to the coffee shop after the early morning class." He paused, his gentle gaze homing in on Cyndi, before continuing, "I was wondering if I might join you sometime."

What could she say? Deciding she must look like the word's softest touch, yet instinctively liking the refined look of him, Cyndi smiled.

"You may join us on one condition. It's a rule we all follow," she said, keeping her tone serious and her expression somber, while avoiding the startled looks on Gwena's and Andy's faces.

"And what is that?" the gentleman asked, frowning and appearing to reconsider his request.

"You must tell us your name."

He chuckled.

Gwena roared.

Andy grinned.

The ice was broken.

"Paul . . ." He extended his right hand to Cyndi. "Paul Wilding."

Grasping his hand, Cyndi offered her name, then introduced her companions.

Paul joined the group for coffee the next morning, and quickly proved himself to be intelligent, congenial, and amusing . . . if in a dry way.

Cyndi warmed to him within minutes, appreciating his wry yet inoffensive humor. Andy gave every indication of liking Paul as well. And, by the second morning, he had won over even the suspicious and usually ascerbic Gwena.

Before the week was out, the threesome had become a foursome.

Talk about your diversity, Cyndi thought one morning, observing her new friends. She couldn't have found three more diverse individuals if she had placed an advertisement in the *Philadelphia Enquirer*.

Gwena was the product of a black and white union.

Andy was Hispanic.

Paul had an English lineage.

And Cyndi, herself, was of German descent.

She amused herself with the thought that, while Cinderella may have had her animal and feathered friends, she had her own mini League of Nations.

With friends to share her trepidation, the scary beginning soon evolved into a routine.

And, if there remained an emptiness in her life, her

soul, and her recently awakened body, if her heart yearned for the unattainable reality of being the center of Ben's existence rather than his convenient partner in deception, Cyndi consoled herself with the thought that at least her schedule was full.

In point of fact, it was so full, Cyndi was developing a healthy respect for the nimble talent of professional jugglers.

She attended classes three mornings a week. On her free afternoons and free days, she was occupied with her studies, Frances, and the companionable pursuit of haunting every library, museum, and art gallery within a few hours' driving distance.

The only time she allowed strictly for herself, was a few hours before bedtime. Those precious hours she kept sacrosanct, losing herself, her problems, between the covers of a book, not to advance her studies, but for pure reading pleasure.

Then, of course, there were the evenings and weekends allotted to Ben, whom she now scrupulously addressed aloud by his full given name.

Naturally, during the course of events, and conversation, Cyndi found herself mentioning her new friends more and more often.

As both Frances and Ruth had shown an interest in everything that interested Cyndi, the topic of her developing friendships came up regularly.

So accustomed had she become to inserting one or more of the names into the conversation, Cyndi began doing so without thinking.

And that was how Ben came to learn about her campus companions.

Late Friday afternoon, he sauntered into the house as if he owned it—which, of course, he did. Not surprisingly, since he had been previously informed, he arrived just in time for Ruth's standing rib roast and baked potatoes.

"I know I promised to drive you to the Wyeth Museum in Brandywine tomorrow, Cynthia," he said, passing the side dish of steamed mixed vegetables to her. "But would you mind if we stopped at the Center City store for a few minutes along the way?"

Cyndi's memories of her one visit to the store being what they were, she was not eager to return to the site, yet, amenable ad nauseum to her agreement with him, she assured him she wouldn't mind.

"Are you still so busy at work, Bennett?" Frances asked with maternal concern.

"Actually, no," he answered, his smile and gaze gentle for her. "There's usually a slack-off in business around this time of year. It gives us a breathing spell before we gear up for the Christmas crush."

Savoring a bite from the tender cut of beef, Cyndi didn't think before she spoke. "Paul said the same thing just yesterday about the men's clothing store where he works."

"Paul?"

Uh-oh, Cyndi thought, alerted by the hard steel hidden within Ben's soft voice.

"And who might Paul be?"

"He might be any man," Cyndi calmly replied, determined not to be intimidated by him—ever again. "But, as it happens, Paul is a man I met at Penn. We're in a couple of the same classes."

"Indeed?" Ben's voice also was calm, too calm; the glitter in his eyes told a different story.

"Yes, isn't it nice?" Frances beamed at Cyndi before shifting her gaze back to Ben. "She's made several new friends at school."

"All of them male?" he inquired with seeming uncon-
cern, while pinning Cyndi with that cold, glittering stare.

"No," she replied, offering him a blatantly false smile.
"There are only two others, one male, one female. We
have coffee together after our first morning class. We
have great discussions," she tacked on, answering the
question she felt certain was coming.

"Hmmm."

That was Ben's only response, but Cyndi felt she could
see his mental wheels spinning with questions and spec-
ulations he was suppressing. She couldn't help but wonder why he hesitated, when he never had before.

Ben chose not to go out that evening, opting instead
to spend time at home with his mother. Naturally, Frances was delighted, but no more so than Cyndi, considering the ever-present constraint between them when they
were alone together.

For Frances's sake, Cyndi gritted her teeth and played
the role of happy fiancée until a little after ten. Then,
pleading tiredness, she escaped to her room—Ben's
room—and submerged herself within the fantasy world
of a sweet, funny Regency romance novel.

After that night in Ben's rare book room, Cyndi had
shied away from the hotter, more sensual historical
romance novels, since she'd caught herself envisioning
Ben as the hero and herself as the heroine.

"Go, run rampant," Ben said when they arrived at
the store the next morning. "I'm going up to my office
to see if the fax I'm expecting is there."

He strode away from her, leaving her standing in the
middle of the store, bemused and rather flattered that
he had remembered her answer to him so many weeks

ago when he had asked her what she would like to do if given the opportunity.

Run rampant through libraries, bookstores, and museums. Cyndi's smile was tinged with sadness as she gazed at the reading feast set out before her.

By the generous consent of Frances, and the use of her Mercedes, Cyndi had been running rampant throughout Philly and its environs.

Why then this dissatisfaction? This longing for more? Cyndi readily acknowledged that she had been given more opportunity than she had ever dared hope would be offered to her.

And yet . . . and yet . . .

However well-meaning, it was all based on a lie, a deceit, perpetrated against the kind and gracious woman Cyndi had come to deeply care for.

There were times, occurring with increasing frequency, when, guilt and shame eating her alive, she longed to rebel, confess all to Frances, then bolt and literally run for the hills.

Torn by her inner conflict, Cyndi still held silent, enduring the proddings of her conscience for one and only one reason, one person.

She had always been a dreamer.

This dream, however, was tearing her apart.

It was getting more difficult with each passing day, but as she had done since her eighteenth year, Cyndi accepted the hand life dealt her, playing her cards to the best of her ability.

She hadn't yet reached the point of folding.

Shrugging off the self-indulgence of worn-out metaphors and misty dreams of the unattainable, Cyndi sent a sweeping glance over the abundant display of reading matter around her, determining to apply herself to reality, to possibility.

One such possibility, in the form of a vague and nebulous idea, presented itself to her while she was in the children's book section, located at the back of the store, in the corner opposite the coffee area.

She was admiring the section, made roomy by the removal of two or three of the center-aisle double-sided shelves. A couple of low, tyke-sized chairs were set in the cleared area. Cyndi had raised her gaze to skim the comprehensive selection of titles and authors when a young, pleading voice drew her attention.

"Please, Mommy, I want to hear this story."

Smiling, Cyndi glanced around in search of the child making the plea.

A little boy, three, maybe four years old, with bright blue eyes and a cap of dark red curls, sat on one of the chairs, a storybook clutched to his small, narrow chest.

Cyndi thought he was adorable; but then, she thought all young children were adorable.

"I don't have time this morning, Sean." A woman's voice, skating on the edge of impatience, wafted on the air from the other side of a center aisle shelf.

"Mommy . . . please," the boy wailed.

"Sean, that's enough," his mother said, getting even closer to the edge. "I must find this da—ah, computer manual your father asked me to pick up for him. You look at the pictures in the book until I find it."

Cyndi gnawed on her lower lip, debating the prudence of voicing her first impulse.

"Oh, Mommy," the boy whimpered. Two fat tears trickled down his cheeks.

End of debate.

"Ah . . . excuse me, ma'am?" she called.

"Yes, what is it?" A head poked around the side of the shelf, a head sporting a riot of even darker red curls and framing a pretty face that would have been beautiful minus the lines of strain around eyes and mouth. "Were you speaking to me?"

"Yes," Cyndi flashed her most ingratiating smile. "I don't mean to intrude, but I would be happy to read the book to your son while you search for the computer manual . . . that is, if you have no objections?"

"Objections!" The woman laughed. "Honey, I would be eternally grateful." She heaved a relieved sigh. "One of the clerks said she'd help me find the dratted book, as soon as she's free. But there were several customers ahead of me." She sighed again, then smiled; it transformed her face. "Thank you."

"I'll enjoy it," Cyndi said, returning the smile before turning to address the boy. "Would you like me to read the book to you?"

"Yes!" he cried, thrusting the book out to her, cover side up.

Noting the title, Cyndi smiled, thinking how apt it was, under the circumstances. Then, perching on a chair next to the child, she opened the book and began reading aloud one of the many adventures of a big red dog.

Ben found her there some ten minutes or so later; Cyndi was halfway through the big dog's third amusing adventure.

Cyndi didn't notice him.

He cleared his throat.

Startled, she glanced up. "Bennet, back so soon? I'll be with you in a moment, as soon as—" She was interrupted by a breathless voice.

"I'm so very sorry!" The redheaded woman came tearing around the shelf and ran smack into Ben, who quickly moved to steady her. She gave him a harried look. "I beg you pardon, but . . ." She shifted her worried look to Cyndi. "I am sorry it's taken me so long, but after I finally located the book, there were long lines of customers at both registers."

"Good," Ben murmured, eliciting a confused look from the woman, and a quelling glare from Cyndi.

"It's all right," Cyndi assured her. "Really, we were having a great time," she looked down at the boy, "Weren't we, Sean?"

Sean nodded vigorously in agreement. "Will you read to me when Mommy brings me to the store again?"

"Now, Sean," his mother said in warning. "Don't pester the nice lady. Just say thank you now, because we have to go."

"But, Mommy!" His lower lip thrust forward in a pout. "I want—"

"Sean!"

Cyndi had heard that exact parental tone before— from her own mother when she was little. She knew it meant business . . . so also did Sean.

His skinny chest heaving on a sigh, he stood up and moved to his mother to clasp her outstretched hand. "Thank you for reading to me," he said, glancing back at Cyndi. "I really, really liked the stories."

"You're welcome, Sean, it was a pleasure," she said. "I liked them too."

With a final thank you, a smile for Cyndi, and a tug on the boy's hand, the woman hurried away.

"Playing librarian, were you?" Ben asked, his eyes alight with teasing intent.

"No." Cyndi smiled. "I'm just a sucker for little kids with red hair." She paused to laugh. "Or any other color, come to that."

"Lucky kids," she thought she heard him murmur. But then he briskly asked, "Ready?" Not waiting for a reply, he took her arm to lead her to the door.

Ben appeared willing to put himself out to be a charming escort. Cyndi loved the Wyeth Museum, and had she been willing to admit it, which she wasn't, every minute of Ben's company.

He gave her a running commentary about the individual works, along with bits and pieces of information about the three artists, N. C., Andrew, and Jamie Wyeth, the first of whom Cyndi had never heard much about, so she hadn't known that he'd been a rather famous illustrator.

Cyndi found it all fascinating, and yet, all the while she spent admiring the artistic ability of the multitalented Wyeths, a vague germ of an idea took root at the back of her mind, sending periodic shoots into her consciousness.

Chapter Seventeen

Within days of her reading session with Sean, the idea flowered into full bloom in Cyndi's mind.

Now, she told herself, all she had to do was cajole Ben into giving his approval, allowing her to bring her idea to fruition.

Sadly, Cyndi had never been very good at cajolery; she was more inclined toward the direct approach. So, she decided she needed an advantage, and she hoped to find it in the company of allies.

She waited until, right on schedule, Ben turned up at the house at dinnertime Friday evening. And still she waited, biding her time while he savored Ruth's delicious breast of chicken a l'orange.

Cyndi broached the subject after helping Ruth serve the coffee and dessert of fresh melon wedges.

"Ahh ... Bennett, I was ... er, wondering if you might be interested in trying an idea I have in the store?"

"I'm always interested in new approaches," he said,

giving her his undivided attention. "And I'm certainly willing to listen to yours." He raised his cup to her in a silent salute.

"Cyndi always has such good ideas," Frances chimed in, encouragingly. "Doesn't she, Ruth?"

"Mmmm," Ruth murmured around the rim of her cup. She swallowed the sip of coffee, then elaborated, "I know it's been a lot easier for me to find exactly what I want ever since she had the idea to alphabetize the canned and dried foods in the pantry."

"Alphabetize?" Ben repeated, choking back laughter. "You *alphabetized* the pantry?"

Cyndi gave him a superior look. "All the better to read the labels, my dear," she paraphrased.

"That's right," Ruth championed, scowling at Ben. "Don't knock it if you haven't tried it."

"Hey," he said, chuckling and raising a hand in the peace sign. "I'm not knocking it. It just . . . well, sounded funny."

"My son was always amused by the oddest things, Cyndi," Frances said, smiling even as she shook her head in despair of him. "Why don't you just ignore him and tell Ruth and me about your idea?"

Reflecting that ignoring Ben would be next to impossible for her, not to mention that it would hardly serve her purpose, Cyndi nevertheless launched into an explanation of her concept, fully aware that, as he was seated next to her, Ben could hardly avoid hearing what she had to say.

"Well, I have to begin by explaining that, last week, when Bennett and I stopped by the store, I offered to read a story to a little boy while his mother located a particular book."

"How thoughtful of you," Frances inserted. "But I'm

not surprised; you are always considerate of others. Isn't she Ruth?"

Cyndi cringed inwardly. She wasn't considerate; she was deceitful. The naked truth hurt, but she persevered.

"Always," Ruth concurred with a positive nod of her head. "And I'd bet that young mother appreciated the gesture."

"She did." Ben offered the information, directing a smile at Cyndi that scrambled her thoughts and erased her guilt for a moment. "She was very grateful to Cynthia for giving her those minutes to finish her shopping."

Cyndi recognized a perfect opening when she heard one, and she jumped into it.

"Yes, she was," she agreed, leaning forward in her desire to hold his attention. "And that ties in with my idea." She drew a quick breath, then took the plunge. "There must be countless numbers of women who, by necessity, shop with their children in tow." She raised her brows. "Right?"

"Yes, of course." Ben nodded.

"And I believe that every one of them would appreciate a few minutes to shop, or simply just browse, without having to keep one eye on a youngster."

"No doubt," he agreed. "So?"

"So . . ." She hastily took another breath, then rushed on. "I was thinking that, if the children's section could be enlarged a bit—maybe by removing one more of the double-sided shelf racks . . ." She faltered.

Ben was frowning. "Remove shelf racks?"

Cyndi had garnered the knowledge of how important shelf space was, to both the store's sales and the books' authors. But she truly believed her idea could improve the volume of business and benefit the children. Her belief lent passion to her argument.

"I understand your reluctance to do that," she hastened on. "But hear me out, Ben, please," she beseeched, unconsciously reverting to his shortened name.

Something flickered to life in his eyes, and then he smiled. "Of course," he murmured.

Sparing an instant for a relieved sigh, she forged ahead. "I suggested the removal of a shelf rack to allow a little more floor space for more small chairs. Then, with your permission," she wet her lips, "I would post a day and time—say Saturday morning from ten until noon—and make myself available to read to the kids."

She held Ben's gaze . . . and her breath.

He smiled.

She breathed again.

"Why, Cyndi!" Frances exclaimed. "I think that is a wonderful idea!"

"So do I," Ruth echoed.

Although Cyndi was grateful for their endorsement, she kept her eyes focused on the only one there with the authority to approve her plan.

"It is not a wonderful idea," Ben said, sending her spirits into decline. "Wonderful is much too mild a term," he went on, reversing the downward spiral of her spirits. "I think it is a brilliant idea, for several reasons. First and foremost, it would be an excellent way to promote literacy. Then, as you said, it would entertain the kids, while giving their parents a break." A smile tilted his lips. "In addition, it would probably increase business substantially."

Cyndi's spirits took flight.

"But . . ."

Nosedive.

"Cynthia, you already have a full schedule. Are you sure you want to do this?"

"Yes," she answered, firmly and at once.

"Okay, I'll look into the possibilities."

It turned out the possibilities of her idea were even better than Cyndi had dared hope.

After spending the weekend in open, sometimes heated, discussions about the project—not the strained and stilted inanities they had been indulging in of late—Cyndi returned to classes on Monday morning, renewed and recharged.

"Hey, what's got you all pepped up, Cyndi?" Gwena asked when they convened for coffee. "You must've had one invigorating weekend."

"Well . . . yes." She laughed as she recalled her planning sessions with Ben.

"You look great," Andy offered shyly.

"Yes, indeed," Paul concurred in dulcet tones. "I'd say glowing, actually."

Gwena rolled her eyes, as she habitually did whenever the Brit, as she referred to him, lapsed into a heavy British accent.

"Yeah, you know, like you're flying or somethin'," she lapsed into the vernacular of the street.

Paul leveled a quelling stare at Gwena.

Gwena met his stare with a serene smile.

Andy choked on his coffee—and his laughter.

Cyndi shook her head in amused despair of them.

"So . . . give, babycakes," Gwena demanded, smirking at Paul. "Clue us in here as to what major event got you up and running?"

"I really don't think—" Paul began, only to be rudely interrupted by the unquailable Gwena.

"Dump it in the trash, Shakespeare," she sweetly

advised. "Spill your guts," she then ordered, grinning at Cyndi.

Excited by the project, Cyndi launched into an enthusiastic account of her idea, the incident which had precipitated it, and Ben's acceptance of it.

All three of them knew about Ben. Not that Cyndi had volunteered the information. She'd just as soon have kept her pretend engagement to herself.

It was the ring—that lovely and unique piece he'd inherited from his grandmother, the ornament that weighed more heavily on her hand with each passing day—that had piqued Gwena's interest and curiosity.

Initially, Cyndi had considered claiming the ring was an heirloom. But she was sick to death of lies and so had owned up to being engaged to Ben.

Paul had immediately offered his solemn and sincere congratulations.

Andy had shyly added his good wishes for her happiness.

Gwena had quipped that she thought it was pretty cool that Cyndi had bagged "an upper middle-class tycoon in the making."

In regard to her explanation for her upbeat mood, Cyndi was pleased but unsurprised by the supportive response she received from the unlikely trio.

"Hey," Gwena exclaimed, "that's a fantastic idea. There are kids out there starving for more than just food, you know. We're talkin' inspiration here, babe. Trust me, this is gonna catch on like a house on fire. If—no, *when*—you get overwhelmed and need help, sing out for Gwena." She flashed a cocky grin. "Don't forget, we're talking about the Center City store here. I just might be able to relate to the brothers and the sisters."

Cyndi was thrilled by Gwena's enthusiasm and her

offer of assistance. "Do you mean it? Not just about helping, but about it working?"

"Can't miss, honeybunch," Gwena said decidedly. "You're going to be crying for help in no time."

"I agree," Andy said, his shyness giving way to eagerness. "And I'd like to help too." He shot a challenging look at Gwena. "I just might be able to relate to the Hispanic kids."

"I'd like to offer my limited talents, as well," Paul intoned quite formally, smiling at Cyndi. He executed an elegant shrug. "Who knows, there just might be some *one* child with whom I could relate."

Utter silence. Gwena and Andy looked appalled and ashamed of themselves. Cyndi stared at Paul from wide, stricken eyes.

Paul's cool and remote gaze rested briefly and in turn on his companions. Then he grinned.

"Gotcha."

There was a stunned moment then, as if cued, they all burst into laughter.

Gwena was the first to gather herself enough to speak, and when she did, she expressed the sentiments held by Cyndi and Andy as well.

"You're all right, Britisher. In fact, in my less than humble opinion, you've just progressed from rigid to rad."

Late that afternoon, Cyndi received a phone call from home; it was her father, and he was calling with both bad and good news.

After they had exchanged greetings, he told her he had recently received letters from her brothers, Carl Jr. and David, both of whom were doing fine and sent their love to all.

"That's good," Cyndi said, then laughed. "Neither of them are great letter writers, are they?"

Carl chuckled. "And they don't write any more legibly than they did in school."

"How's Jess?" Cyndi made a concentrated effort to keep her voice light.

"Says she's in love."

"I know." She swallowed a lump in her throat.

"I believe her," her father said. Then he chuckled again. "And, if appearances mean anything, I'd say Jeffrey Adams is every bit as much in love with her."

"I'm glad," Cyndi replied; lucky girl, she thought.

"Ah . . . Emily's father suffered a heart attack yesterday morning." He sighed on imparting the bad news. Cyndi caught her breath, but he continued, "He died late last night."

"Oh, that's awful. Please tell Emily I send my condolences," she murmured, wondering what this turn of events might portend for the future.

Her father didn't keep her wondering long.

"Umm . . . Cyndi . . . would you be upset if Emily and I were to get married?" he hesitantly asked, then quickly added, "After a respectful interval, of course."

"No, Dad, I wouldn't be," she assured him, tears stinging her eyes. "I can't think of any two people more deserving of happiness than you and Emily," she murmured, blinking against the moisture clouding her vision. "But you must promise me that you will be happy together." She sniffled. "Okay?"

"I promise." Carl's voice carried a suspicious roughness. "There's one other thing." His tone lightened and held a note of excitement that aroused Cyndi's curiosity.

"What, Dad?"

"Emily has a little money . . . Well, quite a bit more

than a little. A sum settled on her after her husband's death, a benefit provided by the construction company he worked for."

Cyndi frowned, concerned her father might allow his pride to cause a rift between him and Emily. She voiced her concern. "Does that bother you, Dad?"

"Bother me? Heck no!" he answered, laughing. "Thing is, Emily and I were discussing our wedding, and well, we don't want any fuss about it."

"Oh." Disappointment colored her tone.

"Don't sound like that, princess," he pleaded. "I'll tell you exactly what I told your sister this morning, and that is that Emily and I . . . well, we're past fuss. We both want a fussless, quiet but . . ."—he paused, then quickly went on—"but romantic wedding."

Dumbfounded, Cyndi pulled the receiver away from her ear and stared at it in stunned silence. Romantic? Her father? Figure that!

"Cyndi?" His voice was faint.

She brought the receiver back to her ear. "Yes, Dad, I'm here. You were saying?"

"Promise you won't laugh."

"Laugh?" There was a note of something almost childlike in his voice. Intriguing, to say the least. "Why would I laugh?"

"Because we've decided to fly to Florida the week before Christmas," he explained in a veritable flood of speech. "Start the New Year right, as man and wife. But that's not all," he rushed on. "I . . . I've always wanted to go and it turns out, so has Emily . . . And well, Cyndi, if you laugh I swear I'll . . . Darn it all! We're going to Disney World for our honeymoon!"

Cyndi didn't laugh; she cried with joy for the couple and at the revelation of the romantic bent her father had never before revealed. Not to her or her siblings.

But somehow she knew that her mother had been both privy to and thrilled by this hidden bent.

Carl Swoyer was a dreamer, too.

Fancy that, Cyndi mused, staring mistily at the phone after they said their goodbyes.

Chapter Eighteen

The place was packed.

From his position before the door to the hallway, off to the side of the coffee bar, Bennett surveyed the shoppers thronging the aisles of his store, the kids jam-packed into the reading areas, both of them.

Who'd have ever imagined . . . ?

His lips curved in a smile of satisfaction. They were racing toward the end of the holiday shopping frenzy, and business was good. Wrong, he corrected himself. Business was fantastic.

Of course, sales were always good at the season of massive giving, had been ever since Bennett opened this, his first store, years ago.

But this year was different. In every one of his stores, the sales were off the charts.

Bennett was man enough, honest enough, secure enough within himself to admit the difference could be attributed to Cynthia's innovative idea to conduct weekly reading sessions in the store.

The idea had been an instantaneous success, had taken off like a rocket, and had very quickly been incorporated into the other stores.

From day one, the interest and response, from employees and customers alike, had been so great, Bennett had been forced to reevaluate the situation pertaining to space.

After the second week of reading sessions, he had removed one more double-sided rack from the center aisle and had added six more little chairs.

The week after that, Cynthia had recruited more readers, a few eager employees, her friends from Penn, and, amazingly, his own mother.

The weeks had literally flown by since then. There were only a few shopping days left before Christmas; Thanksgiving was long past. They had been so busy, he had barely taken note of the holiday.

Yes, Bennett mused, sales receipts proved that Cynthia had every right to feel justifiably proud of her end of September brainstorm.

His roving glance came to rest on the children's section in the opposite corner. A wry smile played at the edges of his mouth.

Every inch of space was stuffed full of wide-eyed, attentive—and quiet—little people. They were in two close, but separate, groups. The tall, snappy-mouthed Gwena held one bunch in thrall, while his mother, looking supremely content, held sway with a younger group sitting on the floor around her.

Bennett's gaze moved on, coming to rest on the area utilized as a coffee bar, except on Saturday mornings, when it was off limits to all but teenagers.

Teenagers for heaven's sake!

Bennett would never have believed it. Hell, he hadn't

believed it when Cynthia had applied to him for permission to use the area for the older kids. He had assured her it would fail from lack of interest.

He'd been dead wrong.

Bennett's bemused gaze rested for a moment on Andy, who had paused in his reading, his eyes soft, his smile shy, as he defined a word for an intense-looking young man, who, Bennett judged, had to be somewhere in the neighborhood of seventeen or eighteen.

Shaking his head in wonder, Bennett shifted his gaze to the group of girls and boys, about middle-school age, all of whom appeared mesmerized by Paul's cultured British accent.

Incredible.

Finally, shifting his gaze once more, Bennett zeroed in on the face in the crowd guaranteed to capture his undivided attention, set his pulses pounding, and constrict his breathing.

Cynthia.

God, he loved her.

A twinge of pain struck his chest. He loved her so much, he could see the weariness behind the smile on her face.

Moments ago, Cynthia had relinquished her chair in the children's section to his mother.

His beloved was tired.

Little wonder, Bennett reflected, his sharpened gaze probing beneath the mask of makeup she had applied to conceal the dark smudges under her eyes; the killer schedule she had been maintaining for months made him tired just thinking about it.

Cynthia hadn't eaten, he knew, but then, there was little about her actions that he didn't know. Still, to his continuing despair, her thoughts, her feelings remained a mystery to him.

As if she could feel his gaze resting on her, Cynthia glanced over at him, smiled, and gave him a thumbs-up gesture, signaling her delight in the success of their venture.

Yes, she could smile at him, and often did so, Bennett thought, smiling back at her. And why shouldn't she? Hadn't he been knocking himself out these past months, playing the charming, easygoing, ever-patient companion?

Bennett experienced an inner ripple of discontent; his stock of patience had about run out.

He had trod lightly, his every step measured, since that night in the rare book room, the night he had acknowledged his true feelings for Cynthia.

Unlike his impetuousness when he'd lost control and taken her innocence, he no longer seized the opportunity to kiss her, deeply, meaningfully, while in the protective company of his mother.

Wanting—needing—Cynthia's trust, he had suppressed his natural impulses, bestowing nothing but chaste kisses on her tempting mouth.

How was she feeling and thinking about him now?

Bennett had to know, because if he didn't, he feared he'd implode.

The irrevocable decision made, he raised a hand, beckoning her to him. His heart thumped in rhythm with her every step as Cynthia made her way to his side.

"Come with me," he said, grasping her hand and turning to the door to the hallway, then heading to the elevator beyond. He inserted the key into the lock.

"Are we going up to your office?" she asked, allowing him to usher her into the lift.

Bennett smiled, shook his head, and activated the elevator. He needed her in his life, he mused. In his bed. He definitely did not need her in his office.

"The rare book room?" she asked, tersely, when the lift shuddered to a stop at the second level.

"No, Cynthia, I'm taking you to my apartment," he said, yanking her now resistant form along as he strode into the hallway to the door to his flat.

"Bennett—

"Where," he said, cutting off her protest without a qualm, "I am going to fix you lunch."

"Oh."

"Oh, indeed," he grumbled, shoving the door open and motioning her to precede him inside. "You look about ready to cave. Have you eaten anything at all today?"

"Sure," she answered, strolling after him into the tiny kitchen. "I grabbed a sweet roll before leaving the house this morning, ate it on the way in."

"Wonderful," he muttered, heading for the fridge. "And so nourishing."

"I was pressed for time," she said defensively. "I overslept."

"You overslept because you're always pressed for time," he growled over his shoulder. "How about a steak?"

"A steak? Good Lord, no." She laughed.

The sound of her laughter shimmered through Bennett, turning him on. Tamping down an urge to forget her need for food in favor of his need for her, he turned to frown at her. "What, then?"

"Do you have any soup? Canned would be fine," she quickly clarified.

"As a matter of fact," he said, shutting the door to the fridge and then pulling open the one to the freezer on the side-by-side unit, "I have here in my hand a single serving of"—he displayed a plastic container—

"Ruth's famous homemade chicken noodle soup. It'll take only a few minutes to nuke it."

"Yummy, nuke away, please," she said, swiping her tongue over her bottom lip.

It required quite an effort, but Bennett held back a groan as he dragged his gaze away from the temptation of her moistened mouth.

Thirty-odd minutes later, Cynthia scooped up the last spoonful of the soup, then sat back with a contented sigh.

"That was sooo good," she said, dabbing her lips with a paper napkin.

Good for her, perhaps, Bennett thought, rising from the chair opposite hers at the table. For him, watching every spoonful she slipped between her lips drew a little more moisture from his throat.

Lord forgive him, but he wanted her mouth, felt starved for the singular taste of her. The simple act of not touching her when he collected her soup bowl and spoon, her still half-full water glass, took every ounce of willpower he possessed.

Enough, he decided, stashing bowl, glass, and spoon in the dishwasher. He had been patient long enough, charming and amiable long enough.

And enough was enough.

Turning from the sink, Bennett paused, his gaze caressing her face. Her appetite satisfied, she looked relaxed, mellow; in her eyes was a vague and sleepy expression.

Moving slowly to her, he lifted her hands from the tabletop, drew her to her feet. She came into his arms like a homing pigeon, sending a thrill of surprise and delight racketing through him.

When Cynthia raised her head to look at him, the

breath lodged in his throat, which was already tight with a mixture of passion and tenderness.

Her eyes. Oh, God, those beautiful green eyes betrayed her; they glowed with an inner fire, the flame of desire.

This time, he vowed, he would not lose control.

Lowering his head, he gently touched his mouth to hers, his intent not ravishment but adoration. Banking the passion threatening to overwhelm him, he slowly caressed her lips, then the tender inner flesh with the tip of his tongue.

She made a soft mewing sound in her throat and curled her arms around his neck, seeking closer contact with his mouth, his body.

Hanging on, Bennett lightly stroked her tongue with his own, claiming her lips with increased pressure. His touch feather-light, he skimmed his hands down the length of her spine, finally molding her body to his. One palm brushed the outer curves of her breast.

She moaned and arched into his caress.

She was his! The realization hummed through Bennett, testing his determination, his control.

But still he hung on, each successive touch light, enticing, eliciting from her ever deepening moans of intensifying desire.

The move was seamless, from the kitchen to the bedroom to his bed. Bits and pieces of clothing—male, female—marked their passage.

Without a word spoken—their murmurs, the agony of their breathing saying volumes more than mere words—they pleasured one another with touches and fused lips.

Clinging to his presence of mind, Bennett stroked, kissed, laved every inch of her satiny skin, until, writhing beneath him, she grasped his hips and brought him to her, inside her.

It was the single most incredible experience of Bennett's life.

Afterward, his body replete, his mind floating, he stirred, confused, when he felt her leave the bed.

"Cynthia?" He opened heavy-lidded eyes, frowning at the sight of her pulling on her clothes, piece by piece, as she backtracked along the trail of strewn garments. "Why . . . ?"

"I've got to go . . . Darn! Where are my shoes?" She tossed him a distracted and frantic look. "Your mother's waiting. I've got to drive her home, Ben."

Ben. She'd called him Ben. Relief shivered through him. He lifted himself up to rest on his elbows, loving her till it hurt.

"We have to talk," he said, aching to pour out his heart to her. "I'll come to the house later this afternoon." He smiled. "Tell Mother, and Ruth, that I'll be there for dinner."

"Yes, okay." She swept a glance the length of her delectable form. "Do I look all right?"

"You look . . . perfect." Retaining some of his wits, he reached over the side of the bed, grabbed his pants, extracted his keys and tossed them to her. "For the elevator. I've got a spare set."

"Oh, right." She caught the keys, stared at him an instant, then gave a strange-sounding half-laugh, half-sob. "I've got to go."

She took off at a run.

Bemused, Bennett dismissed a disturbing niggle of concern aroused by the flat, final note underlying her parting remark.

Cynthia had called him Ben.

Chapter Nineteen

Daybreak. The sky was a leaden gray.

Cyndi stared out the window at the gently falling snow, the sparkle of the flakes prismed by the tears blurring her vision.

She was home, but derived no comfort from the familiar surroundings of her own things, the background of snow-dusted mountains.

She was alone. Jess was at work, with a date for dinner afterward with Jeffrey. Her father and Emily were chasing their dream in Florida.

Yet Cyndi's dream was dead. She had administered the lethal blow with her capitulation, not only to Ben but to the long months of enduring her own clamoring need of him.

She had known what to expect from the moment he had taken hold of her hands, drawn her up from the table. She had known—and hadn't cared. Not then.

Cyndi had reveled in Ben's lovemaking. She had

thrilled to his every kiss, his every touch, his heart-breakingly beautiful possession of her.

She loved him.

The excuse hadn't been good enough to ward off the attack from her conscience after the fact.

Her short-term memory was hazy; everything had happened so fast.

After running from Ben's apartment—what had it looked like?—Cyndi recalled Frances chattering happily on the drive home. She could not remember what that kind woman had talked about—only that Frances was happy.

Cyndi did remember, too clearly, the searing sting of guilt. Frances's happiness was based on a lie, a deliberate deception.

Cyndi knew what she had to do before they had reached the house. She could no longer live with the deception. To her mind, she had but one option.

By confessing to Frances, she would betray Ben.

By remaining silent, she would betray herself.

Since she could do neither, her only option was to leave, return to the home she never should have left in the first place.

Tears running unnoticed down her pale face, Cyndi strove to reconstruct the steps she had taken.

Closing her mind to everything but her intention, she had gone to her room—Ben's room—as soon as they got back to the house. She had called US Air, and booked a seat on the early evening flight out of Philadelphia International to Pittsburgh.

From the phone, Cyndi had gone to the dresser, to count the money she had stashed under her outrageously expensive lingerie. Taking only enough to pay for the plane ticket and the bus fare from Pittsburgh to her home, she shoved what was left, most of the money Ben had given her, into an envelope, along with a note she quickly dashed off.

Writing Ben's name across the front of it, she placed the envelope on the dresser and, removing his ring, laid it on top of the envelope.

Keeping her mind blank, she had taken a quick shower, gotten dressed, then had thrown her clothes, *her* clothes, into *her* suitcase. That done, she had called for a cab.

She had then lied one final time, telling Frances she had talked to her father and he had asked her to come home, due to a family emergency.

The cab had arrived.

Cyndi had left . . . crying.

She was still crying.

Bennett arrived at the house just in time for dinner, hungry for Ruth's good cooking, hungrier still for the sight of the woman he loved.

The house was quiet, too quiet. He could not detect so much as a whiff of the usual mouth-watering aromas of food baking, simmering, or broiling.

"Mother?" he called, walking into the empty living room, apprehension invading his mind. "Ruth?" The quiet was making him restive. "Cynthia?" His voice revealed his expanding uneasiness.

Striding through the dining room, Bennett came to an abrupt halt at the sight that met his concerned gaze. His mother and Ruth sat at the kitchen table, cups of what appeared to be untouched tea in front of them. The dejected look of the two of them set inner alarms to ringing inside his head.

"Mother? Didn't you hear me call?" he asked, moving into the room.

"Oh!" Frances started and then glanced up, blinking at him, as if coming out of a trance. "Bennett, I didn't hear you."

Both women looked lost, confused, which turned his apprehension to dread.

Cynthia. Where was she? Incipient panic crawled up the back of his neck. Mindful of his mother's heart condition, despite the recent glowing progress report from her physician, he contrived to conceal his upset.

"Where's Cynthia?" he asked with deceptive calm, flexing fingers that wanted to curl into fists.

"Oh, Bennett," Frances wailed. "She's gone."

"Gone?" he echoed, more harshly then he'd intended. "Gone where?"

"She was called home," Ruth answered, her thin lips quivering. "She left not even an hour, after bringing your mother home from the bookstore."

And after leaving his bed. The thought beat inside his head.

Frances nodded agreement. "She was fortunate in that, when she called the airline, the ticket agent had just had a cancellation." She glanced at the digital clock set into the microwave. "Her plane was scheduled to depart forty-five minutes ago."

Damn. Damn, goddamn, he had left it too late, Bennett railed at himself in self-disgust. He knew, felt certain, Cynthia had not been called home; she had run . . . from him. Now she would never believe that he had intended to confess to his mother, this very night, to explain the extent of the deception—the bogus engagement—he had lured Cynthia into in an attempt to lull his mother.

"She left a note for you."

Bennett refocused his eyes, and his undivided attention, on his mother. "Where is it?"

"She said she left it on the dresser in your room."

Bennett started for the doorway leading to the hall, the foyer, and the staircase beyond. He took three steps, then stopped, swinging around to peer at her.

"Are you all right?" He examined Frances's face for the tell-tale grayness; she was pale, but not gray. "Have you had dinner?"

"Yes, to both." She worked up a faint smile. "I . . ." She glanced at Ruth. "Ruth and I are just missing her, that's all."

Accepting her assurance, he again started for the doorway, only to pause once more to look back at her with grim determination. "Don't go away, either of you. I have a confession to make." He grimaced. "I'm afraid you're going to be disappointed in me."

Bennett didn't wait for any comment, he was off, running for the stairs and his bedroom.

Cynthia's note was brief and to the point. With his grandmother's ring clenched in one fist, the note clenched in the other hand, Bennett visually skimmed the lines on the page.

> *Ben,*
> *I'm going home, where I belong. I'm sorry . . . for so many things, but I can't—I simply cannot—continue to stay here, lying to everyone, most especially to your mother. I love her, you know, almost as much as I loved my own mother. I must go.*
>
> *Cyndi.*

That was all she had written.

Bennett read, then reread the lines, feeling a measure of relief. There were no words of bitterness or condemnation. Encouraged, more by what she hadn't mentioned than by the sentiments conveyed, he shoved the ring into one pocket, the note into another, then strode purposefully to the phone.

Minutes later, he slammed the receiver into the cradle. There wasn't a seat available on any of the commercial lines. *Didn't he realize that Christmas was one of the busiest times of the year?*

Screw it, he'd drive, Bennett decided, stalking to the closet for a suitcase. After stuffing a couple of changes of clothing and his shaving kit into the valise, he pulled a shearling jacket from the closet and strode from the room.

His mother and Ruth were waiting for him, as per his request, in the kitchen.

Tamping down the sense of urgency playing hell with his patience, Bennett slowly, concisely, and humbly made his confession, not sparing himself, while exonerating Cynthia of any malice aforethought.

His mother's reaction to his self-serving deception of her came as something of a surprise to Bennett. He had expected shock, anger, hurt, and possibly tears from her, if not from the tougher Ruth. He hadn't so much as contemplated a response of sheer exasperation. But that was exactly what he got.

"For heaven's sake, Bennett!" she exclaimed, in a tone he hadn't heard from her since his rebellious teen years. "That is the most idiotic, harebrained scheme I have ever heard. I really thought you were smarter than that!" Jumping up, she planted her hands on her hips and gave him a this-is-your-mother-speaking-so-pay-attention look. "Now, tell me what are you going to do to compensate Cynthia for your idiocy?"

"I'm going after her," he said, hiding an impulse to laugh behind a chastised tone.

"Good," Ruth chimed in. "Get moving."

Bennett did just that. His mother's parting command reached him when he pulled open the front door.

"Bring her back home to us, Bennett."

"Don't worry," he promised. "I will."

By noon, when Cyndi's tears had finally stopped, the snowfall had increased, grown thicker, heavier, and was rapidly piling up on the ground. Jess had already called to say she would not be coming home; she would be staying the night with Jeffrey.

Cyndi hadn't argued with her sister about propriety; she had envied her.

She suddenly jumped, startled by a sudden pounding against the kitchen door. A motorist already stranded in the snow and needing assistance? she wondered, taking a second to peer out the window before answering. There was a car pulled up close to the house, snow covered, yet there was something . . .

The pounding sounded again, harder.

"I'm coming," she shouted, turning from the window and taking off for the kitchen.

Unlocking and then yanking open the door, she began, "There was no need to—" Her voice deserted her as Ben pushed his way past her into the kitchen.

"Christ, it's cold out there," he muttered, turning and swinging the door shut with a bang. "What took you so long?"

Cyndi didn't answer, she couldn't speak past her surprise. Then, her wide-eyed gaze devouring him, she managed to voice the one word revolving inside her mind.

"Ben."

"Who were you expecting . . . Santa Claus?" he

snapped, shrugging out of his jacket and scattering snow all over the floor in the process.

"No . . . I—I . . ." she stuttered, then common sense reasserted itself, along with a protective dose of anger. "What are you doing here?" she demanded. "How did you get here so soon?"

"I drove, obviously. I left last night, drove until I caught myself dozing off around one, then pulled into a motel to catch some sleep. I'd have been here sooner, but the road conditions are worsening by the minute; it's a bitch out there." Tossing his jacket over the back of a chair, he walked to within inches of her.

Cyndi took a step back.

He arched a brow.

"Why did you come?" She took another step back, not because she didn't trust him, but because she didn't trust herself, her strength of resistance.

"To take you back, of course," he answered. He dipped a hand into a pocket, retrieved something, then held it out, displaying the ring lying on his palm. "And to put his back where it belongs." He closed the distance between them.

"I can't, Ben," she whispered, hurting inside, aching with the need to touch him. "I tried to explain in my note . . . I won't. Nothing you say will change—"

"I love you, Cynthia."

Then again . . . Cyndi banished the thought. It wouldn't work. It couldn't. There were too many lies, too much deception. How could she—

"I've told Mother everything," he said, reading her mind as clearly as if her thoughts had been written on her forehead. "She called me an idiot."

Her lips twitched.

"You agree with her, huh?"

She nodded. "It was a bad idea, Ben," she said,

despairing, the sting of tears in her eyes. "We were both idiots. We could have ended by hurting your mother very badly."

"I know," he admitted, sighing. "Instead, all we managed to do was hurt each other." Stepping closer still, he raised a hand to her chin, tilting her face up to stare into her mist-clouded eyes. "Yet I can't force myself to be sorry for what I did." His voice was low, deep with meaning.

Hope quivered to tentative life inside her. "Why . . . why can't you?" she whispered.

"Because, if I hadn't acted on what my mother referred to as my harebrained scheme, I would have driven away from here that day, driven away from you," he murmured. "And that, my love, would have been the biggest mistake of my life."

"Oh, Ben, I . . . I don't know what to say—or do."

"You could say you love me."

"I do. Oh, Ben, I do love you, so very much."

He exhaled, deeply. "Then could you do me the favor of helping me to warm up?"

She smiled. "I'll gladly do that."

"You could even take me to your bed."

She did.

Epilogue

Snow fell throughout the afternoon, lending the land an otherworldly, fairy-tale appearance.

Cocooned beneath a down comforter in Cyndi's bed, in a world of their own, neither Cyndi nor Bennett noticed the official arrival of winter.

Utterly spent by having made love with Cyndi not once, not twice, but three wild and laughing and beautifully tender times, he dozed, her warm body held close within his possessive embrace.

Cyndi, happy and content, idly stroked Ben's lightly haired chest.

He loved her.

The sheer wonder of it floated in her love-beguiled mind. *Ben loved her.*

She yawned; sleep crept around the edges of her consciousness. Hovering in the netherworld, where on occasion, one imagined one heard whispers—Cyndi thought she heard three—she smiled.

No happily ever afters?

Hah!

Live forever, Cinderella.

ABOUT THE AUTHOR

Joan Hohl lives with her family in Pennsylvania and is currently working on her next Zebra contemporary romance, I DO, which will be published in December 2001. Joan loves to hear from readers; you may write to her c/o Zebra Books. Please include a self-addressed, stamped envelope if you wish to receive a response.

Put a Little Romance in Your Life With
Fern Michaels

__Dear Emily	0-8217-5676-1	$6.99US/$8.50CAN
__Sara's Song	0-8217-5856-X	$6.99US/$8.50CAN
__Wish List	0-8217-5228-6	$6.99US/$7.99CAN
__Vegas Rich	0-8217-5594-3	$6.99US/$8.50CAN
__Vegas Heat	0-8217-5758-X	$6.99US/$8.50CAN
__Vegas Sunrise	1-55817-5983-3	$6.99US/$8.50CAN
__Whitefire	0-8217-5638-9	$6.99US/$8.50CAN

DO YOU HAVE THE HOHL COLLECTION?